Between The Ropes

J H Norris

All content © 2025 J H Norris. All rights reserved

jhnorris.co.uk

To all of our warrior Queens and trauma survivors. To everyone who went to hell and walked out with the burns on their backs.

We see you, we hear you, we're with you.

To my soulmate, who navigates this torturous beautiful journey with me. Who gave me life when I had none and breathed life into a soul destined to burn. My safe place, my everything.

About the Author

J. H. Norris writes dark romance that hits like a right hook — raw, obsessive, emotional, and a little bit feral. The team consists of Johno and Fliss.

Johno is lifelong fighter, chaos-bringer, and trauma survivor, Norris weaves together violence, vulnerability, and desire with zero apologies. These characters don't play nice — and neither does the prose.

Between the Ropes is a debut — the opening strike in a wider universe of devotion, depravity, and dominance. It's also a love letter to survival, obsession, and the chaos that shapes us.

When not writing, Norris is usually at the gym, in the corner of a ring, changing nappies, or muttering "one more chapter" at 2am.

Common Sense Disclaimer

This is not a fucking instruction manual.

Between the Ropes is a work of fiction. It blends sex, violence, obsession, trauma, and power dynamics into a gritty, dark romance storyline. Some of what you'll read is messy, extreme, or downright feral — because that's the point.

But let's be clear:

Consent is not optional.

Just because something is sexy on the page doesn't mean it's okay in real life without enthusiastic agreement.

Kink responsibly.

Safe words. Aftercare. Mutual trust. If you're not doing that, you're not doing it right.

Respect your partners.

Don't be a dick. Don't use this book to justify shitty behaviour.

You're here for a filthy, emotional rollercoaster. Treat it as fiction. Enjoy it as fantasy. Live with respect.

This is a debut Title from Indie Authors

We've tried our best, but we are first time independent authors. If you should find a typographical, spelling, or grammatical error in a book that contains morally grey men burning down half of London, forced orgasms, polyamory, graphic violence - and everything else this whirlwind has to offer, we're sure you'll survive.

We're not backed by huge editorial teams and massive marketing budgets. We appreciate you taking the time to read our first book.

This is a work of fiction

Any resemblance to real people — living, dead, or somewhere in between — is purely coincidental. If you think a character sounds like you, that's on you.

No one in this book is based on a real person. Seriously.

Not your ex, not that lad from the gym, not your sketchy mate with a burner phone.

This is make-believe. Messy, chaotic, filthy make-believe.

So don't come for me. I promise — if I had based a character on you, you'd fucking know.

Reader Advisor Warning

This story intentionally explores the blurred lines between fantasy and dysfunction. It does not condone abuse, non-consensual acts, or real-world violence — but it does portray emotionally complex, broken characters navigating love, sex, and survival through a raw and brutal lens.

This work contains themes of religious extremism. It is evident in the narrative and the content that any and all forms of hateful extremism, from any religion is wrong. It should also be evident from the content of this book that religion must be treated with respect, and that all religions are on the premise of love and acceptance.

Trigger Warning

This book contains mature themes and graphic content. Please read responsibly and check the list below if you are sensitive to certain topics. Your mental health matters.

- Kissing and romantic intimacy that may disturb some more hardened readers
- Emotionally intelligent men, which some may find disorientating

- Anal sex
- Asphyxiation and breath play
- BDSM including physical restraint
- Blood and cum play
- Blood, injury, and combat-related violence
- Child abuse & neglect (backstory references)
- Death & murder
- Domestic abuse / emotional abuse (depicted and unpacked)
- Dubious consent / CNC-style dynamics (all contextualised and intentional)
- Fisting and vaginal stretching
- Forced orgasm
- Graphic sex scenes
- Group sex
- Human trafficking / exploitation (referenced, depicted through liberation scenes and backstory explanation)

- Kidnapping
- Knife play
- Male-female, male-male, male-male-female, female-female-male, and group sex scenes
- Masturbation
- Mental health struggles / dissociation
- Pain play with scratching and other implements
- Power imbalances in relationships (emotionally and sexually)
- Psychological torture
- PTSD & trauma responses
- Religious extremism — specifically one antagonist, who voices it consistently
- Religious radicalisation, weaponisation, and related language and behaviours
- Sex in public, in a car, in a burning building, in a gym and in any other place you can possibly have sex
- Sexual assault & coercion (discussed, implied, referenced, not glamorised)
- Sex during death (of someone else)
- Sex in the presence of fresh corpses
- Submissive dynamics - including human coffee tables
- Spanking and caning
- Violence & torture (including graphic scenes)
- Voyeurism (consensual and forced)
- Waterboarding / drowning
- Wax play

Prologue

Fuck You, Find Me

She deeply inhales the steam, mirror fogged, hiding her fear. The near molten water futilely attempting to wash away her anxiety. She glances nervously at the awkwardly placed pink bullet vibrator, right by the sink. She knows she's no pornstar, just a woman; longing to be desired by the man she loves.

The cute basque adorns the back of the bathroom door, hanging hopefully from a coat hanger. Her heart and eyes fill with hope and excitement. It's been weeks, maybe months, who's counting? *He's going to see me in this, and he won't be able to resist.* She pins her eyes closed, allowing her hand to wander with her imagination.

There she is. Sprinting, whole arms pumping, legs fighting for every step, her lungs burning. She stops. Lost. An alleyway, it's dark. Dim streetlights barely aiding her vision. She squints and tries to focus. Stealing cold breath from the night air.

The ominous figure casually strolls towards her. Face shrouded in shadow where his hood overhangs his hairline. Eyes dark as shadows, yet he remains faceless. *"The chase is half the fun, isn't it?"* as he throws his cigarette on the ground. Through Doe's eyes, she looks down at the ground and matches his gaze. Nodding with trembling anticipation. *"Tell me you want it..."* his deep voice lingering on the last syllable. She does. She knows she does. He knows she does. But not admitting it is part of the fun. It's what makes it so exciting. He'll take it anyway. She can't fucking wait.

"Tell me, how much you fucking want it" his mouth in her ear, his voice dangerous and low. His hand around her throat, holding her up as her knees weaken. Pinned to the wall with no way out. He squeezes. The unavailability of air adds to the ache. She refuses. His eyes flash, an inch from hers. He maintains his grip, sliding his other hand up her miniskirt. She chose this skirt for exactly this moment.

His hands feel the excitement he's caused, as he circles over the mesh of her g-string with his middle two fingers. Her gasps betray her, as do her writhing hips. She needs it. It hurts how bad she needs it. Her eyes closed, embracing the feel of his unrelenting hand on her throat. His hands expertly handle her.

Until he takes his hand away. Starkly awakened, pleasure pulsating but not delivered. "... *please*" she manages through a raspy whisper. She tastes herself, her tongue dancing around his fingers. Sucking them clean. Anything. Anything to feel his touch again. Craving the release she knows is imminent.

"There's my good girl" he says, without breaking eye contact, or the grip on her throat.

Using his free hand, he undoes his belt, and ties it around her neck. She doesn't move. If she wanted to escape she could. He loops it and slips it over her head and around her neck, before tightening it to a perfect fit. Pinning her to the wall, he plants his lips on hers. The passion is tangible. He wants her, he *needs* her. She can *feel* it.

The kiss is passionate, almost to the point of violence. Their tongues dance, intertwined. Rolling around one another, interlocked. Every nerve ending on the tips of their tongues alight with the excitement of what's to come.

He pulls away, and she bites his lower lip before opening her eyes. He flashes that dangerous smile. The one she sees every night. *"Knees"* he simply commands. She drops, the cool tarmac of the summer evening grazing her knees. Her leash angled to his face. This time it's her who maintains the gaze. Her hands rub up from the sides of his hips, under his hoodie to feel his chiseled obliques.

Knowing the consequence, she digs her nails in, dragging them, scratching him. The predictable and desirable tightening of the belt around her neck reassures her of who is in control. She brings her hands down to his waistband. Pulling his trousers and boxers down simultaneously, like a gift being unwrapped. She's confronted with it.

Veiny, throbbing, pulsing at her. Silently begging for what only she can give. The tip glistens with a taste of what awaits her. Moving her face to the very base, she drags her tongue, teasingly to his tip, opening her eyes to look up at him once she gets there. His lip curls as he heavily exhales.

She opens, just wide enough, which is already nearly wide enough to dislocate her jaw. Her lips kiss the very tip, and she starts to work her way down. He grows impatient, dropping the end of the belt, he grips her hair from behind. She knows what's coming, and she can't fucking wait.

Then he pushes. He pushes until he hits the back of her throat, her eyes closed. She feels him hit the back of her tongue. The back of her throat. And he keeps going. She doesn't gag, she holds it back. He pulls out slowly, and pushes back in with more force than she's ready for. Holding her hair steady with each thrust, forcing himself in her throat.

She fights her gag reflex, and feels her eyes start to water. As she's accustomed to, he carries on. Her mouth overflowing with saliva and precum. Her chin soaking, he continues. Fucking her face harder. She gasps for air between every thrust. Her laboured breathing audible.

Her hands slip to her own exposed thighs, there are no thoughts in her head. Just ecstasy. Being used like this made her feel so raw, so wanted. Her hand glides to her clit. Pulling her g-string aside, she circles her aching clit. Matching the pressure thrusting at the back of her throat. Frantically her circles became straight lines. Maniacally rubbing before sliding her two middle fingers inside. Her escaping gasps, hiding her moans.

He notices and smirks. He pulls all the way out. Ropes of cum keep her attached to her Dominant, from lips to cock. She looks up at him, longing. Smirk still decorating his face, he pulls her up tenderly by her leash. Comfort in his domination. Feeling beautiful in her chaotic state.

He loosens the belt and slips it into her mouth, tightening it in place. He turns her to the brick outer windowsill of the building that was behind her. He turns her by the jaw to face the darkened window. *"Look how pretty I made you"* she looks at her reflection. As clear as day, the running mascara, glistening chin. Her gag stops her from speaking. He doesn't need her words to know what she wants.

His hands place her forearms on the windowsill. Sliding them, at painstaking pace, down to her thighs. He reaches around, and teases her lips with his finger tip. Her inner thighs. He traces every nerve ending, she trembles with anticipation.

As the climax starts building, her knees shaking and weakening. He brings his hand up and holds her up by her waist. Holding her close to him, not allowing her escape from an earth shattering orgasm. She maintains eye contact throughout, through the reflection in the window. Hips circling, encouraging his hand motions to push past every nerve. Every millimetre of movement is electric. Every nerve in her body is alive.

Then she feels *him*. The heat radiating from his throbbing cock. He rubs it over her clit, making her shake again. She feels him, pressing against her. His hands hold her wrists in place on the windowsill. *"No, please don t"* she whimpers, at the same time as pushing her hips back towards him. Needing to be filled, lost in the moment.

Her mouth drops open and a silent gasp escapes her lips, as he drives his hips forwards. Every inch of him taking her. She nuzzles her head against his forearm on her shoulder, still holding her in place. As he pulls out with aching slowness. And slams himself back in. Over, and over.

She loses grip on the wall, forearms grazing, probably bleeding. The cold soreness an earth shattering contrast to the heat from him. He pushes her further into the wall, pulling her top up to expose her torso. The cold brickwork rubbing sorely against her front, as his heat dominates her back. *Make me bleed, leave me bruised and scarred for you. Fucking own me.*

Pace steady and controlled. He knows exactly what he's doing, teasing her climax. He won't let her cum until he decides its time. He owns her, inside and out. And she's fucking thrilled about it. With every thrust her desperation increases.

"Please let me cum" she manages, through almost tears. An overwhelming need for release. It builds and builds. Panting with every movement. He picks up the pace. Slamming her into the wall now. Holding her in place as he uses her as his toy. His play thing.

"Oh my god...". It's imminent now. Shaking uncontrollably. She's going to explode as he detonates, firing his load inside her at any minute. She can feel the build up. He's harder than granite, filling her completely.

"Fuck..." she breathlessly whispers *"...yes... please"*

The darkness shatters, replaced by white light. The warmth rolling over her body dissipates. The slamming of the door against the wall ruins her moment. The waves of heat rolling over her body replaced with the ice cold gust caused by the bathroom door opening with such force.

"What the fuck is this?" His words boom as the door flies open, it crashes against the wall detonating with fantasy shattering volume. His words and tone cut like a knife. "You think I want you dressing like *that*?", his eyes lock onto the sink, the bullet. "Obviously - honestly, Aria, you make me sick. Wanking in the shower? Classy."

As quickly as he shattered her efforts, the door slams behind him. *Obviously* she didn't get a chance to explain, to voice her needs. She puts her hands on the wall, she's long since given up trying to reason with herself.

With resigned fate, she towels herself dry. The air extractor works to clear the mirror. Her reflection becoming visible, she sees how ridiculous her attempt was. *He's never been into that,* she reminds herself. It was wild to think that she could tempt him with something so cheap, so shallow.

His exposed shoulders lit by the flicker from the TV, he's left the boxing highlights on, and is paying them as much attention as he pays Aria; snoring already. In her dresser she finds pyjamas, definitely not the kind they'd sell at Victoria's Secret or La Senza. Simple bottoms, and a t-shirt she doesn't recognise. Sizes too big for her, but it's comfortable, like a blanket wrapped around her, hiding her from her own gaze.

Defeated, she climbs into bed. Stiffly, uncomfortably. Flicking the TV off, the world falls into silence. A deafening, stifling silence broken only by the low rumbles of his snore. Regret, shame, and despair fill her consciousness.

Rejection is imminent, but the dying drop of hope inspires her. She shuffles towards him, pushing her chest against his back, no response. Sliding a hand around his back to his chest, gently placing a kiss against his shoulder blade. Still nothing. Boldly her hand explores further South, a finger slipping under the elastic of his boxers, tracing the line. He stirs.

His hand takes her wrist, and discards it like litter into a bin. "I've got work in the morning. You're 25, grow up", and he shuffles closer to his edge of the bed.

She sighs, nausea swirling. The weight of her sinuses increasing by the second. Self criticism fills the void between her ears. Her cheeks remain dry, this isn't the first time, she's become accustomed to longing for the attention and affection of the man who supposedly loves her. She stares at the ceiling she can barely see. Sleep evades her for what seems like hours, as she bathes in a deep, rejected sadness.

In sudden and stark contrast, artificial light fills the room, and dissipates as quickly as it came. And again. And again. His phone's going off. Machine gun notifications light the room like the blitz. It drives her to distraction, and she makes her way out of bed and round to his night stand.

Respecting his privacy, she resolves to not check his phone; until she sees the message preview from

Roxy 😽

I can still taste you, Daddy 💦 I guess my little shopping spree was worth it 🔥

Think of me tonight, sleeping next to that fat slug 😄 😮

Every building has a storm it can withstand, and a storm it cannot. Even sand was once a rock, it was just broken enough. She climbs back into bed, but doesn't sleep.

Her eyes open to Cal, presented in the bedroom checking himself in the full length mirror, tying his tie and sipping his coffee. He's in a good mood this morning, but he normally is. He's a morning guy. He downs the last from the mug and sets it down, *"I'm off now babe, see you later"* and kisses her forehead as her eyes adjust to the morning light.

Once upon a time, that would've been enough. That tenderness, calling her babe, kissing her forehead. It would've been enough to convince her of the emotional health and stability of her relationship. But not today. As the front door closes, and the sounds of his car become distant she picks up her phone and finds the contact.

🖤 *Jade*

"Ree? What's up, babe?"

She can't answer, fighting back tears, the only audible noise is her sniffling - leaving snot down her forearm like a slug

"Ree, what's going on?"

"... There's another girl"

"Fucking obviously, that piece of shit wasteman motherfucker, want me to come get you?", every word dripping with that 'South of the River 'charm

"... Please

"I've got you, give me a few hours, are you going to be okay?"

"Mmhhmm, he won't be back until like 8 anyway"

"We'll be long gone by then"

She glances back at the residence that imprisoned her, nothing of her left behind; but a post-it on the TV.

Fuck you, find me

Chapter One

"Home sweet home, Ree" comes Jade's tender voice, as Aria's eyes strain open, the cooling drool drying from the corner of her mouth. Jade kills the car, and the sounds of *Pure Garage Classics* dissipate. The yellowed lighting barely illuminates the compound they're parking in. It's intimidatingly quiet, with alleyways that could lead to danger everywhere. This is *that London*, not the London from *Love Actually*, this is chicken shops and *Top Boy* London.

Heading out onto the high street, neon signs illuminate a vibrant yet deprived night-time economy. It's an intimidating place to be at night, even when you're accompanied by South London's self-proclaimed finest. Next to the chicken shop is a small alcove with an inset metal security door, buzzers for the apartments, Jade fobs their way in. Making their way through the internal staircase, pieces of flaked white paint crunch beneath their feet under the paper-thin carpet as the stench of "we tried" cleaning products invade Aria's nostrils.

Stepping into the warm clean homeliness of Jade's apartment, Aria immediately recognises the smells of cinnamon, coconut oil and a little smoke. The sweet spice of home reminds Aria of when they roomed together in Uni. Jade's unapologetic assumption of self and heritage had always been endearing to someone as self-diagnosed beige as Aria. That feisty, aunty-to-be, fuck around and find out queen was in stark contrast to Aria's timid self. Maybe that's why they worked so well.

She slings a single suitcase, a lifetime of material possessions, into her newly allocated bedroom. Forty-five minutes later, after three spiced rum and cokes and two arguments about which member of So Solid Cru was hottest, they fall into the sofa. The kind of worn-in leather that swallows you, heavy cushions feeling like you're being held. Spicy jollof rice and fried plantain never tasted so much like freedom. The smell of food, combined with Jade's frankincense and myrrh incense sticks (*girl, devil dick be gone, I don't need that energy funking up my yard*), and a very slight buzz from the rum and Aria breathes a sigh of relief. Her shoulders haven't felt so light in years, it almost brings her to tears. Conversation strolls through the casuals, through some lukewarm tea, and eventually gets to what happened, Aria's brittle armour starting to crack as she begins unburdening the emotional toll of her relationship and its eventual demise.

The Queen of her Yard protests with finality: *"Girl, absolutely the fuck not. I ain't sitting here listening to you whine about some broke-ass, tiny-dick, yellow-teeth, no-taste, bitch boy. Get your shit, we out. Get my hoops."*

Somewhere between the glitz and glam of the West End, and the tired middle-aged hopelessness of a Wetherspoons, sits *Clique*. More than a pub, not quite a club; the DJ is probably "paid in exposure", or maybe just likes to have his "choice of the chicas", but it's a vibe. Well, it would've been in 2005. For now, it's a refuge. *Craig David* and *Artful Dodger* thumping through the speakers, gunfingers waving, 2-step on point, and Jaegerbombs (with Monster Original, not Red Bull) are three for a fiver. Naturally they order six.

Dancing the night and their problems away, they spot him. 5 foot 7 balding white guy in blue bootcut jeans, a poorly ironed white shirt and polish deprived black shoes. He can't keep his eyes to himself any more than Jade can help herself from rolling hers out loud.

Intoxicated and emboldened by supermarket-brand whisky chased with warm lager; he makes his way over to Aria, who has turned her back to him to face bestie and continue their night undisturbed. Undeterred, he slides behind Aria. His odour is a war-crime-scale assault of cheap spilled booze, unwashed cheese dick hands, and enough Lynx Temptation to gas a school disco. If intoxicated, "high value male" delusion has a smell, this is it.

The pair reposition on the dancefloor, exchanging the "get a load of this fucking guy" looks, until the second approach comes with trespassing hands. *"You better get your fucking crusty hands off my girl, move from here, man."* whilst squaring firmly to Handsy Andy, bladed hands animated in his face. Before he has chance to even react, his jaw is clutched by a sizable hand, fingers perfectly on the mandible.

"Leave." with a glare of dangerous intensity at terrifying proximity, by South's answer to Kimbo Slice. After maintaining the glare long enough to incite a bit of wee coming out, Handsy Andy is discarded, scurrying like a rat caught in a flashlight.

Simultaneously Jade shrieks *"baybeee"* before throwing her arms around the neck of a slimmer-built, cheshire-cat grinning, skinny jean wearing, effortless cool cat.

"Babe, my mans, Green" Jade introduces the pair dragging them into a drunken besties, cheeks touching, three-way hug. *"That's my boy, Smoke"*, motions Green to SE15 Kimbo. Something tells Aria he's not much of a hugger, as he stoically nods greeting, handing out more Jaegerbombs. *I guess they're still three for a fiver.*

Green is an interesting sight, a light-skinned, slimmer, Carlton from *Fresh Prince,* with squared spectacles that are giving geek-chic, rather than visual impairment. Short king with a big personality, with a vibe and grin that radiates charisma.

By stark contrast, Smoke is huge. A sight to behold, at least six foot four, and probably the same width. Barely any fat in sight, if he was on the door you wouldn't even try to get in with trainers on, let alone a cheeky baggie in your bra. He airs danger and radiates power. His mere presence gives the feeling that violence is never more than a wrong word away.

The rest of the night goes exactly as you'd expect. High heels discarded. Vocal cords and eardrums tortured. Cheesy chips half eaten-left to congeal in Styrofoam. Makeup imprinted on otherwise perfect pillows. Rogue eyelashes adorning the kitchen countertops, whilst lone stilettos seek solace in random-ass places.

Chapter Two

"Save me, Uncle, I'm dying"

"Beta, you know where everything is," Uncle replies in his gentle Indian accent. Stacking cigarettes on the shelves behind the counter, *"I hear you two had a heavy night"* he continues with a chuckle, reaching past his well-loved belly to grab from the back shelf.

"Already seen my boys this morning then?" Jade replies casually

"I see them more than I see my Meena" Ash responds with a smile

She places four giant Red Bells on the countertop, and without asking Uncle places a pack of paracetamol and twenty Lambert and Butler on the counter.

"Green thought you'd be needing these" with a warm and familiar smile, *"is this your new friend?"*

"Uncle, this is Ree, she's stopping with me a while - Ree, meet Uncle Ash, this is his shop, and he knows the boys"

"It's my pleasure to meet you, Ree"

The gentle waft of a warm South Asian home makes its way through the store to the sound of wooden bead curtains touching one another with placid motion. A soft woman, emanating calm, domestic warmth through a tired face. She glows with the quiet kind of strength earned through decades of selfless giving, love, and devotion.

"Ashok, these girls don't want to listen to you all day - let them go" pauses, and continues defeatedly; *"that Liam boy called again, he's not coming to work... Oh, Suniye, I don't think he's coming back",* she stops for breath, considering her next sentence and delivering it softly *"and you've seen too many sunrises"*

Resigned and tired yet somehow still warm, Ash replies *"Meri jaan... I know. But what can I do, haan?"*.

Jade's eyes widen, like the 500ml of Red Bull that would've been slower consumed intravenously had suddenly given her life. *"My girl's looking for work!"* she spurts, Red Bull-laden spittle misting the air.

"Beta, come now, this is heavy work..." Ash begins, before being interrupted by a forceful smack on his arm from Meena.

"Arrey suno, don't be so bloody sexist, haan! You can't be so choosy - she's a strong, independent girl. At least give her a chance na?" interjects Meena, asserting the strength her years

have earned, slapping her *suniye's* arm, using the dangerously bladed hand hanging in midair to berate her beloved.

Stopping to consider his wrongdoing, or perhaps stopping to consider what it was he did wrong this time, he lets out a warm chuckle.

"6.30 tomorrow morning, work for you? Newspapers need shifting and shelves need loading, after that eh, I'm OK" Ashok replies, tilting his head and raising his palms slightly, glancing to check for the approval of his lifelong.

"That's, perfect, thank you so much - 6.30, I'll be here, bright and early" Ree over anxiously replies, with far too much speed and excitement. After a year of unpaid servitude and silent shrinking, this step feels overwhelming. Her beam makes her jaw bones ache.

With the business done, Meena effortlessly flicks back to Aunty mode in an instant; *"Beta, you look skinny, gaunt like a zombie! Have some Chai? Parantha? I can whip up some Khichdi, you're all bone!"*

"Thank you, Auntie, we've good. Love you, bless! Bye Uncle!" Jade shouts over her shoulder, blowing a kiss to the happy pair, with her arm wrapped around Ree's neck in a not-quite-headlock hug as she swags her way back onto the high street.

A few doors down, they find the kind of café where the chairs are bolted to the floor and the smell of "definitely not Heinz" red sauce ominously lingers in the air. This isn't just a greasy spoon, this is literally called *Greasy Spoon Cafe*. *"What you saying bossman? 2 breakfasts with like, fucking everything - and 2 teas, 87 sugars in each, nice one"*, before taking a seat. Ree follows along, she didn't need to read the menu anyway.

A few minutes of silent scrolling for Ree, and a few minutes of a folded-arm as a pillow nap for Jade, later. Two plates appear. The kind of grease that could make the table see-through, is exactly what the doctor ordered. *"You can't drink that in here"* says the barely legal waiter, motioning to Jade's Red Bull, the second of four she's going to sink. A quiet kiss of her teeth and a strong *"do I look like a dickhead?"* rhetorical retort, with a "way too intense for 9am" stare from Jade. Something clatters in the kitchen, which sends the waiter boy shuffling back to wash some dishes or something. A tut and an eye-roll later, Jade is devouring the plate with the kind of ferocity usually reserved for drink spillers and shoe-scuffers.

"I guess you know them, then?" Ree enquires casually of the couple in the shop.

"Yeah, that's Uncle and Auntie, they own the shop. They know Green and Smoke, practically raised them init. You know how it is out here, but the kids never go cold or hungry, 'cause of them, they're real ones"

"Why do they keep calling you Beta? That's kind of rude?"

"Don't be a dickhead, Beta mean 'daughter' in Hindi init", through a semi masticated concoction of sausage, hash brown, and beans

"Aw, that's sweet"

"I told you, girl, real ones... it's like you don't even listen for real"

With an over emphasis on Queen, playing on this faux social hierarchy *"Well, where to next then, Queen"*, raising an eyebrow

"Dev's, the Gym", she gestures with her knife across the street.

It's an old red brick building with window bars, maybe it used to be a workhouse or Victorian punishment block. Flat zero aesthetic charm, the kind of place that looks like the arm chairs will have tattoos, and the first question on the membership form will be "what the fuck are you looking at?".

Still, when you're following Jade around, you do as she says and you'll be alright. BMX's strewn the footpath, belonging to the most undesirable set of roadmen-turn-bouncers you could ask for, and a gleaming BMW parked out the front.

"After eating all this?"

*"Pussy. It's fight fuel, I'm built **different**"* retorts Jade, flexing her arm muscles, before confessing *"and Dev will kill me if I*

miss a day, and if Dev's vexed so is Green and it's a whole fucking thing"

Chapter Three

Leaving the front door to swing behind her, and slinging her bag on the floor, Jade opens her locker. While Ree stands taking in the scene, almost like an alien world.

This place is huge, almost like a warehouse. Though it feels more like a church. It's a shrine to physical fitness, built for the expressed purpose of violence. No frills, just weight benches, a ring, and an assortment of punchbags. A small group of guys walk in, nodding acknowledgement to the desk.

As her eyes adjust, Ree notices the way sounds in here ring like an auditorium. The bassline barely registers beneath the panting, grunting, and that sharp *tss tss* sound of gloves meeting pads. Skipping ropes slap the floor in rhythm. Big lift bars clang in the corners. No one's chatting. No one's posing.

Everyone's dialled in.

This certainly isn't Bannaytnes, David Lloyd, or one of those spa gyms. There are changing rooms off to the side, but mostly people just change their kit at the lockers in the corner.

A few coaches around the room can be heard giving instruction to those they're training. There's a lad who is clearly twice the weight he should be, being verbally pushed by one of the coaches. Through sweat and struggle he perseveres, but surely he's not far from breaking.

In the ring a coach with thai pads works with a lad who looks to be in his late teens or early twenties. He's working relentlessly, and the coach just keeps pushing. Every kick, every punch is delivered with a roar, with audible power and recoil almost unsettling the pad holder's footwork.

"You're late" comes a deep voice from the desk, not looking up. Entirely unphased and unbothered. This must be Dev, his name's above the door. Chest and shoulder muscles bursting through his compression top, as his durag hangs. *"Warm up. Medicine ball slams, 100, get them done"* he commands. Uncharacteristically, there's no retort, no attitude, no sass from Jade at this. She nods and gets to work, leaving Ree unsure what to do.

"You wanna train?" enquiries the coach behind the desk, tone completely shifting from dealing with Jade, to a more customer facing, humanised one for Ree. Before she can answer, a frustrated shout from a distant coach. *"In the bucket, not on the mats!"* followed by the unmistakeable sound of retching. Then what sounds like litres of water hit the bottom of the bucket, as the unfortunate athlete gasps for air. With a dry laugh, the coach adds *"maybe not like that - first week is free, train as much as you want. You ever trained before?"*, a wide eyed Ree stares back, blankly, unanswering. *"Take these, you can borrow them for the week"* as he hands over some ratty looking boxing gloves, the smell - added to her

hangover - nearly makes her puke. *"I'm Dev, need anything give me a shout, I'm sure you can show yourself round".*

Trackies and a t-shirt might not be ideal, but it's good enough to start. Slipping the gloves on, she wanders around looking for an available punchbag. The only one available is huge, the biggest heavy bag in the room. Maybe that means something about what it's for, but just hit it, how hard can it be, right? Feet parallel to the bag, she swings a fist back and hits the bag. It doesn't make any kind of impressive sound, it just kind of, moves a bit. She takes a nervous look around, observing for someone going slow enough for her to copy. She spots someone who looks to be working lighter, maybe they're closer to her ability - which at this precise moment, is exactly zero.

The round timer beeps, and the noise around her quietens. Hands up, she pushes the fingers of her gloves to her chin. One foot in front of the other this time, not together. She unleashes another punch from her rear hand. This one makes a noise, not an impressive noise, but something, and the bag moves a bit. She tries again, this time with the front hand first, following with the back. *I'm not a pro, but this is **fun**.*

She goes again, and again, and again, before she's throwing what feels like hundreds of punches, in a furious flurry, moving the bag more and more, getting more and more into it. Freedom, power, it's all flowing now and it feels amazing. The timer beeps again. She stops to catch her breath. The gym erupts with the sounds of people working, bags being hit, coaches instructing.

Oh my God! Her hands hurt. Like beyond hurt. *What the fuck?* She slips off her gloves and there's no visible damage, but the pain is all too real. She stares at her hands, with no idea what to do next.

A low chuckle, and a huge presence. She sees Smoke approaching. He's worked up a sweat, skin glistening against the lights, towel easily hung around his shoulders. *"First time?"* he asks, already knowing the answer. He takes her hand, in both of his, and feels and massages them one at a time. *"You need these"*, he says, ripping open a new pack of hand wraps.

"You do it like this", gently taking her hand, he puts her thumb through the loop before wrapping her hand, not dissimilar to a bandage. A loop round the back of the hand to above the thumb, then under the thumb and two around the wrist, before working between each of the fingers. Before she knows it she has a hand wrapped. *"It's for support"* he adds, whilst wrapping her second hand.

She appreciates the tenderness and the gesture, but concedes *"I don't know if I'm ready for another round just yet"*, which is, confusingly, met with a lot of laughter. *"You haven't done a round yet, you did the rest between rounds, a cool 60 seconds - but that's your hands sorted for today. Try working nice and slow, basic footwork, just a 1-2 - you don't need power yet, just form"*, he instructs, before demonstrating on the bag.

"Try that bag instead, and keep your hands up" he adds, motioning to a significantly lighter looking punch bag a few stations down. Ree makes her way down, taking on the advice, and starts studiously trying to work and improve. *How did he make so much power, such dents in the bag, without even trying?*

Smoke goes back to where he was working, giant's shoulders rising like mountains from his vest. Headphones on he works a mixture of deadlifts and squats, followed by some rounds on the heavy bag Ree was previously using. Expertly weaving punches and kicks together with devastating power and precision. *How's that even possible? I don't know anything, but I can't see a human surviving being hit like that.*

Mid thought flow, arms heavy and lungs burning an arm hugs its way around Ree's shoulder, it's a considerably fresher looking Jade. *"You good, girl?"* she asks, Ree non-verbally responds; with a shrug and a *"mmhhmm"*. *"Aite, I'll be working"*, and quickly as she came, she disappears.

Against one of the walls is an old, tattered looking sofa. The kind you'd find in a taxi office you stumble into at 3am. It looks like a good place for a rest, and maybe a nap, so Ree heads over there waiting for Jade to finish.

"Yes bro, you good" comes a voice from the entrance, as Green walks in, fist bumping Dev. He must be here for Smoke. There's another guy with him, no fist bumps for him, just a firm and sincere handshake and nod. He's pretty unremarkable really. Dressed in all black, cargos, boots, hoodie; in contrast to Green's skinny jeans and converse and colourful choice of shirt. *"Smoke! Mashallah my brother"*, with a huge grin behind his square specs, this greeting is met with a warm hug and some quiet chat, whilst Dev has his own quiet conversation with the Hoodie.

Smoke and Green head back over to the weights, where Smoke carries on working, Green encouraging him - even though Green looks like he couldn't lift his own bodyweight himself. Mr Hoodie eventually finishes chatting with Dev, who gets back to doing something on his phone, whilst Hoodie walks around the gym, greeting people and seemingly exchanging pleasantries.

Once the bell for the end of the round goes, he effortlessly jumps into the ring, greeted with handshake-hugs, and starts talking to the coach and the fighter-looking fella. They seem eager to listen to what he has to say. He fist bumps the coach and ruffles the fighter's hair before jumping back out of the ring, and heading in the direction of Green and Smoke.

Ree dozes off in situ. She's jolted awake by a huge sigh and Jade dropping herself onto the sofa. She swings her legs to go across Ree's lap, with a stretch and yawn. *"Needed that, notch the bitchometer down a bit - how'd you find it?"*

"Yeah... good... I think" says Ree, looking down at her still-wrapped hands thoughtfully, and looking up just in time to see the Hoodie leaving, with Smoke and Green two steps behind.

Chapter Four

Ree's been moving like a bit of a ghost through the last couple of weeks. She's fallen into a habit, but she doesn't hate it. Early mornings working with Ash, it's nothing exciting, just helping him with the stuff that his body doesn't want him to do any more. Sometimes Meena brings food and snacks in from the house. Delicious treats from foreign lands, made with love.

Followed by afternoons in the gym. Smoke's been helping some more, but she's feeling sore. The expectant triumph isn't coming very quickly, and enthusiasm is fading. *I'm just not getting any better.*

The water just can't seem to heat up enough to take the sting away. From her hands and wrists, shoulders and core. Jade's out with Green, so she's got the place to herself, *finally.*

She stands in the shower and just reflects. Taking a deep breath and massaging everywhere that hurts, so, everywhere. Letting the lather just rinse away.

Smoke's been helping her most days, but the lack of progress is infuriating. Even if he says she's getting better, it doesn't *feel* like it.

*I can see why Jade loves it here though, she's built such a family. She's got Green, and Smoke's like their brother, third wheeling. Ash and Meena giving some parental affection that she's never really had before. That **I've** never had before. OK, so it's not the postcard London. But there's community here. Whether they say it out loud or not, there's love.*

As she rinses the final bubbles of shampoo from her hair, she looks at her hands, the hands that Smoke has dutifully wrapped for her every day, saying things like *"You're going to have to learn to do this yourself, you know?"* with a small smile. *Smoke's smile is so intriguing. His eyes betray his emotions more than his face ever does. He says so very little, but he says it with his whole heart, and his whole chest. I don't fancy sparring with him though. Jade keeps trying to push me to spar, but I'm just not sure I'm ready to be getting punched in the face.* She laughs at the ridiculous notion of having a fight. She managed to avoid it her whole life, why would she now do it for fun, when she's getting hurt hitting a punch bag for fucks sake.

A gentle knocking at the door *"Ree, you in there babes?"* comes Jade's voice, *"Yeah give me a minute, I'll be right out"* Ree hurriedly replies. Jade probably needs the bathroom for something, she can't hog from her. *"No rush, you're good"*.

Ree breathes a sigh of relief. It seems so insignificant, yet so powerful. To have agency over how long to use the shower, when she's ready to come out, and have that physical boundary respected. It's profound in its idiocy. A quick scrub of her face, and a drawn out moment. A breath of steam, a moment of complete embracing autonomy and freedom.

This freedom gives her time and space to think, to breathe. To remember her wants. Her needs. She still has them. Oh God she still has them.

Dried off and in her dressing down, she walks into the living room, Jade's chilling with a root beer watching some Netflix crap on the telly. *'Thinking about ol' Big Smoke in there, were ya?"* Jade retorts with a smirk. Ree doesn't reply. Not because Jade's right, but because she couldn't be more wrong.

Smoke is an attractive guy, in a massive black guy that could tear a bear's head off without sweating, a terrifying kind of way. But he's not that guy, to her. She has an emotional, even intimate connection with him. Just not, like that.

Whilst pondering the connection she actually *does* have with Smoke, Jade grows impatient. *'Excuse me, yeah, hi, back in the room".*

'I don't know exactly how it is, but it's not like that with Smoke" Ree admits, and honestly it's not like she'd gotten any

vibe from Smoke either, there's closeness but no chemistry,

"he's just safe, as fuck". Jade nods, she gets it, *"girl, I feel you, same"*.

"So, got yourself a little job, you've got yourself into the gym. Slay. But what about a man, if it ain't Smoke, then who?"

The audacity of this Queen takes Ree by surprise, no fight no flight, just freeze. No response, but maybe Jade's right. The furrowed brow gives it away to Jade, who seizes the opportunity.

"Girl, find a man, jump on his dick, it ain't that deep... well, unless you're lucky" she laughs carelessly *"gimme your phone, I gotchu"*. The drinks flow through the night as Jade progressively convinces Ree that actually it might be fun to swipe on other humans.

They laugh at the expense of many a poor, desperate man, and they swipe. And they swipe, and they swipe some more. Nearly all left, but there's a few decent choices there, or maybe a few wine-induced lapses in judgement. Jade is the expert coach and apparently now the manager and co-ordinator of Ree's newfound dating freedom. Somehow the driver's seat changes position, as Jade goes from encouraging, to coaching, to just driving herself as Ree's intoxication gives way to fatigue. She opens her eyes only to grunt an approval, grant a smirk or otherwise acknowledge and approve of Jade's antics.

"There you go, Ree. 8pm tomorrow night, at Mario's for Pizza. Nice and casual, nothing to worry about"

Ree awakens and is vaguely aware of what she's told, a little chuckle turns into a deep, wine fuelled snore.

Chapter Five

Day number - who's fucking counting any more. Grey mornings in a grey city, brightened only by Ashok's warmth and Meena's beautifully colourful choice of saris. Uneventful, if you don't count the spectacular cream soda apocalypse courtesy of some kid who thought sprinting in sliders was a good idea.

She clocks out and heads across the road to Dev's. Though this time there's no Smoke to be seen. His absence aches a little, like when your older sibling leaves home. Ree manages, through trial, error and seemingly endless frustration, to wrap her hands herself. She keeps training basic, working on one-twos, leg height roundhouse kicks, and lead hooks in varying combinations. Smoke had told her this was a good way to work, gradually expanding your technical vocabulary, including a new technique or two infrequently, and working them into your arsenal.

She's starting to feel confident in the gym, becoming confident, maybe dangerous. She could probably handle herself in a fight. She's probably done more than most at this point, right? Then it dawns on her; in about 4 hours, she has a date. An actual date, with a man from Tinder. Oh God, what does he even look like? What's Jade done? Anxiety creeps all over her.

Diving into her phone head first, she scrolls back to the messages. Okay, found him. Alright, actually Jade's not done badly here. Darren, he's 40 years old, never married, no kids, ooh he's a solicitor. He's not bad looking either. Alright, this is going to be alright. Or at least, it will be, after a cheeky glass.

Half of the makeup in her tiny bag in the suitcase has never seen the light of day. Maybe it's been applied, to be hurriedly washed off after a nasty word, or just the reverberation of the impact of those words. It takes an embarrassingly long time to get date ready. *Why does **everything** need doing?*

Like seriously, chin and cheek fluff, eyebrows, legs, armpits; it's like mass deforestation. *Greenpeace are going to show up and blame me for global warming soon!* This man had better be worth it. After everywhere, well nearly everywhere, is done she stands. With a razor in one hand, as she thumbs through her pubes in the other. Cal hated it groomed down there, another bit of slut shaming, some weird misplaced infantilisation. But maybe it would be sexy, she always liked it shaved before.

So she does, she inflicts righteous depilation on her pubic vegetation. It's almost vengeful. But it's done, now to bathe in body lotion and spend the next 4-5 working days drying off listening to *Ne-Yo* and *Chris Brown*.

Feeling silky and daring to entertain the idea of feeling, even maybe a little bit sexy. It takes another slightly generous gulp of wine before she steps into her favourite La Senza set. Matching frenchies and a lacy bra. Not too supportive, but when you don't like the picture, you may as well get a pretty frame, right? It's hard for her to exactly pinpoint what she doesn't like, when she sees herself. Sure she can highlight all the imperfections, but even if those imperfections weren't erased, she knows she still wouldn't like what she sees.

Tight, very dark blue, high waisted jeans - hiding the calorific sins that are inevitable in a house where Jade does the cooking. A nice top, white, more low cut than she'd perhaps normally wear but only a little, with loose flared sleeves that scream "I'm a free soul". Well they do until they accidentally hang in a drink, or the sauce... or she accidentally hands them over an open flame.

An open flame, really Ree? Is immolation not a bit far fetched, for a first date?

The mirror nearly de-steamed, and she checks herself out from behind. *It's hard to like your own reflection.* But this view is, well, tolerable. And actually my ass is firming up a bit, it's getting some shape to it. Must be all the kicking and lifting heavy ass boxes of cans and shit. Some nice shoes, respectable heels, only a few inches and chunky. It's been a while and the last thing we need is a *Sandra Bullock Miss Congeniality* moment, flying down the stairs.

Am I over-dressed, for a first date? Eesh, I hope I don't look desperate. No this is fine, girl you look fine. She knows, deep down, it's Cal's criticisms she can hear, and she tries her damnedest to drown them out for what they are - complete bullshit.

Handbag check - right... phone, lipstick, gloss, powder, concealer, mascara and shadow - just in case. Perfume, house key.

Palpitations, her chest goes tight. Breathing gets harder and dizziness begins to set in.

You're just anxious, Aria. Stop, you're okay. 5 things you can see... the front door, the erm, the light switch... vase, coffee table... key bowl. 4 things I can feel... the wallpaper, the rug, sofa fabric, 3 things I can hear... the traffic, the neighbours dog, my own breathing... 2 things I can smell... my perfume, the wine... something I can taste... cherry lip gloss. Jesus, kid. Really, all this, to eat a fucking pizza. Get a grip.

A small chuckle and she closes the door behind her, nothing to it but to do it. It's a pretty short walk to Mario's, even in the short heels. In hindsight flats to get there and then changing into the heels might have been a good idea, but seriously when Google Maps says "0.3 miles" it seems crazy to think you can't walk it. It's fine, not tiring, just a little more time consuming than perhaps we'd like.

She stands outside, waiting for... *crap*... she checks her phone... Darren. *What if he stands me up? Damn, girl, what* would Jade say if she could hear you thinking like this? It's going to be fine.

"Hiya, Air-e-uh?"

"Hey" - she smiles sweetly - "it's Arr-ee-uh, actually, you must be Darren?"

A kind of awkward hug, he plants a kiss on her cheek. *Bit forward I guess, but like, I didn't hate it.*

"Shall we go in?" he suggests, and she politely obliges.

Casual pleasantries flow into such a cascade of conversation, chat is so easy with Darren. He's laid back, intelligent, well informed. He's polite, and thoughtful. Kind to the serving staff. And he shares the garlic bread. Bonus.

Service is slow, but that works for both of them. They're enjoying the company, easy jokes, no really taxing topics of conversation. They actually kind of hit it off, *this guy's nice.* She finds herself growing more attracted to him, and more open to the idea of physical intimacy, as the time goes on. Naturally the courses flow. So does the wine. Before they know it they've talked about everything and nothing for 2 hours, and dessert has arrived.

As they speak, he's not just waiting for his turn to talk. He's actively listening, engaged, with open body language, he recalls what she's said, questions thoughtfully, refers back to it later. *Guys can **listen**, who knew?! Is this what comfortable feels like?*

It's been a couple of hours, but neither of them are ready for tonight to end yet. She starts absent mindedly walking back in the direction of home, he strolls alongside her. As they walk, she notices his hand brush against hers. Flutters, just baby ones, but they're definitely there. She smiles a little, and let's them brush together again before interlacing her fingers with his. They meander vaguely in the direction of home.

Distracted by chat, she nearly steps into the path of a night bus. Luckily he's paying attention, he stops at the crossing, and pulls her back by the hand, saving her from becoming roadkill. *That would've been a bummer. I guess it was lucky he was paying attention, and was holding my hand so tight.*

They cross the street, conversation turning to the best gigs, concerts, or shows they've ever been to, and it almost gets heated for a second. *"If you think the Artful Dodger can really outwork Avicii you need to put the pipe down, that's wild, you cannot be serious"*, this must be one of those really dry senses of humour. It's not that deep, he must be a megafan or something, because he kind of meant that. *"Alright fanboy"*, she laughs, but isn't too sure he's found her particular brand of humour funny. His silence lasts like a second too long for Ree's comfort, but then she's going to be over sensitive, her ex was a class A cunt, and she never saw that coming, *obviously she's going to be weary and see shit that isn't there. Bro just **really** likes Avicii, and like he is dead now.*

They continue walking, and the little awkward speed bump dissipates. They talk about music and movies, they really have the same tastes in a lot of stuff. They share stories from childhood, juvenile antics and they laugh over mutual experiences - even if they didn't know each other back then.

Before even realising it, they're in front of the chicken shop and walk together to the door as Ree fobs them through the main door. Conversation continues flowing as they crunch through the old paint, flaking onto the floor. They stop while Ree fumbles her keys into the old Yale lock, when she realises she never told Darren where she lives, yet he seemed familiar. *Well, he was probably just walking with me. You're being crazy. Not everyone's a psycho.*

"Make yourself comfy. Is red okay?" she asks, dropping her keys onto the side and making her way round the kitchen countertop.

"Actually, could I have water? The wine's going straight to my head tonight" he replies easily. Glasses in hand she makes her way to the sofa, where he's sat himself down and made

space for her under his wing. It looks so inviting, inevitable in its comfort. She cozies in, and snuggles in under his arm.

Idly flipping through the channels, he pulls her gently closer, kissing the side of her head. Flutters, as she melts into him some more, closing her eyes. Enjoying the affection and closeness, just for a moment.

He shuffles slightly, turning to face her, as his opposite hand sits on her thigh. It doesn't linger long, before making it's way over her top to her face. He cups her cheek, so gently. *Flutters!* Involuntarily, she bites her lip. Raising her eyes to meet his, passing from his chest to his chin, and finally meeting his gaze. He leans in, she doesn't pull away.

His lips meet hers, and they're intertwined. Heart racing, hands shaking. Gently at first, then more forceful, passionate, explosive. *A bit much, actually.* She pulls away slightly catching her breath, his hands reach to the bottom of her top and she instinctively raises her arms for him to remove her top for her.

Taking a moment to admire her newly revealed body, he looks her up and down, before licking his lips. What happens next can only be described as some terrible attempt at wrestling, as he attempts to dive directly on top of her, pushing her to her back. *That's... enthusiastic.*

His weight starting to press down on her, his mouth fully invading hers. With his left hand to the side of her head, his right hand makes its way to her jean button. It's unbuttoned and unzipped a little too quickly for her liking. She manages to wiggle her head away from the oral invasion and to the side, *"slow down baby"*.

But he's preoccupied, his hand playing around the top of her matching bottoms. Mouth magnetically reattached to hers. As his finger tip grazes her hood, she realises how not ready she is. Physically and emotionally. *"Darren.. wait"*.

Like a freight train, and undeterred he persists. *"Get off me!"* as her knees come up between their chests and she pushes him off with her legs and hands.

Leaning back in, he negotiates *"Oh come on Air-e-uh, we both know you want it. You've teased me all night... and wore those..."* hungry eyes devouring her bra and the top of her frenchies.

"Get the fuck out" but his looming approach, and intended violation, evident she does that which she's never done before. Her hands raise, face protected behind her forearms. Those forearms are her shield now. Her hands clench and with a battle cry of *"No!"* she feels teeth on her right fist.

Eyes widening, she realises what she's done. Blood appears on his now split lip, his eyes widen before narrowing. He pulls his hand back, she braces behind her arms. Then the weight is gone, and carnage ensues. She can't hear a thing, adrenaline whistling through her ears.

In what seemed like slow motion Jade has gotten home, and seemingly realising what's going on; straight up speared this prick from his upright position, into some kind of chaotic bundle at the opposite end of the sofa on the floor by the wall. In a display of feral femininity Jade rains unholy fury on Darren's curled up body.

"That'll do, babes" comes Green's somehow still calm voice. Jade clambers to her feet, sticking one final punt in. As if approaching a wounded bird, she takes the seat next to Ree. *"You're okay, girl we gotchu"* holding her tight, encasing Ree's head into an absolute bear grip.

Green calmly strolls to the still panicked and now beaten Darren. A hunting knife appears from the back of his skinny jeans. He expertly chambers his knee and stomps a kick onto Darren's pitiful skull. Three or four more. Then Green crouches in front of him. His hand on Darren's forehead, holding it steady. His right hand pointing the knife firmly at Darren's face. *"Forget this address and forget Ree. You understand? You don't want this smoke, big man."* When Darren fails to respond, Green hits him with the butte of the knife to the temple. *"Yo big man, don't ignore me, it's rude. Ya understand me?"*.

Darren manages not much more than a nod, before clambering to his feet, certainly unsteady, certainly rocked. As fast as his legs can carry him he's out the door. Whether he ran or fell down the stairs is anyone's guess. But he was gone.

Slowly Green paces his way to the front door, locks and bolts it. Without a word, he returns to the sofa, with Ree in the middle, and Jade to her left. He lowers himself beside them, and wraps his arms around the pair of them. Jade still shaking with rage - maybe even fear, Ree frozen in disbelief and shock. Under his arms, the pair of them exhale their tension and melt into one another further.

An uneasy peace settles amongst the trio over the next 10 minutes or so. Then the door knocks. Loud, but not intimidating. Green jumps up and bounds his way to the door, not even checking the spy hole to see who it is. Smoke makes his way in slowly, with two unmarked carrier bags.

*"Motherfucker where's **my** chicken?"* Green teases, to an eyebrow raise and an eye roll from Smoke.

Green takes his place back on the sofa with Jade, as Smoke pulls a beanbag from under the coffee table and sits himself down. Bucket of chicken between his legs like a toddler, and he dives in face first like he's never seen food before. Not feral, but certainly not paced. He gulps Diet Pepsi straight from the 2 litre bottle. When he catches his breath he looks up at Ree, who is clearly aghast at the rate of chicken consumption. He simply shrugs and answers her unasked question *"Cheat day"* before returning to demolishing the family sized bucket.

Ten thousand calories of chicken later, Smoke takes out the wet wipe from its packaging and cleans his hands and fingers, and pats his mouth dry with a serviette. *What a distinguished gentleman.* An internal chuckle. His presence, as quietly comical as it is, is deeply reassuring. Everyone seems to settle when he's around.

"Bro, watch this..." suggests Green to Smoke, gesturing to the now paused live-TV. It's *One Championship*, Green hits play to show an action replay of a devastating flying knee, landing flush on a poor, already rocked, opponent. He's out like a light" *"Boom! Get wrecked, diiiickhead"* laughs Green, to an impressed Smoke.

The evening continues on, highlight reals of the Kickboxing. Fight-porn from TikTok and Insta Reels. Generally just chilling, safe in one another's company. Maybe not quite as central to the group as the other three, Ree is deeply thankful for their presence.

As they chill and relax, the mood lifts. Ree is mindlessly scrolling her phone, disturbed by a low chuckle, and the sound of kissing. Raising her head from her phone, she risks a peak at the lovers sharing her sofa. Jade is curled up to Green, whispering something in his ear. He's smiling slightly, his eyes not leaving Jade's, whilst hers look him up and down. Ree's gaze naturally follows Jade's, to realise she has a hand down the front of his jeans. She's not working, just holding. Jade carries on punctuating kisses with short sentences in his ear.

Sliding her hand out from his jeans, Jade mounts her partner. His hands instinctively take hold of her arse, as she places a passionate kiss on his lips. She grinds backwards and forwards in his hand, her crotch on his. Tease complete, she climbs off and takes his hand. Leading him to the bedroom.

Paralysed by the rawness of their affections, Ree helplessly glances at Smoke. He just makes a face and shrugs that says *"same shit, different day"* and makes his way to the kitchenette, sorting his rubbish into waste, recyclable, and dry cardboard. He makes his way back to Ree, who hasn't moved an inch.

Standing a few inches from her, he takes the back of her neck and gives her a tight hug, pulling her to his abdomen, for no more than a second. *"Tomorrow, kid"* and places the lightest of kisses on the very top of her head *"bolt the door behind me"*, casually making his exit.

She does as instructed, and bolts the door. Turning to lean backwards on it after his departure. A man feeling *so safe* is a world rocking culture shock, and she's *here for it*.

"That knife.... it's going in someone tonight...." Jade's breathy fantasies whispered, carrying effortlessly through the now near-silent apartment *"oh God, yes"* after a couple of seconds.

Three guesses what's going on in there, the wide eyed revelation that *hopefully the handle* is now inside her bestie. *That's kinda, fucked, right?*

55

Only having the soundtrack to go by left a lot to the imagination.

Jade's quiet whispers turn into audible moans. *She's not the type to fake it, he must be **good**. "It's yours daddy, fucking make me take it, you wreck my pussy so good"*. The speed and strength of the headboard hitting the wall increases. With definitive pause between slams and creaks. Probably giving her half a second to feel his full length before he rips it out and slams it in again.

With absolutely no desire for Green, the thought *lucky bitch* finds its way intrusively into the front of Ree's mind.

Seasoned tastefully on top of their clearly filthy sex, was the sounds of flesh hitting skin. *That sounds fucking hard* as Jade's moans start to reach their crescendo, and Green's grunting moans add to the mix. And then the end. The vocal sigh. They collapse onto the mattress and the bed frame gives a final triumphant creek.

A few moments later, Jade emerges, bare legged. In nothing but pants and Green's oversized hoodie. He follows her out, his arm over her shoulder. Shirtless, but at least with his jeans on. Still breathing slightly heavier than normal, and with definite, deep scratch marks across his chest.

Clocking eyes with Ree, a cheeky smile and a *"girl"* with a lip bite, followed by *"sorry not sorry"* from Jade, and his signature grin with *"gotta do what ya gotta do"* from Green as they grab Diet Cokes from the fridge.

Blushing and smiling from the awkwardness, eyes to the floor Ree makes her way to her own bedroom. Closing the door behind her, and laying on her bed. Mixed emotions run rampant.

*What a fucking **dick** Darren is. What the actual fuck is Jade into? Dirty bitch..... Smoke never did share that fucking chicken.*

Chapter Six

"Here again? You're dedicated, I'll give you that" comes Dev's voice from behind the desk as Ree makes her way through the doors to the lockers. There's another man at the desk today. Mediterranean looking, not too tall, black hair. He probably used to be an absolute unit, but has eased up on the calorie control by the looks of it. Crisp white shirt, maybe one too many buttons undone but it works for him. Thick, yellow gold chains adorn his olive neck and wrist. Raybans hang from his top button. He looks like he's plenty of money, but would haggle you over €1 on a €1,000 purchase, whilst checking the time on his gold Rolex.

Wrapping her hands is effortless now, as she recites her training plan..

12 rounds of work today. 3 on skipping for stamina and bounce, 8 rounds on the light bag broken into 4 sets of 2 rounds. 2 rounds of Boxing combos, 2 rounds of kickboxing combos, 2 rounds of mixing, and 2 rounds of mixing out the fast shots for the power shots. Then a final maximum effort round on the heavy bag - 60/40 split on hands and feet. 36 minutes, 11 minutes of rest. Light work. She can almost hear Smoke's voice telling her it's easy.

It's not going to be easy, I'm going to die.

The timer goes. Her heart rate settles. She gets skipping. All in a day's work. Working at this intensity has become her peace -

her paradise in Peck-'nam. She recognises regulars as she moves between bags and walks off the stiffness in the rest rounds. Mostly it's casual nods. The occasional fist bump. The *first* fist bump made her feel like an absolute G. Now? All part of the game. *"They're all here for the same thing, to work".*

She recalls Dev's attempt at comfort after a particularly devastating session near the beginning.

Five rounds in. Rhythm building. Flow arriving. Hamstrings loosening up with the motion. Dev appears over her shoulder, but she doesn't allow herself to be distracted. *"Good work, champ. There we go, if you can't do anything else, move. Every move sets up the next, don't get caught dead on your heels"* he punctuates in her drills, his rhythm layered on top of her.

*Why the hell is it always scarier working when **he's** watching?*

The round timer goes off. *"Alright kid, you're warm. Go get some rest, new day, new challenge. Don't go anywhere. Stay warm"*, and he leaves. Dev always instructs, he never negotiates or suggests. *What the hell am I meant to do now?* Ree heads to her locker. *He said stay warm.* She throws her hoodie on. She recognises the ridiculousness of being in a baggy hoodie and tiny Thai shorts, but whatever. She half-effort shadow spars, light jogs on the spot, side strides, usual movement stuff that she guesses is right, based on watching other people do it around the gym.

Jade comes through the door, quickly followed by Green and Smoke - deep in conversation about which era of *Dr Dre* was the best - and followed by the hoodie. He never seems to be all that far away from Green and Smoke.

"Kalispera, Rizzy, my friend! Come, let me show you!" booms the Greek voice from behind the desk to the hoody. Rizzy smiles warmly, his handshake turning into a bro's embrace. *"Dimos, good to see you brother"* before Dimos 'phone is thrust under Rizzy's nose. Rizzy silently watches. *"I'm telling you, it's legit, it's all money, those looks won't last forever, eh?"* he grins, playfully slapping Rizzy's cheek a few times.

"Girl" Jade greets Ree with a tight embrace, before stripping her hoodie, and wrapping her hands, pacing and bouncing a little. Just getting loose.

"Jade, bad news. Chantel's not coming" Dev delivers the news before finishing his coolly paced approach, to be met by a cold stare and silence from Jade. Dev's far too confident to be intimidated in his own gym, so he just returns the glare.

Jade allows a singular, under-breathed, grunt of frustration. She said so much, without using a single syllable. *"You know I've always got a plan, not quite Plan A, but something"* Dev continues flatly before glancing at Ree.

He doesn't need to see if anyone's interested before delivering the plan, he knows Jade's on board. *"Kid, you're doing great on the bags and the pads. But they don't hit back. 3 rounds. That's six minutes of work, two minutes rest. You'll be done before my Deliveroo gets here"*.

If Ree's eyes opened any further, she'd be able to see inside her own damned fivehead.

In the absence of protest, Dev slaps Ree on top of the shoulder. He may as well have dusted off his hands - decision made, day saved - and heads back to his desk to order his curried goat.

Practically skipping, Green with his trademark way-too-big smile, bounds towards them impersonating a cheap boxing caller *"Ladies ladies ladies! The show of the season, the Queen of Mean! 3 rounds of chaaaaampionship kickboxing action, let's get ready to ruuuuumbleeeeee"*. Smoke walks casually behind, focus mitts on his hands. He's rolled up the sleeves on his hoodie. He means business today.

A quick hug, close and strong, from Jade and she leaves with Green. Bobbing and bouncing on the balls of her feet, just loosening off.

Smoke nods towards a corner of the gym, for Ree to follow him. Ree still has no real idea what's going on, Smoke senses it, so explains *"don't worry. It's just another day in the office.*

It's just sparring. Keep moving, keep your hands up, keep it simple. Don't overthink it." and then he raises his focus mitts running the usual drills. 1-2-leg kick. 1-2-roll-2. 1-2-roll-2-lead hook. Subtle encouragement, no corrections today. *I must be killing it.* Sets of five on the round kicks against the mitts, and the sound slaps. *Yes, let's go.*

"Time, ladies. Let's get to work" booms the Greek across the hall. *I guess he didn't need to use the PA for us to hear him, eh?*

Stomach drops. Smoke notices, hands on the back of Ree's shoulders as she walks towards the ring, giving gentle reassuring massages. *"You've got this, you'll be fine, just* **move***".*

Awkwardly, Ree climbs between the 1st and 2nd rope and stands frozen. Jade, by contrast, slips between the 3rd and 4th. Jade walks into the centre of the ring, brings her hands together in her gloves like she's praying, and gives a small bow - like a nod - to Smoke. She turns and does the same to Dev, and to Green. Finally, she faces Ree and bows again - the same, nothing less.

Ree has no idea what to do, so tries to return the bow. Awkward and uncomfortable, and painfully aware of it. To Ree, this is foreign. To Jade, it's ritual and sacred. She treats the ring with reverence, and her opponent the respect they deserve.

Dimos climbs into the ring. Far too confident for a man whose belly barely squeezes between the ropes. The confidence comes from somewhere, but it sure isn't his physique - or shouldn't be.

"Ladies, we're all friends here. Friendly sparring, but that doesn't mean it's not serious. Stick to the rules, protect yourselves at all times"

Jade heads to Green, so Ree copies and does the same. A quick squirt of water into her mouth, and Smoke slips her gumshield in, and fastens the strap on her headguard. He turns her by her shoulders and gives her the gentlest of nudges towards the middle of the ring, where Jade is already waiting, focused.

A quick nod to both ladies from Dimos, and the round timer goes. Jade holds a glove extended, and Ree recognises this, she taps the glove with her own. A fist bump of respect.

After the bump, Jade inhales through her nose and gets on the balls of her feet. Ree copies and does the same. 1-2, swift but not heavy, they land on Ree's high guard. *But like, I still punched **myself** in the face - how's that better?!* Jade's floating now, changing angles it's impossible to aim at her, and as soon as Ree is facing her, she gets jabbed and Jade's gone.. again.

"Wake up now - do something" calls Smoke from the corner, though Ree can barely make his words out through the headguard and the adrenaline.

Okay, something, do something and she bounces forwards, just like she practiced. She lets out a 1-2 of her own, which Jade effortlessly avoids. *Bounce and strike* - she tries again. Jade's head moves like it's not even attached to her body; it's so hard to hit, but this time Ree catches a counter, a lead hook to her ribs. *Why didn't it **hurt**?* Obviously, Jade's gone again before Ree can respond.

Undeterred, Ree tries again. She gets close enough, but gets interrupted, she throws the jab but her body wobbles off balance horrendously. *What the **fuck**?!* As her leg detonates in pain, she can barely stand. As Ree had thrown the second punch, Jade had pivoted out and landed an absolute bomb of a kick on Ree's thigh.

Jade's on the front foot now, coming in. Ree recognises the pattern as soon as the jab comes, and attempts to avoid the inevitable second punch. The second punch never comes, instead another absolute stinger to the leg. *Same fucking spot, bitch.* Like a fog, Jade's out of range before Ree can respond.

Ree can barely put weight on her lead leg now, like Bambi's mum just waiting to be finished off. But it's not over yet. Bouncing her front foot on the floor, guard high to not get tagged in the face again. Jade comes forwards, and Ree throws that front foot out with everything she's got. She feels the ball of her foot hit Jade's solid abdominals. It doesn't do much, but it does pause this attack and make Jade back out. *Aha! Yes, get it girl.*

Jade comes in again, reads the kick coming again, and swiftly scoops Ree's grounded leg out from underneath her with her own. It takes Ree a second to figure out why the fuck she's looking at the ceiling, to the sounds of clapping and an excited "*oowee*" from the outer ropes.

Ree clambers back to her feet, just in time for the timer to beep the end of the round, as the fighters head to their corners. She falls onto her stool, waiting for some sage wisdom, or a *gun* or *something* from Smoke.

"You're doing well out there. Caught her with the teep. Keep it simple, but you've gotta get some pressure on her, you can't let her fly in and out scoring when she wants okay. Either get in there, or wait for her shots, then throw something back - weather the storm."

Another squirt of water, gumshield back in and they head back out. Dimos dramatically poses pointing to both fighters, one with each arm. Timer beeps and he motions them to go before stepping out of their way.

Alright, pressure on, we can do that and in she goes. Hands up and getting closer and closer, as soon as she can nearly reach, she starts throwing as many punches as she possibly can 1-2-1-2-1-2-1-2-1-2-1-2. Ree feels the impact on the side of her headguard, as it turns her whole body with its force, following the turning of her head. It doesn't hurt. It just feels heavy. Ree turns back to face Jade, her eyeballs take an extra second to find their target and focus up.

Jade could've gone in for the kill right then and there, she chose not to. Instead she offers a glove touch. That doesn't stop Ree wanting to get her back. She touches gloves and gets ready to go again. Edging forward a foot at a time with as many jabs as she can manage before unleashing the absolute best overhand she can muster. And getting caught with a roundhouse kick to the face for her troubles. But she doesn't back out.

Now they are stood, toe to toe, against the ropes. Ree won't let her out, no matter how many times she's getting hit. *Weather the storm.* Now she unleashes some body hooks of her own. Almost definitely 500% less effective than she thinks, but at least they're hitting.

The success is short lived before Ree notices, out of nowhere, a forearm on each of her shoulders and behind her headguard. A series of devastating knees to her abdomen and chest have her moving backwards, and rapidly losing oxygen. One forearm disappears, giving some release, until an elbow crashes into the side of her head, dizzying Ree and making her very unstable on her feet.

The beeper beeps. The coaches coach. Ree's too tired to care. *Just another 2 minutes.*

This time Jade's off the line like a short, straight in Ree's face.

"Pressure on, don't let off baby, win the round, this is what we do, all day, get to work" excitedly encourages Green as Jade backs Ree up into the corner - landing so many shots, but none of them with damage, none with intent, not really.

Ree can't do much, she keeps her guard up. *"If you can't do anything else, move. Don't be a target, Ree, MOVE"* comes Smoke's own instruction. *All I want to do is sleep, and cry. I'm **exhausted**. C'mon girl, move.* By some beginner's fluke or something, Ree manages to pivot out on her front foot, and holds Jade off with her lead forearm. Just like she practiced with Smoke. Somewhere, out of nowhere, Ree's hand flies upwards. It lands. It lands clean. Ree's eyes widen with realisation, victory. Jade's head settles back to its usual angle, blood starting to appear in her nostril. *Ooh, I fucked up.*

Jade launches forwards with a 1-2, forcing Ree back half way across the ring before flying forwards with a front kick that lands. Flush. Snatching the air from Ree's lungs, the violent expulsion of air causes an involuntary gasp for air as another jab lands flush on Ree's face. Using all this momentum, Jade throws a hellfire missile of an overhand to Ree's unguarded temple. Jade pulls all the power at the last second, landing the overhand with a fraction of its power, leaning fully over her front leg, knee completely bent, she fires a lead hook into Ree's exposed body.

The room goes dark. Ree's legs disappear. Her body won't respond. Fighting to keep her eyes open. It's futile. She blinks and she's sat against the ropes. The world coming back into focus. She looks up to see Smoke, offering her a hand to pull her up, which he does with ease.

Dimos has Ree stand to one side of him, Jade to the other, all 3 facing Rizzy, and Dev. He raises Jade's glove as the victor. There's polite applause, and Jade turns to hug a very confused Ree, who doesn't hug back so much as lean into Jade to be held up.

"C'mon girls, break it up. We need the ring. Good fight" comes Dev's voice. Ree isn't really cognitively functioning right now, thankfully Smoke guides her out of the ring and to the sofas where he helps her get out of her headguard, gloves, and handwraps.

"You did good, kid" he reassures. It falls on deaf ears

"Really, 'cause it feels like I just got battered" - sarcasm hangs on every syllable.

"She's an amateur with a few fights under her belt. She played nice, you're just in different places" - there's that sage wisdom, *so helpful, so useful*

"She knocked me out"

"She could've, she just dug your liver, don't be a pussy"

"Why though? She's meant to be my friend, what the fuck even was that"

"She was showing you respect, you'd rather her let you think you won, like a toddler on Mario Kart? You don't get better like that"

The others make their way over to the sofas, Jade makes a point of sitting on the arm of the sofa next to Ree, hanging her arm round her and planting a kiss on the top of her head, with a little squeeze.

With Jade in position, Green sits on an adjacent arm. Dimos and Dev take comfy positions on the other sofa. Rizzy stays standing, arms folded.

"Good fight girls, not a bad first proper round at all for you" compliments Dev

"Eh, the girl's a natural" responds Dimos with a friendly shrug

"Jade, you still fixed for the end of the month" interjects Rizzy, all business

Jade silently nods, acknowledgement of the serious next fight ahead of her, today was fine tuning

"We've gotta work that close quarter boxing, long and mid range is good - kicks are working well, clinch work is tight, but you're staying too close for too long without going into the clinch, you'll get tagged" Rizzy carries on

"To be fair babes, you did get tagged" comes a brave Green, adding some salt into the wound, with a chuckle

"A first round newbie, tagged you and drew blood kid, you gotta do better than that against these girls, they'll hurt you for it" all business from Rizzy, once again

"Don't be harsh, she did well" comes Dev, trying to level the playing field for Ree

"Did well? We should call her Bee, the way she bumbled around in there, bumping into stuff and then taking a little nap - way to go, kid" finishes Rizzy, with a sarcastic clap

There's a tension in the air, not an angst, more of a sadness at the harshness of Rizzy's words

"My friend, you can't buy heart, she's got plenty. And a pretty solid chin. You trust me, she'll be great" Dimos, the unlikely defender, but Ree will take it, *"I'll take her to Rhodes with me, bring her back to fight, you'll see"*

Everyone pauses at this, gauging the reactions of everyone else in the room. Nobody even gives Ree a chance to say she likes training with Smoke.

"Oh really?" After a pause, comes Rizzy's smirking response. Dimos remains stoic, maintains eye contact. A subtle challenge, alpha to alpha, ego to ego. *"No need to pay for flights. I'll train her."* he turns to face Ree *"You work with Uncle in the mornings right?"* she nods, and he continues *"be here at 5, and be ready and serious"*.

"Girl, you on the early shifts with me now" affirms Jade, ruffling Ree's sweat-matted, headguard shaped hair *"Another girl in here taking it serious is gunna be lit. Maybe we can do something 'bout the smell now, maybe our own locker room, eh Devvy?"* chirps Jade with comical optimism, to be met with a single raised eyebrow - no words needed

Whether it was out of ego, professional courtesy and respect, or something else, it doesn't really matter. *But I liked training with Smoke,* she thinks, but doesn't verbalise.

"I'm here at that time, too" Smoke answers without being asked

"You bet you are you fat fuck, you've gotta make weight at the end of the month" laughs Rizzy. The group all laughs, as Smoke stands, pulls up his hoodie and shirt to expose ripped, lean abdominals, which he rubs and shakes as if he had a big beer belly *"too much Ackee and Saltfish!"* Rizzy drops the punchline.

Chapter Seven

Morning light streams through the window. The first day of her serious career. The day after her first beatdown. Sore, but somehow triumphant, Ree sits on the end of her bed - wrapped in warm, damp towels, with zero inclination to move.

Something shifted in those rounds. The physical punishment of those rounds unlocked something. There's a power in knowing you're not fragile, and in knowing you're not invincible. Acknowledging that somehow made her visible, feel *alive* in a way she's never felt before.

She reaches onto her night stand, and pulls the card.

Dimos Petrakis
Fight Promoter +30 690 123 4567

Ree recalls the strange moment she got the card. The boys had left, Jade was busy swooning with Green, and Dimos came to sit next to her on the sofa. A bit close, but more like *dude, personal space* close than *ew, get away from me* close. *Perhaps he's unfamiliar with his newly-ish found width.*

"My girl, you showed heart in there, and we have distinctly not enough decent girl fighters in Rhodes. You could make a good living. I tell Rizzy too, it's all money. The tourists, they love it. He should come out there, work with me on the promotion. But anyway, if he is dickhead to you, or if you want to see the islands. Give me a call."

She thumbs the card and turns it over, it's very generic. Probably deliberately so.

What a strange man. Imagine thinking I have talent after seeing that particular show.

She chuckles to herself, puts the card in the dresser and glances herself in the mirror. Surprisingly few battle scars are visible. But *Christ* can she feel them.

Chapter Eight

"Morning Bumble Bee!" - Rizzy's words dripping with disdain *"This is the early morning shift, and we aren't fucking around, there are rules here, this isn't public training. We start at 5, rule number 1, don't be fucking late".*

Jesus, I was here 10 minutes early, ready 5 minutes early, and I've barely finished wrapping my fucking hands and he's giving me shit already?

He carries on *"Rule number 2, don't cry. That's bitch shit, and not what we're here for. And before you get all woke about it - that rules for the boys, too, and I tell them exactly the same"*

A raised eyebrow in response to that one. *"Rule number 3 - trust the process, we're here to work, and the people you train with are either fighters, or used to be. Don't fuck around. Can't hack it, the doors that way we won't miss you."*

Harsh, but okay, I get it, you're the boss man. Christ.

Rizzy turns to address the room, jumping onto the flooring of the ring bringing him physically above the crowd.

"Alright guys circle up. You know the drill, pair up; circuits for warmup. After that, free sparring. Full kit, no injuries.

Don't take the piss on the head contact, we don't need concussions so close to fight night, and CTE is real. After warmup Smoke, you're in for rounds with me. Bumble Bee, you'll be in afterwards".

It was a weird choice to pull Ree into the ring. She wasn't fighting or preparing to fight. Maybe he just wanted to use her embarrassing nickname in front of everyone, or maybe he wanted to get her to quit on day one. Smoke made sense, he's fighting soon. But Bee? Something didn't add up there.

The circuits were brutal. Relentless. Harsh. Unforgiving. Ree partnered with Smoke, with them being the first two in the ring. He was quietly encouraging whilst putting in his own graft. The man was unbreakable. Kettle bell swings, battle rope slams, agility ladder footwork drills, heavy bag drills, tyre flips. Every station designed expertly to improve a strength, sharpen the fighter, or forge unbreakable mental resilience.

Everything hurt, every muscle burned. Her lungs were on fire. This was beyond hell on earth. With the exception of the occasional retching, vomiting. Everyone works unapologetically. Pushing as hard as they possibly could.

Between the movements came retching. Gasping for breath. Gulping water. Strained groans and shouted counts. Everybody pushed to its limit, no apologies, no complaints. The soundtrack of training for war in a gym.

"Time! Stretch off, take on some fluids, get wrapped and padded" Rizzy's voice cuts through the room like a whipcrack. No applause, no praise, just the next command. Everyone moves. Marching to their kit bags like worker ants on the scent of sugar.

Ree is still approaching the ring when the timer buzzes. Without ceremony, the pair touch gloves and begin their chess game. Footwork. Head movement. Feints. No strikes thrown, none received—just two tacticians reading each other, testing patterns, laying mental traps. This isn't brawling. It's something far more dangerous.

It's hypnotising to watch - so much spoken between two warriors without a single word. It moves like slow motion. Then, after a flicker of tactical foreplay, Smoke bursts into life. He springs forward on a double jab, then hurls an overhand at Rizzy's temple. With a slip left and a roll right Rizzy is out of danger - he drives his right knee to Smoke's stomach before vanishing out of Smoke's sight and range.

With an acknowledging shrug, smile and fist bump, they reset. This time Smoke throws the leg kick. Rizzy's lead shin snaps up to block. He taps the ball of his foot on the floor and it bounces effortlessly catching a blink of a gap in Smoke's guard, touching his temple.

No frustration - only determination. Smoke gets his guard back up and carries on walking down his man. With surprising elegance and agility, y'know, for someone Smoke's size, he sends a flying knee at a cornered Rizzy.

As if it was scripted, Rizzy dodges to the side, pivots "on the circle" and has Smoke cornered. Then it happens, he ignites. With the righteous fury of a Knights Templar he unloads. In the time it takes Smoke to turn to his partner Rizzy has detonated. Landing a flurry of body shots and alternating up to head shots. Wherever Smoke's hands and arms are not, shots land. This is the kind of speed that commentators use VAR to unpick between rounds.

Even mid-combination, everything's aligned—Rizzy's head never stays still more than half a second, his off-hand always guarding, his stance perfect. There's nowhere to hit. No target exposed. Just movement, pressure, punishment. Smoke may as well be trying to hit a ghost.

Then, almost imperceptibly, Rizzy steps in—close enough, fast enough—and sweeps. Smoke hits the canvas like a felled tree, thudding into the centre of the ring. *"Timber!"* Rizzy laughs *"c'mon big fella, it's only the first round, up you get"*.

Through an eye roll and an acknowledging chuckle, Smoke jumps back to his feet. Gloves up. They touch gloves and go again. This time, Smoke is cautious. He doesn't chase—he claims the centre of the ring, stalking Rizzy, picking his angles. "There we go," Rizzy calls, approving. "Sit on your basics. Sit back on that jab. Use the teep."

Smoke nods. Rizzy comes in fast—side kick first. Smoke blocks, pivots, fires back with a jab. It lands. Rizzy whips a roundhouse at his head—Smoke teeps to the stomach. Neither shot hurts, but it halts Rizzy's advance. Smoke holds his ground. Centre ring is his now.

Rizzy picks up the pace. A front-leg kick. Then a hop-switch, back-leg strike. Smoke sees his moment—he charges. But Rizzy's ready. The raised leg drops like bait fulfilled. Rizzy's arms snap behind Smoke's neck, locking in a tight clinch. His right foot steps behind Smoke's left—he sweeps. Smoke hits the canvas again, just as the timer beeps.

Rizzy offers a hand to his fallen comrade, helping him up - Smoke takes it, dignity intact. Smoke gathers himself and takes on some water. Rizzy faux-skips and shadow spars, limbering up for the next round. Focused and precise.

The next couple of rounds are more of the same. Complete technical dominance from Rizzy - without insult or offence - punctuated by calm, clinical coaching. Plenty of laughs, whoops, fist bumps, and *"oh for fucks sake"* eye rolls. Guidance without ego, and precision without mercy.

Ree is awestruck. Smoke is *good*. Size and weight are on his side. His presence and power are terrifying. But Rizzy just outclassed him. Surgically. Repeatedly. Smoke looks spent. Rizzy barely looks warm.

"Bumble Bee, step into my office" Rizzy calls. The way he says it, not cruel, not playful, just flatly inevitable - like tax returns.

He's not going to do that to me, surely? Ree starts to panic, chest tightening, heart racing.

The fuck am I gunna do with this kid? Rizzy wonders, already bored at the very thought of it.

To her absolute relief, Rizzy has undone his gloves and dropped them outside the ring. Replacing them with thai pads.

"First thing's first. No point being able to throw anything, if you're getting tagged by everything" Rizzy explains *"your guard is always intentional. Long distance, lower, wider guard. Shorter distance, higher tighter guard, unless you're expecting body shots"*. Ree nods. Her hands come up high. She's a few feet from Rizzy. Rizzy sighs, and jolts forward.

Before she can react he's kicked her in the ribs. Under her guard. More tap than strike. No pain, no punishment, just a point proven - *"too far for that guard, you can't see me"* - his eyes locked to hers. She lowers her hands to be closer to shoulder height, in roughly the same position. He throws a round kick to her head, and she raises a glove and blocks it. *"See?"* he confirms smugly. He follows up with a series of, admittedly kind, round kicks. Different heights, different sides. She's blocking most of them fairly effectively.

"Mistakes deserve punishment - I miss, or you block, you counter, sharp"- she nods. He throws a kick, slowly. Blocks

with the right, counters with the left. It's not hard but it touches. He nods, they run this drill a few more times.

"We can't stand still. Moving targets are harder to hit" she starts bouncing on the balls of her feet, like Smoke showed her. An arcing round kick to the head. She moves away. Her hands come too high. He puts in a body kick. She freezes, he puts another one in. She gasps and freezes, he puts another one in. She brings her hands down to her body. He puts a kick onto her lead thigh, followed by one to the head. *"Move, Bumble, move"* raining tactical strikes. She doesn't move. *"You can't block, fucking move"* she starts backing away. It's futile. The shots are becoming a storm now. *"You gotta fucking do something"* her front foot flings out in a weak teep. He kicks out the grounded leg. She lands on her back. *Fuck.* She does not bounce up. She stays there. *What the fuck am I even doing?*

Rizzy takes a knee, by Ree's shoulder. *"Nope, not in here. We don't quit. Trust the process. On your feet. Finish your round"*. Although physically speaking downwards, this is exactly how Rizzy would talk to any fighter. Her head rolls to the side, where she sees Smoke. Silently he wills her on. She clambers to her feet, and starts to bounce.

"Keep fucking working. The fight doesn't let up, neither does the training" - he leads in with a couple of kicks before getting closer. Head moving. Boxing combos flowing. She does her

best. Guarding as much as possible. Eating as few shots as possible.

"Appear strong when you're weak and weak when you're strong - The Art of War" Rizzy recites as they dance around, not really throwing. *Did this motherfucker just quote Sun Tzu, fucking unbelievable.* Gaining her breath and rhythm back, Rizzy takes the opportunity *"Bumble Bee, you're blowing out your arse. Let's see what you've got"* and he holds his guard way too high, behind his head, exposing his torso. She hesitates. *"Stop fucking around and hit me"* - so she does. In a moment of sheer determination, she hits, and she hits, and she keeps going. *"30 seconds - don't stop - PRESSURE"* she throws everything she has. Nothing left in her arms, shoulders, or gloves. She gives him everything she's got. He doesn't even flinch.

Round timer beeps. Vision starts to blur. Head starts to spin. Stomach... *Shit...* she runs to the ropes. Smoke's ready, bucket in hand. *Bleurgh.* The violent reappearance of her hydration. Eyes teary. Lungs empty. Inhalation damn near impossible. *Beep.* Goes the timer. She turns, hands up, not even wiping her mouth. She can barely see. But she'll be fucked if she quits and gives Rizzy that satisfaction.

Smoke laughs, a small but deep chuckle, from his belly. *"Gwan, gyal"*.

Rizzy raises an eyebrow, and starts to play. A kick on the leg. A spinning kick scrapes past her face. A round kick to her head, she rolls under it, hands staying high. Rizzy's gloves come up and he starts walking her down. She jabs out on her back step, catching his guard. Same again, but she throws the lead hook with the jab. It doesn't connect, but Rizzy has to react. He throws a lead hook, she reacts. He taps the other side of her headguard with the other hand. This cat and mouse game goes on. *"Keep working, stick with it".*

Nobody would call it a "good round". But she did survive it. He might have played, danced around, landed audacious shots. But she kept working. She finished the round. And another. The occasional short sentence. A bit of encouragement. A bit of advice.

*"Well you 're not **totally** hopeless - shower off Bumble Bee, you 're done for the day"*

Ree takes a squat. She breathes deeply. She survived. *And, was that a compliment?* She doubts it. But it was better than how he started the morning. *Ah man. I hope Ash's deliveries haven't turned up so I can just sleep in the store room.* She stops for a second, and realises how hard she's grinning. And how hard Smoke is grinning back at her. *Why am I grinning like a twat?* Quickly followed by *Why do I give a fuck what that dick thinks of me anyway?*

Chapter Nine

Bzzz. It's her phone. Not that it makes or receives calls these days. Just fucking training and nutrition reminders.

Reminder: Fridge Raiders + 1l water

With a faux-Rizzy voice Ree mocks *gotta be hydrated, gotta do your protein, you fight on your stomach, blah blah fuck you Rizzy... dick*

Still, she does as the reminder says, and somehow chokes down more fucking chicken, then downs the litre of water. Training this last few weeks has been intense, it's not calmed down and it always stays 25% above what she can do.

Physically she might not look too different, or at least she can't see it in the mirror. But comfort in the ring? Technical fluency? Definitely improving. *Progress, not perfection* she recites, another Rizzy-quote.

This man is in my fucking head 24/7... but he does get the results, to be fair

He'd complemented her leg block return head kick the other day, and it's her new absolute favourite technique.

She's so thankful for her new family. Honestly she *loves* them. Ash is the most supportive and understanding uncle ever. He gets it, and because he gets it, so does Meena. And because

Meena gets it, and she's fed a tonne of fighters before, she keeps bringing food out.

The food is delicious, it's right on the nutrients that Rizzy mandates, and it's so damn tasty. But a little hot. And hot is kind of okay when it goes in. But kinda burny when it comes out.

They are the absolute sweetest, against a backdrop of pushing your body to its absolute limits. The warmth of Meena's *"Beta, you break bones out there — I break bread in here"* whilst damn near force feeding her butter chicken, jeera rice, or piping hot rotis props up the strength needed to forge a mind and body out of Damascus steel.

Walking into work, after a brutal session with Rizzy, to see his warm smile and his knowing eyes. *I feel like I'm working in my family's shop, it's hardly work, it's more like aunty's house.*

Though she can't help but to stop and wonder if Ash and Meena *really* know about Rizzy, in his entirety. It's not something she can, or would, ever question. But what do they know, really?

With a quick punch of protein, but not enough to throw up - nobody wants that reputation - and some hydration. She's out the door and over to the gym. Another standard start.

Rizzy expertly commands the room, delegates the training plans and everyone gets to work.

Ree is minding her business, practicing thrusting side kicks on a heavy bag. She's had some tips from Smoke, Rizzy, and Dev about how to get maximum thrust and damage on someone walking her down. She swings the bag away, and times the kick as it comes back - emulating someone throwing their body weight at her. She practices, again, and again, and again.

Meanwhile, in the ring, Rizzy is running padwork drills with Smoke. Mostly keeping him moving and countering. Smoke is ominous and dangerous, but *"hit the other guy, and don't get hit"* is Rizzy's motto, and they're working on it. Smoke is becoming more elusive by the session. He's living and training by his own motto *"henched and drenched"* usually with some signature bodybuilding pose.

"Rizz" comes a quiet, nervous voice from the ropes. It's startling in its protocol breakage. Nobody interrupts a round in the ring. *What the fuck?* Almost impatiently, Rizzy is borderline irritated, he approaches the youngster at the ropes. The youngster nods in the direction of the benches, where one of the younger lads on the squad, Liam, sits. He's holding an icepack over his eye, blood soaked tampon hanging from his nose. *"Probably fractured,"* the whistleblower, Will, continues.

"Who?" immediately interrogates Rizzy - skipping courtesy and formalities - Will nods in the direction of one of the sparring pairs, where a young hotshot is being viciously over enthused in his round. Teeping his partner onto their back. The first thing Rizzy notices is the clear weight class discrepancy between this kid, and his abused partners. *"Who is he?"*

"His name's Charlie, comes from Joey's gym, been training a week or so. He's a bit heavy handed, Rizz"

Fucking Joey's. Typical muscle head, dickheads gym. They love tuning people up until they're well matched. Then it all goes to shit for them. Egotistical scumbags. And Joey's a prick to boot. There's been some bad blood at a fight night before, Joey's lads got pasted in fair fights. Joey complained about foul play - *obviously.*

The round timer beeps. *"Charlie! Fancy a round?"* - it was not a question. Nobody in the gym thought it was. *"Corner"* Rizzy commands Smoke, who happily obliges. *"Set the timer to 3 minutes"* comes the next instruction, aimed at Will.

Charlie is way too confident. Balls to the wall toxic masculinity. He walks like Connor McGregor. Tension in the gym is palpable as everyone pretends to not be eagerly awaiting this round. If Bible Belt White Trash had a British counterpart, this is it. He likes his Lager Belgian, his Kebabs

Turkish, but *"not them fucking immigrants"*. Peak protein-shake-personality dickhead energy. Head shaved cos he's Britney era batshit.

Chinese whispers spread around the gym to anybody who is still actually focusing, including Ree, who makes her way ring side. Too full of intrigue to care if anyone knows she's stopped working.

The timer goes. Rizzy's normal stoic expression turns to a full grin.

"C'mon kid, let's have it then" he jokes, taunting the serious expression Charlie is wearing.

Charlie wastes no time flurrying at Rizzy, who's already on the balls of his feet. A boxing combination expertly avoided. A head kick with malicious intent, and Rizzy just isn't there to be hit.

He dances and avoids everything, the silence of every missed strike is deafening. Charlie's frustration climbing. He throws vicious kick combos and just can't land them. He exhausts all his tactical options in less than 30 seconds. He charges forward and Rizzy claps him, hard, with a 1-2. One to the nose, two to the eye. Blood from the nose and swelling from the eye are imminent.

A hard grunt from Charlie and he rages in again. This time he throws a leg kick, which Rizz blocks with his shin, before tapping up and round kicking Charlie in the face. He doesn't follow the kick through, he just hurts him a bit. Rizzy's evident amusement only adds to Charlie's frustration. A guttural road and he tries again. This time Rizzy lands a side kick flush into his solar plexus. It's like a fucking spear, doubling Charlie over and emptying his lungs.

Charlie fires back with a lazy, heavy round kick up high, and Rizz takes the moment to sweep him. Landing Charlie flat on his back, winded again from landing so hard, looking up at Rizzy - who's stayed stood almost on top of Charlie, looking down on him.

2 seconds of hard eye contact and visible dominance later, Charlie rolls onto his front. He punches the canvas in frustration and climbs back to hit feet. There's no glove touch.

Then Rizzy goes to work.

Rizz expertly shuffles forward, feinting the jab, and landing a scorcher of a right to Charlie's temple, sending him staggering back. Rizz doesn't let up, stepping over the lead leg to deliver a thunderous lead hook to his body and then to the left side of his jaw. Charlie's gumshield flies out. Nobody notices, or maybe just nobody cares. The fight doesn't stop. Still reeling and against the ropes, Rizzy's onslaught continues, and he throws a right straight to Charlie's floating ribs.

Charlie barely has time to scream in agony before Rizz has delivered another deliberate strike, like a baseball bat he throws a kick to Charlie's calf. He tries to limp away, one legged, trying to keep his hands up. From the other leg a straight kick lands flush on his torso. He's going down.

Rizz isn't allowing it, he grabs him into the clinch and starts delivering message-sending knees to his torso. Physically holding Charlie up to take his punishment at this point, he doesn't let up. There's no mercy to be found here. Releasing one hand, Rizz throws 3 elbows in quick succession to Charlie's skull; temple, jaw, and cheekbone.

Putting his forearms back into the clinch, he pulls Charlie's skull down into one final knee, landing flush in the middle of his face. His nose explodes, and there's probably bits of teeth everywhere.

Mercifully, Rizz let's go. Allowing his victim to slump to the floor.

Looking at the canvas, and snarling his nose slightly at the blood spillages, *'we need a mop... and a towel for this bum"*.

"Pussy" the word drops like venom at his fallen opponent. There's no respect here.

"It is what it is" Smoke's words as Rizz walks back to his corner.

Wide-eyed ring side, Ree is awestruck. *"Don't worry, sweetheart, he'll live"* with a wink.

"Might talk a bit funny for a while" comes Smoke's dry sense of humour, with an overzealous broken jaw imitation.

Ree barely hears it. As Rizzy removes his blood covered gloves. His body glistens with sweat, he doesn't drip, but he's done some work. It's like slow motion. He drops the gloves and grabs the bottom of his vest. Pulling it over his head to reveal the body of a Greek God. Every muscle is perfectly sculpted. Splashes of blood still cover his arms, and face. The veins in his forearms protrude, as if they're dripping with violence.

He uses his vest to wipe the blood from his face. Which serves to show off just how sculpted his shoulders and abs are.

Not a word in her mind. She watches. In awe.

Thud. Comes the sound of the defeated Charlie, who has managed to roll himself under the ropes, and fall to the ground.

The tension evaporates, and Rizzy laughs. Really laughs. A complete release. Torso muscles flexing with every chuckle. All she can do is stare. After much needed comic relief, Rizzy stretches off. He doesn't bother replacing his shirt. Ree doesn't bother reminding him. As Rizzy turns facing the other direction, Ree notices just how ripped Rizz's back muscles are.

Christ I'd read him like braille. Then she notices the scars. Old and faded now, about half a dozen long thin scars, and a couple thicker and much shorter.

Rizzy notices, climbs out the ropes and jumps down to the floor. He lifts Ree's jaw with his finger. Apparently her mouth was hanging open. He leans in close, and whispers in her ear, slowly, intentionally *"shouldn't you be working?"* with a sly smile and a wink.

In a trance, she mindlessly wanders back towards the bag. *"Hey Bumble Bee... don't be like that fucking kid, he's a dick"*

Rizz laughs at her *"you're better than that"*, contrasting to deadpan seriousness. As if having his own internal realisation.

Back at the bag, she can't think straight. With all her might she tries. But her mind keeps flashing back. The abs. The blood. The loyalty. She'd never seen him like that. Calculated, violent. Always skilful, but he *meant* to hurt that boy. Because that boy hurt his boys.

*I knew he could fight. I didn't know he could do **that**. That's.... that's... fucking hot.*

Physically salivating thinking about him. And maybe, kinda... kinda wet. Fuck. I've gotta train in these pants.

Rizzy, back at the ring. Focus mitts back on working some drills. Technically challenging for his partner, *same shit different day* for Rizz. Thinking back to her. The way she looked at him. That wasn't fear. *But what was it?*

Watching her walk away. She's a pretty girl, sure. Maybe even sexy if she weren't in gym kit all the fucking time. But when did she get hot?

In disbelief, at the end of the round, he turns to his most trusted friend, Smoke. He can see the cogs turning in Rizzy. He already knows the next question, but Smoke makes him say it anyway.

"Bro, tell me about the Bumble Bee"

Chapter Ten

"It's team bonding" Smoke coolly explains, Ree looks to Jade. With Ree distracted, Green gives Smoke a knowing wink

"Girl, it's a night out, don't be boring" interjects Jade

"It's a place we know, it's chill" Smoke continues

"And you can try your new fit!" finished Jade, knowing how to sell it

Well I guess that's decided then. Ree is excited to go out. Covered in bruises and dripping with fatigue or not. Excited, but nervous. *£20 says Rizzy'll be there.* She is desperate to see him. And desperate to not seem desperate. He just radiates something. Something terrifying, alluring, something deeply dangerous and deeply erotic. *He's probably gay* she laughs to herself, realising she's just broken her heart a bit.

Ready to go out, she's gone edgy tonight. Combat boots, skater skirt (red and black, obviously) and fishnets, an off the shoulder, chesty top - black, *it's slimming*. Winged eyeliner, obviously. *Maybe he likes Avril Lavigne and mid 2010s Scene Queens* with a mock Hail Mary to Emma Roberts, *we're channeling Coven* in reference to her *favorite* TV show - American Horror Story.

Fuck it, if he doesn't like.. I do and she gives herself a twirl in the mirror.

They all meet outside the club, Ree, Smoke, Green, Jade, and of course, Rizzy. Green in his trademark skinny jeans and checkered shirt. Smoke wears a plain white t-shirt, gold chain and a chunky watch; very much giving Biggie Smalls with his flat cap. Rizzy is in boots, black jeans, a grey t-shirt, and a leather jacket. No jewellery, just a nice watch, material strap.

Jade's gone with a timeless classic: barely dressed ghet-ho. Green is *feeling it*. Their vibe is immaculate, and Ree is *feeling it*.

Rizzy goes ahead, he doesn't bother to ask if everyone's ready or following. He knows. Even in this dingy back alley, there's a gen-pop queue, and a VIP queue. Rizzy cuts the VIP queue. *Because why wouldn't he?*

The security are all smiles and handshakes for Rizzy, Smoke, and Green. Straight through the VIP entrance, no hand stamps, no pat downs. Rizzy melts through the crowd to the bar, the staff don't ask for his order before he's got a Black Label on the rocks in hand. Smoke's Hennessy and Coke. And then 1, then 2, Pornstar Martinis. One for Green, one for Jade.

"Chin chin motherfuckers" Green laughs, raising a toast to the crew - Ree's the only one without a drink. Rizzy doesn't say a word, a hand on Green's arm halts the toast. Rizzy looks

expectantly at Ree, he doesn't *ask* what she wants to drink, well at least not with words.

"Double SoCo" she tries to mouth across the group, but it's futile, it's too loud in there. Rizzy seizes the opportunity to take her by the wrist, and pull her close, so she can whisper in his ear. Naturally placing his hand on the small of her back - you know, so he can hear her better. She repeats her order and he passes it to the bar staff. She has her drink in hand quicker than she could get nuggies from McDs'.

Rizzy raises his glass, Green takes the cue, and the group toast - to a night just started.

They walk through the curtain to the VIP area, and sit in a booth. Space to drink, to talk, and a dedicated space to dance; overlooking the peasants in the club. Everyone's having a good time, even Rizzy cracks the occasional smile. Normally to a setup-punchline combo from comedic duo Green and Smoke - who are funnier the more they drink.

Jade hasn't sat down yet. She started dancing the moment they got in, and hasn't stopped yet. *She's.... enthusiastic.*

Green is picking up every last bit of sexual energy she's putting down. The guys all give her a wide berth, which makes the approaching white shirts completely irrelevant, until they approach the booth.

This time Rizzy stands, he greets the men with a handshake and a hug. Green and Smoke follow suit. They seem tight, but not close. Both in dark grey trousers, crisp white shirts, and waistcoats, no ties. Rizzy introduces them to Ree; *"Bumble, meet Chiz... and Ali"*. They could be brothers, Chiz kisses her hand in a slimy kind of manner. It doesn't outright give the ick, but it's not far off. Ali shakes it dismissively. No friendliness or warmth, just social obligation.

"Well boys, enjoy your evening. Any problems, let us know. We always love seeing you in here. Ladies, stay fabulous" Chiz politely bids adieu, and leaves; with Ali close in tow, like a lapdog.

Looking somewhat perplexed, behind a slight fog of drink and another unknown social interaction, Rizzy leans in and explains *'we do some business together, they like how our boys behave, that's why they work the doors... and tend to fill the dance floor... we like the music here"* he laughs over *Usher - Yeah*.

Uncomfortably watching their departure, before the door shuts, Ree is interrupted by a well dressed waiter. He's holding a large metal bucket of ice, with a bottle of Champagne. Rizzy rolls his eyes *'they know we don't drink the bubbly stuff"* he laughs, but is caught off guard slightly by a second bucket, this one containing a bottle of Johnny Walker Black Label, and a bottle of Hennessy, and a series of cans of full fat and diet Coke. *"Now we're talking"* Smoke comments, rubbing his hands together.

Then Jade comes teetering over, tray in hand. Full of Jaegerbombs. Proper ones. Green is as enthusiastic as Jade. Ree doesn't wanna seem cold, so grabs one from the tray. Smoke takes one with his signature *"fuck it"* shrug. Rizzy doesn't reach for one.

Double powered by her SoCos, Ree takes a second, and slides into the booth next to Rizzy. She puts one down in front of him. He looks at her and subtly shakes his head. *"Not gunna happen"*.

"Oh don't be boring" she insists, a smile cracks across his face, but he doesn't take the bomb. *"Aw big Mr Rizzy scared of a little Jaegermeister?"* in a childlike voice. *Did I just do the fucking, oh fuck sake*. She could facepalm if she wasn't still holding her drink. *Smooth, dork*.

His smile widens, and he picks up the glass. The group all toast to each other and bomb their drinks. Rizzy toasts towards Ree, and drinks his much slower, never taking his eyes off of her. Whether she noticed or not, until she did.

Ree decides not to leave his side. Rizzy isn't much of a talker until he is. Mostly he shares fight anecdotes with Smoke. Smoke is far less humble about Rizzy's exploits than Rizzy is about them. Rizzy doesn't blush or tell Smoke to shut up, but nobody's sure how Rizzy's feeling about the spotlight that Smoke's giving him.

Smoke knows exactly what he's doing. *Just call him Goose, he's wing manning so hard right now.*

Then she pauses for a second *wait,* **why** *is he wing manning for Rizzy?*

Eyes widen in realisation. She must've squirmed or given some sign of discomfort, as Rizzy's hand firmly sits on her thigh. He looks her dead in the eye before leaning to her ear, *"you okay?"* he asks. She swallows, hard. *"Uhuh"* she nods, her eyes scream at Jade to save her.

Jade doesn't notice, but Green does, and he gives her a little elbow nudge and a head nod. *"I need to powder my nose - you coming?"* - Jade throws the best used life ring in the world at Ree, who clambers out and follows her.

After a breath, a cigarette, a release of fluid build up, an eyeliner and powder touch up. They're back. Jade back to owning the dance floor, and Ree waiting at the bar for water. She's hardly *trying* to get served. Barely looking at the bar staff. She's more *at* the bar, than *waiting* at the bar.

Then he appears, like a conker in her throat. Leaning coolly on the bar facing her. *"I just wanted... water, it's hot in here"* her botched explanation escapes her lips without being asked anything. Rizzy raises a hand, two fingers relaxed but extended, within seconds *"what can I get you Rizzy?"* flirts the barmaid, bleach blond, breasts bursting out of her poloshirt. He doesn't even look at her, *'ice water, please"*, she returns quickly, though seemingly disappointed by his interest in Ree. Rizzy sincerely thanks the girl, but barely looks in her direction.

He takes an ice cube in his hand, and places it on the side of Ree's neck. She gasps ever so slightly, as he rolls it round to the nape of her neck. It's dual purpose. Sensory as fuck, and will serve to cool her down quickly. He knows what he's doing. His exterior might not crack, but he's just as nervous as she is.

Emboldened by units of alcohol, she tilts her chin upwards, mouth slightly open. Internally dying at being vulnerable enough to be rejected. *He doesn't want to kiss you, you fucking idiot.* Until he does. With the ice cube melted under the heat of his hand, he takes the base of her head and holds her. His top lip brushing under hers, before their heads tilt and their mouths connect.

Fireworks. The room disappears. The music is gone. The smoke from the machines now engulfing them in a timeless universe of pure lust and desire. His tongue in her mouth, and hers willingly accepting it. His other hand holding her waist. Nothing forced, the most natural, passionate kiss either of them had ever experienced. Lost in the moment completely.

Then a glass smashes, the world comes back into focus, she flinches and pulls away from the sound. He looks at her lips and smiles. She's gasping for breath. He pulls her in and rests his forehead on hers. For one glorious moment, they saviour each other.

Before there's time for anything to get awkward, Rizzy moves back to the booth, and Jade ambushes Ree. *'Bestie, what the FUCK'*.

They laugh, they giggle, they get giddy and do silly dances. They do more shots. Rizzy and Ree keep catching each other's eyes, but he's with the boys and she's with Jade. *There HAS to be more coming. Right?!*

Then a hand, on her hip. It's not Rizzy's. She turns sharply to see him. She blinks hard. *Surely fucking not.*

It's Cal. Dressed to the nines. Stood in front of her. Way too close.

'Baby, I found you'

No reply. *The fuck do I even say to this dude?* Jade stands, confused. Violent reactions delayed by the non-response from Ree, and her own intoxication.

After a moment, a brief visit to the place in her head where she once lived. She comes out fighting. *'Get the fuck away from me'* she roars, shoving him with both hands in his chest, with everything she's got. He staggers several steps backwards, face completely blank with disbelief. Then he steps in, a bad move. Rizzy's already there.

"The fuck is this?" Smoke calmly asks, interjecting logic where Rizzy's eyes radiate crazed danger, behind his still exterior.

"Smoke... this, it's erm.. Cal". Smoke's eyes now fill with the same danger as Rizzy's. Green standing between the ladies and the men; chin up, chest out. Smoke and Rizzy exchange exactly one glance.

Smoke throws his arm around Cal's shoulders and starts leading him to the booth. *"My guy... let's get you a drink, you like Henny?"*. Cal does not have the physicality to resist, and is stalked by Rizzy on the other side.

Green leans over the bar and speaks to the staff, checks in with the girls. Then heads over to the lads, who are now sat in the booth. Boxed in, Cal's got nowhere to go. The conversation does not look comfortable, at all.

Rizzy puts a hand in the air, signalling Ree from the end of the booth. The girls head over. Cautiously, aware of the danger in the air. Rizzy gets out of the booth, leaving Cal boxed in by Green and Smoke.

Calmly, slowly, Rizzy takes a breath. *"Smoke says this is your ex, is that true?"*

Ree gulps, and nods.

"And what Smoke and Green tell me, that's all true, too?"

She doesn't look up from the floor this time. That's all the confirmation he needed.

"Do you like bullying girls, Cally?" he questions, menacingly, right in Cal's ear. His lips brushing the skin of his ears. Cal is frozen, terrified. *"What, no mean words for me? I wonder why that might be..."* his words trail off.

With all the precision of a professional underground fighter, he grabs the back of Cal's head, and smashes it on the table. On a metal table, that's bolted to the floor. Once. Twice. Three times.

When he brings his head back up, Cal can barely keep it steady atop his shoulders.

"I think you owe our girl here an apology, don't you?" the dizzied probably concussed former "lover" doesn't reply. Rizzy snaps his fingers in front of his face and slaps his cheek. *"Oi, hey, hello. Talking to you, focus, there we go... I was just saying, I think you owe our girl here an apology, don't you?"*

With that he drags him, by his shirt, to the ground, and forces him to his knees.

"I.... I.... I'm...."

"Sorry?" Rizzy impatiently finishes his sentence

"I'm sorry" through tears

"For....?" Rizzy questions

"For......."

"For being a piece of shit? For not loving you like you deserved....?" continues Rizzy, not realising what he's giving away to Ree with this sentence

"For being a piece of shit, and for not loving you like you deserved" hysterically cries Cal.

"Aria, do you accept this snivelling cunt's apology?" Rizzy asks

Horrified, awestruck, and kinda turned on, but ultimately frozen, Ree doesn't respond.

"Tough break, kid" comes Smoke's voice, as he pries Cal's jaw open, planting his overbite on the steel table *"don't fucking move"* - not that he could, with Smoke so close, and so physically imposing.

Rizz looks around, and Ree notices the whole VIP section is empty now. Rizzy takes Ree by the chin, firmly, but gently. Like he's cradling a baby bird. He plants the lightest of kisses on her lips, before turning to Cal.

Calculatedly planting a hand on each side of the booth table, behind Cal, he winds his leg back up, drawing his leg behind him. Then thrusts his knee purposefully at the back of Cal's skull. Shattering his jaw instantly.

His screams can't be heard over the deafeningly loud *Beast* by *Rob Bailey et al.*

Writhing in pain, he's fireman-lifted by Smoke. Who carries him unemotionally to the fire exit, which has already been opened, leading out to a set of steel stairs - an outdoor fire escape.

Unceremoniously, Smoke drops him, head first, down the stairs. Turning to come back in, Green places a "Wet Floor" sign down, and shuts the door behind Smoke as he comes back in.

"Health and safety hazard, that balcony you know? Someone's gunna fall down those stairs one day" Smoke deadpan quips to the group when he gets back.

"It's okay, I put the sign down" laughs Green, who then motions a thumbs up to the bar staff before continuing *"they need to sue their security company. Y'know the cameras in here are so sketchy, always going down **just** when you need them"*

"Well, shit happens to shit people" Smoke comments

Rizzy has already sat back down, fixed himself another Black Label on the rocks, and is enjoying the music.

Ree is in a daze. Never before has she been surrounded by such danger. Never felt safer. Never felt more loyalty. Never felt *so fucking turned on. Goddamn. I've just witnessed a seriously violent crime.* Then giggling almost hysterically.

"Drink?" asks Jade

"Fucking. Yes".

The girls unwind, the drinks flow, the dance moves start coming out. The rest of the night is pretty uneventful. Which is, fucking odd.

"Baby gyal, look atchu...." Green flirts with Jade *"... you like a Christmas present, I'm gunna get you home and cut you out of that fit still"* rubbing his hands together and biting his lip. He's deliberately playing to the social cliché but Jade's feeling it, and quips back

"Baby, call me Kawasaki, 'cause you can ride me all fucking night" with a wink, blowing him a kiss.

It takes a literal second before they're all over each other, and making their way out.

Smoke's next, *"til one, I'm out, it's been real"* with a big man hug *"you good?"* while holding her tight.

"Yeah..." she says, glancing at Rizzy. Smoke chuckles

"He's good people. He's got you" he says, knowing she already knows, and with that he's out

The club's still busy, but it's just the two of them in the room now. Rizzy, and Ree. Hunter, and deer in headlights.

She smiles at the violent psychopath at the other end of the VIP section. He makes his way over, she tries to walk towards him and stumbles. Steadying herself on the bar. It's not the shoes. It's the shots, all the shots.

It's my fucking chance. I need this man, and I need him inside me, and I need him inside me fucking tonight. I'm shooting my fucking shot.

He laughs at her unsteadiness. *"I'm gunna take you home, okay?"* he says, voice cool and calm.

Oh I bet you are. She leans in, to kiss him.

He leans back and pulls away. *What the FUCK.* Undeterred, and cognitively delayed from the concoction of cocktails and shots, she tries again. This time throwing her whole body at him. He holds her close, stopping her from falling, but keeps his face out of range of hers. Dodging her advances.

"Come on, let's get you home" a taxi ride later, he walks her into their building, and carries her to her room.

Laid on her bed, a final act of desperation, she tries to pull him in. He resists.

"You're wasted. I'm not doing it like this" he plants a kiss on her forehead, then puts his forehead firmly on hers, holding it there for a few seconds. Long enough for her to feel the safest she's ever experienced, and fall asleep.

He leaves a bottle of water and a pack of painkillers on the bedside unit. With a final glance back at her, he leaves.

Chapter Eleven

No training on Sundays. *Thank fuck for that.* She wishes last night was a blur. Some moments are painfully vivid.

There's so much there to process. But right now? Cuppa.

On autopilot, and opening her eyes as little as humanly possible. Ree heads to the kitchenette and makes a very strong, very sugary cup of tea. Climbing back into her duvet, cuddling the mug and sipping.

Was that even a good night out? It's chill they said, it'll be fun. Team bonding. Mmhhmm. Well actually there was team bonding... kinda.

Then it dawned on her.

Oh my fuck. I'm a co-conspirator. I'm an accessory. I'm joint venture in a serious assault. Or a murder. Oh fuck oh fuck.

She replayed the scene in her head. Somehow finding absolutely zero sympathy for Cal.

Cunt.

As she replayed the scene again; *he kissed me... Right before he knee-fucked Cal's skull.* Excitement peaking in the first part, stomach dropping in the second.

Then squirms thinking about it. *Oh my God the ice cube.*

It all floats back, piece by piece. *Shit me sideways, this man.*

A few more cups of tea, a little more confusion, and finally a *nah fuck this* later. She climbs into the shower. The bright light hurts her head, but she squints a bit and it's fine.

It's 1pm, if the Police were coming, they'd be here by now. It was a serious thing.

Logic prevailing, she finally relaxes. She remembers Jade's wild dance moves, Smoke and Green's comedy duo. The ice cube. All the stories about Rizzy in the ring. Cal's face when he realised he'd fucked up. The ice cube. Green and that fucking wet floor sign, she cracks up remembering it. Oh and the ice cube.

Hands on the wall, hot water falling on the top of her head. Washing away her sins. Most of them, anyway.

Her eyes close and her mind wanders. His face is there. His smile. His foreboding eye contact. The way his hand felt on her thigh makes her body react as if he's there again.

He was there. In my room. I threw myself at him... he didn't want me

As her emotional memory comes back in, trauma repeating itself this time, logic prevails. *No you dumb bitch, you were*

wasted - *you can't consent that pissed. He wouldn't have had sex with you, he would've raped you.*

The realisation dawns on her. She *couldn't* really want it, so although he could take it, he *refused*. Of all the things this man will do to other humans, he won't do that to you.

I need him. I need all of him.

Her body's reacting now, nipples hardened to a point. The very thought of him excites her. Her clit pulses thinking about him. She can't help herself but bring a hand to herself, to start to circle with her middle finger. Teasing it out. Breathing speeds up. She's rubbing harder now.

All she can think about is him. Taking her. Owning her. Forcing her. Every ounce of power he's got, she wants it. *Own me. I'll give you everything. Give me everything you've got.*

With two fingers inside herself now, barely half way in. She's so turned on just thinking about him. Until, sweet release. Body shaking, knees nearly giving way. The water in her face makes it hard to breathe. *"Oh, Rizzy"*.

Two words betray her innermost thoughts out loud for the first time. In awkward nervous sensory release she giggles like a child.

Wrapped in warm towels fresh from the radiator, she heads from the bathroom through the living room, where Jade's sitting with a red bull. Trackies and a hoodie, and a bit of *Sean Paul* in the background.

"Good morning, sunshine" she smirks.

Why do I feel so naughty? I didn't even do anything.

"Girl, debrief"

"Let me get my dressing gown"

They sit together, now both on the Red Bulls.

"So, what happened last night? Like there's obviously tea, you gotta spill"

"You mean outside of the 15 year minimum GBH?"

"Don't trip, that's a standard Saturday night - well maybe a bit more than standard - but it ain't special. Rizz gets like that when someone threatens his own"

"I'm sorry, what? He does that shit, what, all the time?"

"Not all the time, but if you threaten his people, sure. You've not heard the stories?"

"Clearly fucking not"

"Right girl, I gotta fill you in. Especially if you're gunna, y'know...

The man's no joke, and actually girl, I've known him to fuck, but not like... be with anyone

But anyway, so you know he's got love for the boys and for Ash and Meena. Well way back when, Smoke was a bit of a fat boy. That's where the jokes come from. Anyway, the boys fucking tortured him at school. They were only about 15, in secondary school. Rizz found out. He went skiiiitz brev. Banged bro in his face, and when he pulled a knife on Rizz, he put him through a glass fire door. That was the end of his academic journey.

But that doesn't sound so bad... shit got real deep, when the boys were in their late teens. They'd always rode together. Green's family are Muslim, they didn't really approve of who he was riding with. Smoke's mum was working three jobs and was never home to make him behave. And you know Rizzy's back story.

Anyway Ash had kind of taken them all in, kept them out of trouble. He sent them over to his brother's, what's now Dev's.

Dev is Ash's nephew, Ash's brother, Sanjay, used to run the gym. Ashok sent the boys to Sanjay's to train.

Jay was a bit too nice, he was a hard coach, but he believed everyone could be saved. Not too different to Ash really. Anyway the rude boys moved in. Before you know it everyone's embroiled in their bullshit.

Well Green wasn't too smart back then. They took his money and his goods. And he still owed for them. Rizzy tried to talk it down, and realised it was the rude boys that done it. They'd given him the shit on tick, robbed him, then made him owe for the food and the lost revenue.

Rizz tried to truce it out, but they weren't having it. They threatened Ash and Jay's places, then they jumped Green.

They stomped my mans to within an inch of his life. Bros 'up in fucking ICU and they aint backing down.

Rizz fucking flipped. Between Jay, Ash, and Green he just lost his shit. Him and Smoke rolled hard. Taxed like 4 of their dealers, raided a couple of bandos, went wild. It caught up to them. They got jumped. Rizzy made sure Smoke got away, but they carved Rizz up pretty good.

They made him agree to work for them, earn off the debt.

Anyway, everyone thinks that's the end of it, but he spends a year or doing a bit of this, bit of that. Ends up working for the brothers that were running the show.

Then out of fucking nowhere, he torches their car, with them in it. In the middle of their estate. In front of their boys. Him and Smoke just stand there, listening to their screams, guns in hand - refusing to let anyone help, and refusing to put them out of their misery. They let them fucking burn.

He's got a long fucking memory and a short fuse.

Nobody wanted to fuck with them after that. They just didn't want it, and let them walk away.

Nowadays though, he just organises fights. No violence for those who ain't consenting. He's got enough money, people chip him some here and there, bit of this bit of that. He mostly keeps his nose clean, and Feds couldn't give a fuck about a few boys from the ends banging each other up on a Saturday night and a few illegal bets kicking around."

Ree sits, taking it all in. Rizzy's true character is coming into focus. And it makes a lot of sense. But it's still a lot to take in.

How much of this shit is he still into?

As if any answer would be enough to pull her away now.

"And that's it, just the fights?" Ree asks, sceptical that he could be that clean with that kind of history.

"I mean, pretty much. They know heavy people, but Rizz isn't greedy. He does favours here and there, calls them in occasionally. But honestly it's mostly just fight - train - fight - train."

"Okay, so one more question, it's been fucking chewing me girl"

"Shoot"

"Their names, obviously aren't their actual names"

Jade laughs, kind of an obvious question really.

"Well my mans. He reckons they call him Green because he's 'all about that paper'" Jade mocks *"but actually nobody's too sure. Maybe it's that, or 'cause he likes a puff, or maybe because his dumb 'green' ass got himself taxed in the ends"*

Ree laughs at the last point, all are plausible really, *"and Smoke?"*

"Well, he reckons it's because he heads up North a bit, up there they call London 'the Big Smoke' and that's where it

comes from. Rizz reckons it's 'cause he's very quiet but fucking deadly. Green says it's 'cause" - with a Green impression - 'you don't want this Smoke, my guy"

Jade waits to be asked, but Ree refuses to give her the satisfaction, so Jade continues

"Rizzy, well that's short for Rizvar. Again there's different stories, Green will tell you it's because of all that 'rizz' but that wouldn't have made sense 15 years ago, so he's full of shit. Smoke says it's 'cause he goes up like a fucking Rizzla. Either way Green says that if you've got Green and Rizzla, Smoke will never be far behind"

She half takes the piss, and half laughs, clearly fond of the yarns that Green spins her.

Ree sits and contemplates all of that. Trauma, bonding in violence, yet somehow she understands everything they've done for each other. She starts to understand the positions they've been in. *Legality and morality ain't the same. You're really on your own out here if you don't have your brothers.*

"They've... really been through it together huh?"

"Yeah, those boys would kill for each other, fuck they'd die for each other. And Rizzy doing that for you, with Smoke playing *his part.... I'd say you've got him, girl.... mmm you ain't shaking that boy now, you know that, right?"*

Why the ever loving clusterfuck is that so exciting?

Chapter Twelve

A few weeks of hyper-focused training fly by. She's consumed by her need for Rizzy's approval—earning it the only way she knows: bare-faced balls in the gym. All grit, no shit.

Face Down by The Red Jumpsuit Apparatus blares through her headphones. She's firing at the pads, all cylinders. All intent, all snap, all power. It's a friendly interclub spar, not even a proper fight. *I'll be fucked if some bitch from Joey's embarrasses my Rizz.*

"You good, lil one?" Smoke asks, it's rhetorical, and he continues *"you're ready, you've got this"*

It's an interclub fight, so there's no entrance music. No ceremony. But she climbs into the ring fucking ready.

"Keep it simple, sit on your basics, float, and don't get hit" sage advice from Rizz, *"be patient, wait for her mistakes, and then fucking punish her"*

Focused and in the zone, Ree nods. Bounces on the spot. Shakes her hands out. Ready to go. Dev motions them both forwards.

The other girl looks mean. No—*she looks like she's got a temper. Like she's waiting to be provoked.*

Sit on the basics, be patient, wait for the mistake

Dev says some shit. Ree's not listening, she is staring into the soul of this bitch. She's not sure why she has inherited this beef with Joey's Gym. But she's not losing. Dev motions them to their corners. *"Relax, move, punish"* Rizzy says, putting Ree's gumshield in for her.

They've worked their game plan, Ree knows what to do. Joey's fight *all temper, no tactics*. It's all intimidation and bullshit, not skill and not finesse. Ree can't even remember the name of this girl, she just calls her *Joey*.

When they come out into the centre ring for the start, Ree extends her hand to touch gloves. Joey doesn't. Instead opting to launch straight in with a cross off the back hand. Slipped, *easy work. No opportunities, just move.*

Joey tries walking her down, it's intimidation. Ree sits on a jab, it hits glove, but the low kick lands. Ree bounces out again. Still walking forwards like the terminator, Ree blocks the jab and slips the cross, before landing a lead hook to her body. No flinch, no effect. Undeterred, Ree moves out again.

The rest of the round carries on much of the same. Basics. Slipping, rolling, blocking and parrying. Returning tactical counters and moving. Joey just keeps coming forward. The end of the round beeps and Ree heads back to her corner.

"Listen Bumbles, you're doing well. Tactical work, winning on the score card 100%. Joey's going to be giving her shit now, because she's not scared or hurt you. She's going to get sloppy, just stay fucking clean, don't get impatient, wait for it. It's coming". A squirt of water in her mouth, and she's out again for the next round.

Joey's eyes are narrower now, she's stepping on that bounce a bit more, and the first jab tells the tale. It's much harder, more intent, overloaded. Easily avoided, but the frustration is showing.

Ree carries on avoiding and countering, nothing powerful. Except chopping wood. She's slowing Joey down with every leg kick, her legs are starting to redden, and she's not putting as much weight on the front leg. Still, she marches forwards. Frustration building with every slip, every roll, every avoidance. Every time she intends to hurt, and hits nothing but glove or air.

Ree's walking on clouds, Joey's stomping the canvas. Desperation is leading her to try wilder and wilder techniques, with lessening precision and finesse. *It's coming.* Time slows down as Joey overloads on a roundkick from the rear leg. Ree reads it a mile off. Just like they practiced, Ree's knee is chambered and a rib splitting side kick lands squarely in Joey's midriff while she's mid turn, one leg in the air.

She drops instantly, flat on her back. Landing with a thud. And a familiar grunt of frustration. The veneer cracks. She bounds back onto her feet. Frustration turns to anger, Ree can see it all on her face.

Ree smiles and winks at her, *let's see what you've got, bitch.*

And she does. Joey rushes forwards like some kind of anime character, with the wildest punches Ree had ever seen. Easy to avoid, and after about 3 of them Joey's *gassed*. Barely anything in the tank. She rushes forwards again and Ree lands a beauty of a teep, sending Joey back with even more damage to her abdomen. She's seeing red, she can't think or fight straight now. *Easy pickings.* Rushing in again she catches a teep from the lead leg, followed by a swift leg kick, torso kick combo off of the right.

Catching body shots when you're already gassing out isn't the one. But Joey's too enraged to see it. Ree's enjoying this.

Joey closes her guard like a boxer and comes forward again, stalking. Fucking idiot. Ball of the foot to the chin, and firing in a side kick to the stomach. Sends Joey backwards, and brings her head forwards. Met with absolute precision, Ree goes in for the kill. Flying knee to the face. She doesn't drop yet, so Ree tees the fuck off. Close range boxing. Uppercuts, hooks, doubling up from side to side. *Don't gas while you're in there, get out.* It's hard to tell whose voice is her own, and what's Rizzy's coaching now.

Ree dives in for a clinch, lands a knee to the ribs before going for the throw. As Joey lays exhausted and splattered on the floor, Ree stands over her. Staring down at her fallen prey. Gloves down, just making her look up at her. *Bitch.*

Ree backs off, but she's in flow state now. Joey makes her way to her feet, but she's unsteady. There's nothing friendly about an interclub friendly fight. Especially between rival gyms.

Joey tries to shake it off, bouncing around the ring. Now it's Ree's turn to walk her down. Joey's too slow now, between the body shots, the leg kicks, and getting dropped on her arse. A bit of a head movement and a couple of feints later the jab lands flush, it stuns.

The overhand comes in hard to the temple, she uses it expertly to close distance before loading absolutely everything to the left of Joey's body. Kidney shot. Right on the money. Joey retches and takes a knee.

Being a friendly interclub, that's all she wrote. Dev steps in and the fight is done.

Ree stops in centre ring, brings her hands together, and bows to Joey, to her coach, to Dev, and to Rizzy. She walks slowly, purposefully, confidently back to Rizzy. He takes her headguard off, and takes her gumshield.

'Good girl" quietly in her ear. That's all she needed to hear. *'I guess you've got some sting after all, eh Bee"* with a smile and a wink.

Bee takes her walk into the middle of the ring, to have her glove raised. Triumphant victor. She turns and hugs her opponent, then shakes hands with Joey's corner.

Coach Joey and Rizz make their way into centre ring. *'Fair fucks. It is what it is"* comes Coach Joey's opener, handing over a small wad of cash to Rizz. They shake hands and everyone heads back to their corners, before climbing out the ring.

'Your girl's banging now, huh Rizz?" one of the lads jokes from the sidelines.

*Your girl. How can something so non-chalant be **everything?** I don't know, but it is. He didn't correct them either. What he didn't say, says so fucking much.*

'Great work Bee, hit the showers" Rizzy instructs, after unwrapping and checking her hands and giving her a quick check for concussion.

Come with me? She pleads internally. She walks towards the changing rooms, buzzing from her fight. More buzzing from his approval. Even more buzzing for her being claimed as his.

Giddy, she glances back - and he's still watching. *Fuck.*

Way to play it cool, Bee. Fucking well done. You nerrrrd.

Chapter Thirteen

Figure You Out by *VOILÁ* screams through the speakers. Rizzy's here, alone. His music, his training, his time, his space. Dev's away on a training camp with some of the lads. It's 10pm. He's alone and free.

He's worked through his shit tonight. Personal bests on deadlifts, squat bar, chest press and lat pull down. Nothing's releasing the tension. Rizz is alone, in the gym, with his thoughts.

Maximum effort rounds, until vomit. Full commitment. Full tear up. Let it go. Get it fucking out.

Round timer beeps, 3 minute rounds, 1 minute rest. And all hell breaks loose. *This fucking girl.* He works through another round, the fifth so far.

The Ice Cube, really?

They'd barely spoken about anything except training since the night in the club.

Why didn't you just fuck her?

Agonisingly silent arguments rage in his head.

You probably scared her off, she didn't need to see that. You could've handled cunt features outside. Why show off? You put everyone at risk you fucking idiot.

He shakes the wrought iron frame with the force of his round kick. Sweat drips from his brow, stinging his eyes. He will not stop.

Why watch her walk away like a fucking creep? Honestly, are you trying to put her off? Fucking melt.

Grunting, almost shouting, with every single strike. Better than therapy. *Pain in the body quiets the mind.*

Body hook after body hook. Shaking the bag. Denting and swinging it with every shot. Full hip. Full body weight. Maximum effort. *"Ruuuagh"* as he puts the final hook in, his agonised voice echoes through the empty hall, even through the blaring music.

She's a nice girl, she can't handle you.... even if she wants you... "your girl", why didn't you correct him? The world can see you're going soft

Beep for the end of the round. Burpees. Non-stop. Between rounds. *I'll vomit out this ridiculous obsession if I have to.*

Weightless and airborne, with each jump, it all flashes back. Her throwing back the Jaegerbomb. His hand on her thigh. Their kiss at the bar. The horror on her face as he kissed her before finishing Cal. Holding her up, trusting him completely. Her curled up in bed as he left.

Every torturous moment he didn't give in to his desire for her. His need for her. His rage at the world for not having her.

You'd fucking ruin her. She deserves better than that.

50 leg kicks, each side, heavy bag. And he gets to work. The heavy thuds landing to the beat of *BACKBONE - Chase & Status x Stormzy*

A warrior's shout with every single shot. After so many rounds of punishment, his shins are swelling, on the verge of splitting.

Body unable to take much more physical punishment. Shins fucked, hands sore and swollen, despite being wrapped and wearing big gloves. Time to cool down. Not feeling much tension released, but at least knackered. A few rounds of skipping in the ring to finish the session.

The playlist loops round again. *Figure You Out* is back on. He lays on his back in mid-ring. Staring at the flickering lights. Everything is still. Everything quietens. Just a man, the music, and his mind.

This fucking girl.

Eyes closed, trying to find some semblance of peace. To think about *anything* else. He feels the canvas bounce underneath him. Someone's climbing into the ring. His eyes shoot open, fixated on the direction of the movement.

Dehydration dream?

His eyes focus and blur repeatedly as he tries to understand what the fuck is going on.

But there she stands. An angel there, to rescue him from his pit of despair? A demon sent to torment him endlessly?

In any case. A fucking sight to behold.

Chapter Fourteen

Rizzy's pulse spikes. *It's her, she's here. The fuck?*

A painful pause.

"Hey" she starts, suddenly less confident than when she climbed into the ring

"What are you here for?" he asks, maybe a bit more confrontationally than he meant it

Another painful pause.

"You" she admits

They just sit in the silent aftermath of that world changing admission for a second.

"How?"

"Ash gave me a key" she concedes

"...why?"

"What's with all the questions? And seriously. You kiss me like that, take me home, handle Cal, we have a real moment. Then what, you're back to Mr Grumpy coach? That's it? Had your fill, changed your mind, what the fuck?"

He's stunned. He wishes he could tell her as much as she needs to know. His eyes scan her, trying to figure out how to respond.

"I won for you" she presses on, he knows *"I don't know why, but I fucking need you. And you can barely speak to me. Is this some weird power play or psycho babble bullshit game or what?"*

"It's not what you think" is all he can manage. It's stammering, bleeding his self assurance with every syllable

They sit in an uncomfortable silence. A void between them. Full of emotion, raw, potent and dangerous. Barely a coherent sentence. Christ, barely a conversation shared between them. But it hangs in the air. Combustible gas, ready to detonate.

"Oh what kind of bullshit's that, Rizz?"

Like a scolded child he sits, where she stands. Looking up at her.

"I don't love like they do... I'll hurt you... you don't deserve that" his words slow and deliberately, regaining that Rizzy rizz. Climbing to his feet, towering over her. His presence becoming intimidating. *"I don't do games, and funny lines. Bee, I'm not the one"*

An intense rage, an unrighteous rejection, hellfire burns with the force of a thousand suns, scorching her soul. She shoves him, with both hands with absolutely every pound of strength she possesses.

"Who the FUCK are you? Not the fucking one? You drive me fucking crazy. You're insane. You break someone's jaw for shit they did BEFORE you even met me. You let people call me yours. You let me bleed for you. Aww you're not the one. FUCK YOU, you don't get to decide FOR me!"

"Bee, don't" he warns, stepping back towards her *"you don't get it"*, eyes locking with hers. *"I will fucking destroy you"*

"... do it" she dares, stepping to match his advance, two inches from his face. Feeling the pace of his breathing on her face.

She swallows, *it's now or never*. And she does it. She leans in, and plants a kiss on his unflinching lips. He doesn't crack, he doesn't respond, and she refuses to stop.

He ignites. Ice melted. Mountains shifting. The gates of hell burst open as he loses the strength to keep them closed. He kisses her back. It's not enough. He needs more. He instinctively and almost instantaneously grabs her by the throat, and marches her backwards to the corner post. Her feet barely touch the floor. Losing her footing he holds her up against the corner, and lets go.

Every second spent obsessing over her. She feels it all. In an instant she's aware that this can't be stopped. This tsunami is inevitable, it's an unstoppable force, and she's the immovable object.

"You're fucking mine now" he growls, moving his mouth to her neck, and biting her, sampling her taste

"Prove it" she gasps back

That was all the challenge he needed, before he ripped her vest top upwards. Exposing her braless form. Discarding it fuck knows where. He pushes himself against her on the ropes. She feels his heat, feels his heart pounding through his chest. She wraps her arms around him, and digs her bitten nails across his shoulder blades and down to his ribs. She can mark him, too.

Taking his hand from her throat to her jaw, running his thumb on her chin, he kisses her again. Claiming her mouth. *It's mine to fucking ruin.*

Without warning, he puts his arms between her legs, and lifts her by the back of her thighs to perch atop the corner post. She lifts her hips to allow him to tear her shorts and pants down in one swift movement, her legs outstretched in front of her, destabilising her balance. *He won't let me fall.*

A foot on the middle ropes. Legs apart. Completely naked. Upon a pedestal. He admires her. Devouring every inch from her knees to her naval, to her nipples. He looks up at God's greatest creation. The cause of his insanity. The object of his obsession. His perfect prize. The woman who'll wreck his life. Her scent drives him wild. Her taste. The softness of her skin. The way her body shakes with anticipation.

He can wait no longer. She needs him not to. She's completely open for him in every sense. By the moment his tongue electrifies her, she's aching. She needs this. The sweet release. The guilt free pleasure. Her obsession, requited.

His tongue dances with her fantasies, her whole body is erogenous now. It *belongs* to him. It hurts to need him so desperately. He does not disappoint. His whole mouth over her. Tongue skimming her lips. From bottom to top. Teasing its way. Agonising. Detouring. He fucking knows what he's doing. She grips his hair with both hands.

"Please" she almost sobs, nearly ripping his hair out. He gives her that which she craves. Taking her clit on the end of his tongue, varying his pressure, building a rhythm, until his matches hers. Her hips and his tongue in absolute harmony. Her breathing, agonises. Giving away her desperation for release. Pure pleasure.

He reaches a hand up to her bare breast, he dances the tip of his finger and thumb around her areola brushing over her nipple, rubbing around it.

Approaching climax now, pleasure unbearable. He adds pain to the mix, he takes her nipple between the tip of his thumb and the edge of his trigger finger. She gasps, she nearly screams. She pulls his head into her lap harder now. Grinding her hips on his face.

The earth shatters. Her body convulses. Her breathing erratic. Her heart palpitates.

He stands, placing his forehead on hers. She wraps her arms around his shoulders. Her heavy breathing calmed by his proximity. They share this moment. Sweat soaked flesh, on sweat soaked flesh.

After a minute or two, her eyes open. She catches him. His jaw clenched. His painful tension is evident. He's holding back.

Her softest hand rests on his cheek, she leans up and kisses him. Softly, gently. Lovingly. *"What about you?"*

He doesn't respond. Restraint intact. He looks into her eyes. His gaze penetrates her soul, but his remains guarded. Her mind throws back to his earlier comment. He'll hurt her.

That's what's holding him back.

Taking a second to fully understand her decision, she owns it.

"I can take it"

His hands under her thighs he lowers her down to the floor. He pulls the stool from beside the corner and places it in front. Grabbing her hips, he sits her down on it. Making her the perfect height.

He towers over her now, cupping her jaw in both his hands, kissing her once more. He places her hands on the ropes. Her legs together, he stands one foot either side.

In the final moments of calm, he reaches down, and pulls himself from his trousers. His passion already leaking from the tip.

"All you've got to do is fly away, little Bee"

The weight of the words sit with her, grounded on the stool. Hands holding the ropes. Steadfast, she looks up to him, one last time, before everything changes. *"Never"*.

With that, she places her tongue at the very base of his twitching, eager cock. She runs it along the underside. Tracing, feeling, revering every feature, every vein. A firm, sucking kiss placed on the very end. Teasing his control. Igniting his nerve endings. She feels him harden even more. She guides her lips expertly over his head. Making him feel every millimetre. She only gets halfway before running out of mouth. Her eyes shoot open with the realisation.

His. Control. Runs. Out.

He takes her by her hair, pinning her head at the corner post. He honours her depth, but not her pace. As he viciously hits the back of her mouth. Over and over. Her lips almost numb with the relentless pace. Then he pushes. He pushes deeper. She stops herself from gagging. If it's her throat he needs, he can have it.

Realising the depth he needs, he starts to pull away, and she pushes forwards. She keeps pushing, until she feels the sweat of his pubis on her face. She grips his naked cheeks. Digs her nails in, feeling him tense, she drives her mouth back to his hip bone. With absolute defiance.

She looks up, past his chiselled pecks. She nods as best as she can, with an "uhuh" hummed out over his throbbing member occupying her mouth. It's a red rag to a bull.

He nails her back to her position. He takes full advantage, she knows what she signed up for. Every thrust bruising her throat. Eyes streaming for him. Body aching. He drives into her. Over and over again. Deep into her throat. The pain lets her know she's alive. Her pain adds to the intensity for him. He feels her throat tightening. He hears her fighting back the gags. He knows she's giving herself completely. But it's not enough.

He needs *her*.

He pulls out of her throat, leaving her gasping. Fighting for her breath. She has no voice to use. He takes her hand, and guides her to the multi-machines. Taking his sweat dripped, blood stained hand wraps. He ties her wrists to the handles, leaving her in a near-crucifix. Mouth still dripping. Still barely breathing.

The handles are too high, she has to tiptoe to maintain contact with the floor. He stands, chest to chest. Grabs her legs, and wraps them around him. He takes her weight from her legs and hips, she holds what she can with her arms. With the only control he has, he pushes firmly inside her. She gasps, unable to do anything but accept him. All of him. Raw, brutal, bloody, crazy, obsessive, and fucking hot.

She grinds her hips, finding his full depth. A moan escapes her lips. She tries to pull herself up, to escape the pain of his size.

It's hopeless. He wraps his arms around her waist, holding her in place, and drives in. She grits her teeth as a guttural groan sits in her aching throat.

An animal behind his eyes. They lock. She finally sees the extent of the fire in this man. She accepts it. All of it.

"Make me take it"

And he does. For a Valhallan's eternity. A warrior's death.

Blissful carnage as he rips her wide open. Unapologetic. Unflinching. Unwavering. She rides with him, as he desecrates her. The beautiful destruction of his obsession.

Their violent crescendo peaks together. He holds her close, tight, intertwined as he delivers his final strokes. Signs his deal with the devil, his fate sealed as she screams his name. Pump after ethereal pump. His flame dissipating with his fluids.

He steps back and admires his perfect Pompeii. He drips from her, bruised and abused. Her subjugation complete. She hasn't looked away the whole time, save to throw her head back and embrace her own intense release.

Pulling the bench forwards for her to stand on, alleviating the pressure from her wrists and shoulders, he unties her. Once required to support her own weight, she falls forwards onto him. Wrapping a leg either side of him. His forearms beneath her rear. Bearing her weight. Her head rests on his shoulder. Almost lifeless.

He carries her back into the ring. Taking a seat on the floor, with his back against the corner he turns her to face the same way as him. Her back against his chest. His arms around her like a seatbelt. He kisses her neck, and strokes her hair into place away from her face. *"I've got you, Bee, forever"*. She can't talk, exhausted from the night. Instead, she kisses his forearm, pushes herself back, and turns her cheek to pillow his arm. Completely relaxed.

Desecrated, yes, but still revered. The most precious thing in his universe. It hurts to hurt her, but it feels too damn good not to.

Fuck sacrificing her to save the world. He'd burn the world to save her.

Chapter Fifteen

Meena waits at the front door. Beating the knock is her favourite game. And it's a point of pride that she never loses. It's not intuition, it's intention.

Jade's the first of the procession. *"Amma!"* she exclaims, throwing her arms around Meena pushing her cheek to Meena's. Meena hugs around Jade's torso, with a squeeze. Before cupping her face *"Beta - my noise in human form! And too skinny! Go get a samosa before you disappear!"*

Naturally, after Jade always comes Green. His usual wild grin, replaced with a sincere smile. *"Salaam, Amma"* voice gentle and deeply respectful, Meena is quieter with Green. Warm in a different way. She rubs his upper arm and returns a warm smile, looking in his eye before giving him a quick squeeze. No words or teasing needed.

Smoke's imposing figure is the next to grace the doorway -

"Auntie" with a wide, warm smile. Which is met with a faux-cold side eye, before she takes his cheeks in her hands, forcefully turning his jaw checking him for bruises *"my naughtiest adopted son - still causing mischief - it's all I hear!"*.

Rizzy bows his head as he crosses the threshold, *"Hey, ma"* he pauses. *"What kind of a bloody son doesn't call for two weeks, huh? Plenty of time for business, none for me? Aye, you drive me to distraction - let me look at you"* she roughly takes his jaw and inspects him, harsher and more thoroughly than she did Smoke *"look at these baggies, boy you're not sleeping - what do I tell you?".* Then her smile cracks, she hugs him high. She pushes her cheek on his and holds him for seconds.

"And you bring me another stray, eh?" says Meena, looking between Rizzy and Bee, who hasn't yet dared cross the threshold. She's met Meena a hundred times. Meena's shown her care, fed her, but never invited her into her home.

"Beta..." letting the weight of the word sit for a second *"why do you wait on the cobbles, are you trying to heat the street?"* Bee cautiously enters, unsure of what reception to expect. *"Is he looking after you, this 'son' of mine? He's bloody careless, you know?"* Meena inspects Bee from head to toe *"and that training diet, it's no good for you, bones are for the dog!"*

One by one, with a nod and smile, maybe a fist bump from Ash, they make their way from the entrance hallway into the dining room. Bee watches this undocumented ceremony, acutely aware of her newfound place, marred with uncertainty.

The warmth and homely smells confront her as she walks through the doorway herself. Noticing the ornate, dark wooden table in the centre of the room. Decorated beautifully with steel and ceramic serving plates bearing traditional appetisers and starters.

The kitchen is off to the left of this room, and another room to the right. Light streams in from the room on the right, and through the kitchen doorway, though the dining room itself is landlocked. The opposing wall is masterfully organised with dozens of framed photographs. Moments caught in time. A family's history documented in photo form.

She notices older photos first, their browning tones catching her eye. A very young Ashok and Sanjay stand proudly next to a Bedford Rascal, parked in the street between the gym and the shop. An adorably young, and a little chunky, Smoke stands fists raised next to a cool looking Rizzy in the same pose. Sanjay standing behind them, hands on their shoulders.

They must've only been about 16 in the photos. A very young Ash embraces Meena in the doorway to their shop, circa the 1980s. A beautiful face to face photo on their wedding day, Ash and Meena - blissfully in love. A photo of the three boys - Rizz, Smoke, and Green on BMXs in the summer. Countless photos of Rizz with prize belts, medals, and trophies. Always flanked by Jay and Ash. Proud as punch. The boys often grouped into the photo. A photo in a ring, with Jay behind Smoke and Rizz, and an older Pakistani man in front of what looks like a young Chiz and Ali. In their boxing shorts and hands wrapped, fight-posing for the camera. A photo of the whole group, Green's arm around Jade, celebrating something.

Meena bustles to the kitchen and back. *"Chhotu"* Green rolls his eyes at being addressed like this *"my little one, take this - vegetarian samosas"*. Bee observes this little ritual, remembering Green's faith, and appreciating Meena's deep, silent respect for it.

After polite, quietened small talk, and plenty of samosas, seekh kebabs, pakoras, and paneer tikka. Meena rises and begins clearing the table. Jade spots the cue and instinctively follows suit. Bee observes and hesitates for a moment too long, before trying to make herself useful.

Meena doesn't look up, but moves to the side to allow Bee to collect plates that she could have carried herself. Meena waits a hot second, to allow Bee to follow her into her kitchen.

The busy hum of the kitchen settles as the final cleaned plate stacks. Bee has barely spoken. She's observed, followed, learned, copied. With a triumphant sigh, Meena nods to Bee with a small smile. The tiniest sentiment. The biggest stamp of approval. She has a seat at the table and a space in the room, not a place on the wall, yet. *One day.*

There's been a lot to learn, a lot of rules unsaid. Topics of conversation that are not suitable for the dinner table. Anything involving money, fighting, or business. We don't speak ill at the table, of anyone, ever. Instead, Ash simply gives a disapproving sign or grunt at the mention of their name, and conversation moves on. What Amma Meena says, goes. It's not questioned, ever. Ashok is the boss in the shop.

Rizzy is the boss in the gym. Meena's the boss here. Woe betide anybody who forgets it.

The feeling that Bee just can't shake, however. Is the intimate trust and safety in this home. These are dangerous dudes. Doing as Aunty tells them. Sure, they could tear the place up if they wanted to. But they never, ever would. They'd die before they let someone dirty Meena's carpet.

Chapter Sixteen

Another night, another adventure.

"We all have darkness inside us. Some of us show that darkness to the world. But true evil, that comes from repression" Rizz matter-of-factly explains to Bee.

That's a bit fucking cryptic, but okay.

They meet at *The Tower*, an old castle/keep looking building. The exterior illuminated with spot lights and red neons, making the structure glow. Low, thudding bass resonates through the grounds.

There's no queue, but plenty of security on the doors. As always, they waltz through to the bar. This whole place is VIP, as is everyone's dress code. There's no peasant queue this time. Rizz's hand never leaves her. Holding her hand, or his hand on the small of her back. He's never far enough to lose touch. She can feel him, and she can feel his eyes.

They bump into some familiar faces, Chiz and Ali. Chiz does the talking, as always;

"Salam alaikum my brother" to Rizz, ignoring the rest of the entourage, including Bee

"Wa alaikum salam" he replies, stoically

"Business good?"

"We move"

"Ma sha Allah. Uncle Hassan was very happy this month, he's happy, everyone's happy." he stops to take a look at Bee, pausing. His gaze engulfs her. Discomfort be upon her. *"New talent? Respect".* Chiz looks as though he may continue his slimy not-so-subtle narrative. He's deterred by a subtle arm fold and cold-as-ice stare from Smoke, incited by a subtle tension from Rizzy.

Chiz continues *"anyway, brother. Enjoy your evening. I hear it's popping downstairs tonight"* and he makes his way, Ali shadowing him as always.

A couple of glances exchanged between Rizz, Smoke, and Green. And between Jade and Bee, and the group get their drinks.

The group enjoy their drinks, talking amongst themselves. Pulling Bee close, Rizz explains *"What you're going to experience tonight, it's different... everyone's going to go their separate ways... you'll be all mine... like always".* The hairs stand up on the back of Bee's neck. *What the fuck have I signed up for?* Rizz watches her reaction with excited anticipation.

Rizz finishes his sentence just as a pair of very dishevelled businessmen - very red faced and out of breath - leave via the downstairs door, straight to the exit.

A small group of chatty, excitable women pass them. They're straight out of the Playboy Mansion. Lingerie, centrefold perfection. They head downstairs. As the sound-deadening doors open, the volume of the thumping bass dramatically increases. In a lull in the beat, a cacophony of explicit sounds are barely audible.

Jade's eyes are glued to where the playboy girls once were. She vibrates with excitement, practically squeaking. Her eyes don't leave the door as she grabs Green's hand and pulls him, like a puppy on a training leash, to the door. He doesn't resist, at all, he's just ever so slightly cooler.

Two gulps later, Smoke gives his signature shrug and slight smile, and heads down himself. With ever so slightly more swag in his step than usual. Popping his collar.

"Your turn Bee, all you've got to do is fly away... or dare to find freedom behind the bars" Rizz slowly and deliberately whispers in her ear. He continues with the kind of vague yet alluring warning that makes her shiver *"I can't promise what you will or won't find down there, that's your choice to make..."*

Ominously making her way down the stairs, staccato stiletto clicks cut through the ambience. Breath unsteady, comforted by Rizzy's solid presence. She grips and releases the hand rail with her decent., feeling the rough imperfections of the paint. Scraping her knuckles on the bare, warm brickwork.

As they reach the sub level, the brickwork opens up to reveal a lounge. Men in three piece suits. Women in lingerie, some completely topless. Exposed brickwork illuminated red with clever, warming, lusting lighting. The air feels thick like a fog. The aroma of whisky and cigar smoke hide the deeper sins that await. The bar is stacked with optics, top calibre drink. The oak box of cigars available for all guests. Refined are the partakers in the erotic.

"May I take your coats?" comes the exquisitely polite voice from a playboy blonde. Topless, in a waist clinching corset and fishnet holdups, with patent leather stilettos. Rizz helps Bee out of her faux-fur jacket, whilst removing his own tuxedo and handing them to the bunny. *"Have a sinsual evening"* she smiles sweetly. Her perfume decorates the air, wafted by the flick of her hair as she turns to the cloak room.

Taking another look around, everything seems surprisingly normal. Black wood sofas with luxurious red cushioning. Ornate stock shelves with dark wooden boxes, with ornate golden features. A coffee table, a futon. This is just a lounge. She starts to relax. The sounds of whips are somewhat unnerving. They're counterbalanced by giggles, and the occasional groan.

How did she squeeze into that? Bee wonders, looking at a busty red head in a black latex catsuit, smoking a cigarette through a holder. Her outstretched legs give way to 8 inch heels. Under the heels, however, is flesh. A man. In nothing but a gimp mask. On all fours. He's her footstool. She leans forward, ashes her cigarette on him, and utters two words which make him shudder. *"Good boy"*.

The only thing out of place, in the decorum of the deranged, is a single black sign, with red lettering. "No phones. No photography."

"Ready?" Rizz asks, her silence is consent. Her footsteps are compliance. As they approach a brick archway, they both drop their phones into the faraday box offered by the huge security guard.

How big is this place? As the archway gives way to a series of corridors in the dungeon. Clearly these used to be cells. Now, they're decorated differently, for every taste, every perversion.

"I have reserved us a space, take your time. I'll be at the end of the hallway" and he walks away. Leaving her. Stranded. Isolated. An island in a sea of seduction, sin, and sodomy. She turns, the exit is just there. *Fly away little Bee? Not a fucking chance.* She gulps at her own audacity.

Slowly, she walks. Some curtains, doors, and separators have been left open. There's secrecy, but no shame.

Walking from door to door, some rooms are empty, some have people, but no action.

Then there's the throne room. There he sits. Dark tattooed chest bare. It's Green. He says nothing, enjoying his paradise as Jade, and a curvy caramel beauty expertly, passionately, desperately working their mouths in unison up and down him.

He admires their nudity. Their dedication to their servitude. Their eye contact with one another, and Jade's with Green.

Bee can almost hear her *"see how good we make you feel, Daddy?"*. Jade goes from all fours to kneeling up, kissing his nipple. She grabs the back of Caramel's head, and forces her down. Green's head throws back. The forced gags and vocalisations from Caramel turning both of them on more. *See how good I made you fuck her face?*

Jade and Green's eye contact barely falters, as she uses another's throat to please him. Sensing him tense, and release imminent, Jade pulls Caramel's head away from the near-imminent ejaculate. Green stands, unimpeded. He takes his Queen to the table, and lays her on her back. Spreading her legs. She's the perfect height and angle, as he pushes himself into her. Slowly, purposefully.

He leads Caramel by her hand, to Jade's side. Then he encourages Caramel's oral worship of his queen, whilst he's slowly working his cock in and out of her.

She writhes, she squeals, she thanks him, praises him, repeatedly. Jade could sing to the world how good her King is at owning her pussy. How much she adores him. Caramel can't be left out. Neither King nor Queen would allow it. So she is encouraged by the hands and arms of her dominants to perch atop Jade's face.

Jade enjoys giving this pleasure as much as receiving what she has been. Caramel groans and grinds. Jade grips Caramel's hips, while Green grips Jade's. The three of them ride the climax together endlessly.

Bee takes her leave, and steps away. Processing what she's seen, how she feels, and how her body is reacting.

It sounds like there's some kind of show going on down the corridor. She follows the sound, and peeks around the corner. The room is darkened, but mostly empty. There's a crowd of naked bodies, she can barely see through.

When the bare flesh parts enough for her to catch a glimpse, her eyes can hardly catch everything in time. On all fours, in the middle of the floor. Completely naked, riding a cock and loving it.

All the bodies blend to one, as another man steps in behind her, slipping himself into her ass. By the ease of entry, that's not the first thing that has been in there tonight. Watching as she's roughly invaded in both holes, and masterfully multitasking, switching cocks in her hands and mouth.

Everyone gets their turn.

The central man, head end removed himself from her throat, and walks to the other end. Where he replaces the anal penetrator. When one man's had his fill, with or without covering her in yet more sticky reward - which she **loves**, by the way - he's simply replaced with another. With so much movement it's difficult to track how many there are, or where they've all been.

But she doesn't care. She's in bliss pleasuring so many cocks all at once. Her enthusiasm is unmatched, and her dedication to the extraction of cum second to none. They cheer and celebrate her, united in their pursuit of being pleased by the woman there to please them all.

"Make - him - bleed" comes a firm, feminine, strong command. Followed by a hard slap. Intrigue captures Bee, and her footsteps give away her position, not that anybody cares.

She leans on another brick archway, resting her cheek on the inside of the arch. Almost unable to consume what her senses perceive.

A huge, muscle bound white man lays, legs akimbo, on a bench. A small smear of blood trails from the corner of his mouth, next to his reddened cheek. Completely naked, covered in marks, scratches, and whelps. Blood rushing to the surface of his skin, desperate to repair the physical damage his soul's desires have done. His body rhythmically jolts and jars away from the body of his penetrator, to the sound of hard muscle hitting hard muscle. A carnal, Smoke, possessed by passion and power. *"See he bleeds for you, how you bleed for me"* comes the voice of the femme fatale. Carving Smoke's chest, bloody drips from the trail her nails leave. *"Thank him"* her instruction continues, to the submissive.

"Thank you...." he pants between thrusts. *"For...."* She instructs his continuation, as he struggles under the sheer force with which he's being defiled. *"Thank you mistress, thank you sir, thank you for fucking me, for making me bleed, for setting me free"* the last part his own creative license.

"Aww, he's getting sentimental, hit him.. again" and Smoke does as commanded, without hesitation. He leans further forward, deepening his penetration, and slaps his submissive's face. It's hard. Rapidly increasing the speed at which blood pools at the corner of his mouth, causing him to spit it out to

the side. *"Thank you"* the submissive whispers without prompt.

"You love it, don't you, boy. Being abused and beaten, wrecked by that big... black... cock, that I control. Making you my toys, my play things. Your suffering belongs to me. You can't unfuck that pretty little ass, can you boy?" She expertly weaves her words. She reaches down to the submissive, and chokes him, talking down to him. *"Are you ready? To be filled, to have cum dripping from your gaping asshole?"* she doesn't wait for a response. The erotic horror in his eyes has achieved the desired effect, and sensing she may get close to a *yellow flag* from her bottom.

"Cum for me, baby" she turns her attention to Smoke. She spanks his ass, hard, forcing a deeper, involuntary thrust into their Bottom. *"Do it now, what the fuck are you waiting for.... fill him"* he thrusts harder, faster, desperate to release. His face portrays his frustration.

She stands behind him, sliding her hand to his throat and gripping it, hard. He audibly chokes for breath, and she doesn't release. *"Hurt him, hurt him like I hurt you"* and she digs her nails in again. Hard, dragging them from between his shoulder blades all the way to the small of his back. Blood runs down his back, the involuntary arch pushing him over the edge. He grabs the legs of the bottom and forces his knees towards his chest. With his whole bodyweight pushed onto their submissive bottom, he drives like a pneumatic drill. Thrust after agonising thrust, the pair of them yell, as she cackles maniacally. With the primal vocalisation of a man wrestling a bear, he delivers his final thrusts. Fulfilling on his promise to both of them.

Smoke stands, releasing the bottom from his power hold. *"Clean - him - now"*, she instructs. Immediately he rolls from the bench, crawls to Smoke's feet and kneels. Carefully, affectionately cleaning him. Inch by inch. His face, mouth, tongue, and chin now expertly decorated with cum, lube, and blood. Her tone changes now *"my good boys, you play so well."* her harsh hands now stroking and softening.

What the fuck did I just see. In a daze, pushing herself away from the wall.

The next she hears is screaming. Not the usual moaning. Actual screaming. As if someone is being tortured. Becoming accustomed to the *Ripley's Believe It Or Not* of sexual tastes Bee ventures onwards.

The next room is darkened again, for deliberate sensory deprivation. The object of the room, however, is perfectly illuminated. She's voluptuous. The largest all real tits Bee had ever seen. Pleasure radiates from her. That pleasure is being extracted forcefully. Over, and over again.

Encased in ornate Shibari, arms behind her, mounted atop a ride-on vibrator. She smiles gleefully, throwing her head around, rejoicing in her lack of choice about how she's forced to climax this time. With a dildo attached to some kind of power tool, the masked man managing the scene goes to work on her back passage.

The crowd, barely visible in the shadows, sat politely in rows, like an orgasmic auditorium, thoroughly approving of his choice of tools.

She lets out another involuntary howl, as she erupts - covering the plastic sheeting in what seems like gallons of squirt. She cries through laughter, possessed by the orgasms she's forced to endure; again and again.

With tits bouncing, as the masked man selects a dildo pole. Our voluptuous vixen gives a nod, and two more masked men enter the scene. One stood behind her, one kneeling in front.

The first of our masked dominants takes his dildo pole, and begins to fuck her mercilessly with it as she leans forward. The kneeling man does not take his eyes off of her face, watching her with great focus.

"I'm cumming" she begins to cry, tears running down her face.

At that exact moment, the third masked man suddenly and quickly hoods her with a plastic bag, pulling tight around her face, preventing her breathing completely. She wriggles, squirms, silently screams, her chest heaves and she releases one final squirt, leaning backwards - the well choreographed original administrator having already removed his pole - she squirts in the air like a fountain.

As soon as the squirt finishes, the bag is removed. She rolls onto the floor, bathing in the remnants of her orgasms. The crowd whoop and holler. She laughs, maniacally. *"Thank you, thank you"*, like a thespian, to her adoring fans. She lays and embraces the moment, the love from her audience.

Before sitting up, a queef escaping her. She doesn't even care.

She lets out a chuckle. *"Well, you've all just seen a lot worse from me than some escaping air"*. Completely naked, as the lights come up slightly. *"That was amazing, thank you all, and thank you three..."* she does a chef's kiss gesture. Still breathing heavily, radiating her confidence. She leans back onto her forearms and catches her breath as the audience begin to leave, many complimenting her on their way past.

She continues her quest down the corridor. To be greeted by an ajar, dark wood, decorated with wrought iron, door. Red lighting bleeding through the opening. It opens slowly, intentionally.

He stands there. White shirt, sleeves rolled up, only half buttoned. Still tucked. Trousers fixed in place by his over shoulder braces. And a smile that says *"I'm glad you made it. I hope you're ready"*. His cigar stands erect, held between his teeth. His whisky, on the rocks, in his hand. The picture of refined dominance.

He offers her champagne. She takes the cigar from his mouth, takes a long drag and swirls it, before blowing it in his face. Distracted, he doesn't resist when she takes his glass, and takes a *fuck-you* size mouthful - savouring the flavour - of his very rich, smoky, peaty scotch. Swallowing smoothly, with an approving facial expression; and not a damn hint of the burn.

Once he's over her sheer audacity, he pours himself another.

The whole vibe in here tells her she's about to give up her options, so she takes another whilst she has the choice. Turned on by everything she's seen - though not by their kinks and shows and acts, but by their freedom and rejoice.

By the time he's replenished his beverage and turned to face her, she stands, unapologetically, completely naked. Feet together, hands behind her back. Playing her final card of the night. Despite the warmth of the room, every hair on her body stands on end. Her nipples betray her readiness.

The rich red, soft, deep carpet feels luxurious under her toes. She can't help but make little foot fists and grab it. *This would be a real nice hotel room.* Looking around, the devil is in the details. Again the ornate boxes, hiding something. The wall behind her, where the door is, houses a wall of torture implements. Tools to provide pleasure and pain. Glancing back to Rizzy, she notices, hiding in plain sight, runners on the floor.

The runners lead to medieval stocks. Currently open. With holes for her neck and wrists. There are holes in the floor running parallel to the runners. Behind the stocks is a curtain, from the ceiling to the floor.

Noticing her examination of the room, Rizzy approaches her. He takes her jaw in his hand, and kisses her. It's different. It's controlled, it's dominant, it's aggressive. Everything from the way his mouth makes contact with hers, to the way his tongue finds its way inside her mouth, drips with *'Tonight, I do what I want with you"*

He slides the stocks back on their rails, and guides her head and wrists into them, before closing them, and bolting them in place.

The deafening click of the lock bolting in sends shivers. *What the fuck am I doing?* She gulps.

The purpose of the holes in the floor becomes evident, as he places her ankles in a spreader bar. The inside is fluffy and makes the restraint feel comforting. He then pins the bar to the floor.

And there we have it, no escape now. What have you done, girl?

She wriggles and tests the restraints. Nothing budges. Her hands, feet, and head, fixed in place. Completely at his mercy. She couldn't get away if she wanted to. For his next act, he places his ice cold glass on her back, and leaves it there.

I'm bent over and exposed like this, and you use me as a fucking coffee table? Unbelievable.

He's in no rush, every act is intentional, it's slow. It builds her anticipation as she realises she still doesn't know what he's actually going to do with, or to, her. *Is it gunna hurt?*

He pulls the velvet chord, and the curtains - now dead in front of her - open, to reveal a mirror. She's confronted with the vision of herself. Well, her head and hands. Completely immobile, waiting to be used by her... *shit, what even is he? My coach? My boyfriend? Master/owner?* She laughs out loud at the last thought. *As if I'm gunna call him "sir"*.

He's unfazed by her reaction, as he rolls up the carpet between the rails. Revealing another mirror. No matter where she gazes, she'll have to see herself. In whatever state he deems fit.

Underneath the mirror beneath her is a small bronze placard. *Please Play Responsibly - Traffic lights: Red - Stop. Amber - Ease Off. Can't speak? Double tap.*

He removes his glass, and runs his hand from the stocks down to her ass. He grabs a handful, as much as he can. He shakes it for his own enjoyment before spanking it, hard enough to leave a mark. Not so hard to make her flinch. He gauges her reaction in the mirror.

She looks his reflection dead in the eye, as if to say *"is that all you've got?"*

Her defiance ignites something in him, he grabs a handful of ice, freezing her ass cheek. It doesn't take long before the cold starts to really bite. Discarding it into a drinks bucket, he slaps again. This time it hurts. She winces. So he goes again. The ice cold rawness of her skin, with the sudden impact creates instant handprints. Despite her flinching eyes, she maintains eye contact with him. A few more spanks and winces, he moves on.

To the side is a lit candle, he takes it and strolls back to her. It's not like she can go anywhere, so he takes all the time he wants. He allows a single drop of wax to fall on her back, off centre, avoiding her spine. She squirms at this, just a little. A big enough reaction to know she felt it, and liked how it hurt, small enough that she thinks she's safe.

So he pours some more. Making her inhale sharply as he burns her skin. *"Oh you like that one don't you, little Bee?"*

She refuses to answer, so he pours some more. The heat ignites her senses. It hurts, so good. Like a pantomime player, he overacts being about to pour, she braces for it. The burn that doesn't come. A second later than expected, he dumps a smattering of wet-hot droplets across her back.

He brings the candle in front of her face, close enough that she can feel its heat - and fear for her hair. *"Blow it out"* he instructs, she looks at him as if to say *fucking really?* And he maintains his position. So she does as instructed, and blows it out. His *"Good girl"* praise elicits an eye roll. This is not acceptable, so he slaps her across the face, causing instant marking to her cheek.

He places the extinguished candle down, and unzips his trousers. Whether she realises it or not, she'd been waiting for this. She's dreamt, fantasised, masturbated over his brutal face fucking. Sliding himself out of her boxers, she eagerly opens wide, tongue out. Waiting for him.

He gets just close enough for her to lick his tip, straining to take more of him in her mouth. With an agony defying, throbbing ache inducing, control. He puts himself away, denying her the usage. Stepping to the side, so that when her eyes open - she sees herself, cock hungry.

Her confusion is palpable. His response, clinical. *"You don't get that yet"*. She tries to stomp her feet in protest, before remembering that she can't. *That diabolical bastard.* *"Beg for it"*

"What?"

"Did I stutter?"

"Fuck you"

He tuts a few times in quick succession. Slowly walking away. She watches him like a hawk as he makes a show of selecting an item from the wall. Finally, after brushing nearly every implement with his finger tips, he selects a multiple-bamboo cane.

He stands behind her, menace in his eyes. Tracing the tip of the cane across her back and ass cheeks.

"You were saying...?"

She's terrified of how excited she is.

"Fuck..." and he cuts her off before the second word, thrashing her ass cheek hard *"...you"* she whimpers, defiantly

"Try again. The sentence you're looking for starts with please'" he instructs with a smirk

She closes her mouth tightly, cinching her lips.

"They weren't closed that tightly a minute ago, were they?" he mocks, giving her another - lesser - hit with the cane. She tenses with the impact and relaxes again in an instant. *"You love how it hurts don't you? My little slut"*

He's right, but she'll be fucked if she's going to admit it. So he hits her again, harder this time. *"Do you have any idea how pretty your ass looks, bruised for me?"* tracing his hand over the red raised markings he's left, admiring his art.

He lets his hand explore her, running his middle finger directly over her ass hole, causing her to tense completely, nearly enclosing it between her sore cheeks. He runs his hand over her perfectly smooth, quivering pussy. She can't close her legs, she's powerless to prevent his touch. She tries to invert her knees, but that does nothing to deny him.

He plays with her, moistening his finger between her entrance and her clit. She squirms in anticipation. It takes him no time at all to tease the nerve endings under her hood and have her breathing heavily. Gyrating for him. *"Let's try again, say my name"* he commands.

This is an easy one for her, she does as she's asked. It doesn't feel like a submission.

He ups the temperature. Increasing the pace. Varying the pressure, finding that sweet spot.

"Say it again" - and she does. *"Now try, please, Rizzy"*

She pauses. *Bastard*. He tricked her into it, whilst dangling a climax in front of her.

"Please, Rizzy"

"That's my girl, I knew you could do it". He rewards her efforts, reading every micro-movement, he brings her to the very edge, before ripping his hand away, denying her release, and spanking her again.

She hears his footsteps before opening her eyes. He takes a microphone stand of sorts, and what looks like a small microphone from an ornate box. He fixes it in position. *It's a wand.* She realises. He plays with his phone for a moment, before playing *Maneskin - I wanna be your slave*. The wand, positioned perfectly on her clit, vibrates to the beat.

Leaving her aching for him he fetches another implement, it's a marbled glass dildo. As soon as it touches, the cold shocks. It's perfectly smooth and lubed. But it still bites on it's way into her ass. He works it in and out, allowing her to stretch. To ache. He stretches and tests her depth some more. She struggles with the size, and the motion. She takes it anyway. Soon, however, he's done working through toys and stretching her. He inserts a plug to keep her filled, and moves on.

He walks back to the front, and takes his cock out again. Cum dripping from the end. Once again, she opens wide, tongue hanging, eyes closed. This time he rewards her, he lets her taste the tip. She tries with everything she's got to take more into her mouth. He lets her strain against her restraints for a few seconds, before pushing in. He feels her mouth, she feels him hit the back of her tongue, and push into her throat.

Fucking yes.

He braces against the stocks, and holds himself, at full depth, until she wriggles, unable to breathe. Pulling himself out, letting her catch her breath; just for a second. He does the same again. He repeats this for an eternity. Her brain, starved of oxygen, completely lost in the moment. He ups the pace. The stocks shake. She gasps for air in the moments it's available. Short of breath the pressure builds in her head. Released only by her tears.

The intensity of the throat fucking and the ever present, unpredictable vibrations from the wand are too much to bear. As she releases a knee weakening orgasm. Luckily, the stocks are holding her up, so she doesn't miss a single thrust of Rizzy's cock in her throat. He feels the throbbing hardening, recognising he's going to cum. He pulls out before he does.

She knows what he's going to do before he does it. She's powerless to stop him. As he fires her well earned load all over her face. Decorating her with the pain and pleasure she's endured. Something tells her its not over yet, but for now, she allows herself to relax. She drops her head.

A single drop of his cum falls from her face onto the mirror below. She can't avoid her reflection. She looks so used. She feels it too. But it's more empowering than the word implies. She's *his* play thing, and she's living for it. The wand has stopped now, and she aches. She needs to be filled. He's perceptive. He knows this, too.

Before she can recuperate, she feels his hand cupping her. He slides his middle finger in, it barely enters. He's preparing her. Sliding in and out intentionally. Motioning with his finger, finding the spots he's going to ruin later. A second easily pushes in and carries on the motion. She can do nothing but feel him, and try to push back, desperate to be *fuller*.

She feels him with the third, and the edges of her hole start to tighten. He's pushing the edge of the girth she can take. He works faster now, with more firmness, more thrust. He's reaching the limit of depth, because of his pinky. So it joins the party too. Applying gentle pressure with his thumb to her asshole, he motions his fingers inside her. She can't hide her pleasure, and frankly she doesn't want to.

"Oh my God" she allows herself to express her pleasure, he's speeding up now. The internal motions joined by simultaneous in-out thrusts - adding to her building sensations. When he's nearly all the way out, he teases her with his thumb. Threatening to push it in.

She's never been fisted before, and he's pretty sure this is the case.

"Rizzy, don't...". She knows the language she's using. *How far will **he** go?*

He slips the tip of his thumb in, alongside his fingers. No response, but a very subtle push back. He pushes in further, his whole thumb now. He can feel her working to take it. So he pushes in more. Subtle noises, internal feelings, give way that she needs this. So he continues on, working his hand inside her.

When he feels her tighten, with no more slack to take. He works back out and in, using his fingers to hyper sensitise *everything* inside her. She's nearly screaming now. Watching him in the mirror, they don't break eye contact as she takes it.

He doesn't push the depth and girth any further. But he does increase the violence with which his hand wrecks her. And she fucking loves it.

Another completely restrained, can't go anywhere, orgasm shatters her world. She lets the stocks take her weight as she leans forward on them. Head bowed. Catching her breath. Maybe not a full fist, but fuck it was close.

"I'm impressed, little Bee". Her heart stops. He walks back to the front *"open wide"*, this time she dumbly does as she's told, trusting him to make every decision for her. He puts his hand in her mouth, and she instinctively sucks it clean. Working her tongue between his fingers, and up and down each one individually, before locking her lips around his whole hand and sucking it clean. He squats down, bringing his head level with hers.

Eye contact a couple of inches away. He takes her chin in his hand, and kisses her on the lips, and then on the head. The affection she didn't know she was craving. He lingers on the forehead kiss for a few seconds. Straightens himself, and walks away.

"Only one violation left, little Bee…"

"No, don't you fucking dare" - she let's her head relax, catching sight of the whore's reflection.

"Don't pretend you've got a choice - you'll thank me before I'm done" with a slap onto an existing welt that has her cry out. *"Breathe"* he commands, slowly pulling the plug from her ass hole. Stopping to enjoy her gape for a second.

The ice cold lube adorns her hole, expertly aimed. The shock and the cooling sensation feels amazing. The head of his cock feels even hotter when it breaks through the ice-lube layer.

"Please don't ruin my ass" she pleads

"Whose ass is it to ruin?". Of course, she refuses to reply. So he continues *"I'll wreck it until you admit it's mine"*.

With that, he lines up perfectly, and pushes his head inside her. Feeling her tightness begin to give way. Quarter inch by quarter inch, holding her at the hips, he pushes in, and retreats. Preparing the way for the destruction that's to come.

With a surprising lack of pain for her, he's all the way in. His hips touching her ass cheeks. He pushes against her cheeks, making her feel the full depth. Her quiet utterances of *"no"* and *"please don't"* add to the tension of his erection. Even if she could move, she wouldn't.

Long, deliberate strokes have her breath short, grunting at full depth as he continues his torturous exacerbation of the anticipation he forces her to endure.

"Just fucking do it!" her impatience cracks

"Do what?"

She can't backtrack now. So she commits to her truth.

"Destroy me, make me yours. Make me take it all, make me beg for mercy"

He pauses completely, with every inch inside of her. Staring her in the eyes through the mirror. They hold the stare for several seconds, him twitching inside of her. Her trying to wriggle, trying to do anything to simulate movement and stimulate her insides. She craves him, and she's over

pretending she doesn't.

He pulls out completely. Lulling her into a false sense of security, subtly dousing himself in lube. Leaving her gaping waiting for him.

"Please, please fuck my ass" she whimpers.

With that, he slams inside of her. From nothing to full depth, with every ounce of power he can muster. He releases the demon inside him, and goes to work. With relentless strength, propped by him gripping the top of the stocks, he relentlessly fucks her ass. Long, hard strokes, at unbelievable pace.

She feels her ass lose all grip, nearly all ability to clench, nothing left to resist. He doesn't let up when he commands her, the pace is constant, unwavering, relentless. This is brutality.

"Thank me"

"Thank you, thank you, thank you for fucking my ass"

"For making you my whore"

"For making me your whore, I'm your whore. Use me"

"You're such a good fucking whore"

"I'm such a good whore, I love it when you fuck my ass"

Her eye contact now with herself, as she recites his instructions. He keeps going, her strength long since gone.

"Tell me again"

"I'm your dirty whore, I love it when you fuck my ass and use me, when you destroy me. I fucking love it, please don't stop, please don't stop"

Crying now, not from pain, but from intensity. As the full force of his girth, depth, and physicality combined with her inability to move overwhelms her. She has no choice but to take every inch of every thrust with complete submission. She's never been more restrained, more violated, yet more proud and more free.

The stocks shake through their steel fastenings with the force that he fucks her with now. Her screams resonate through their own private dungeon. He grips her hips so hard he bruises them almost instantly, as he gets every extra bit of depth. The ending imminent. Savouring every thrust, making her feel his desire.

Her screams meet his yells. Her hips meet his thrusts. His climax meets hers. With blinding force, he finishes. He manages a few more convulsing thrusts as he leaves his remains in her hollowed asshole. Their sweat soaked bodies meld together, his chest on her back. Perfectly still they remain, until reality sets in.

He pulls what's left of his shrinking self from her. Gently. And takes a second to admire the bruised, open, gaping wreckages of her body. He undoes the bolt and opens the stocks, so she can stand, then unpins, then unfastens her spreader. She almost immediately falls backwards into his arms.

He walks them backwards, his back against the door. The iron scrapes his back as he pushes back on the door to allow a controlled descent to the ground. She turns in the foetal position, her cheek on his chest. Feeling his heart beat. As he brushes her hair out of her face. She lays, not asleep, but collapsed into him as he starts to pick the pieces of wax from her back, and kisses her on the head.

Not rushing, piece by piece, he cleans and restores her. She snuggles into him, letting him. She loves it when he destroys her, and loves it when he rebuilds her, in equal amounts.

Chapter Seventeen

Another night, and again hardly any sleep. More a night of naps, separated by vivid recollections of the dungeons a few nights before. Each inciting and inspiring reactions from her still raw body. Every movement causes a painful reminder of her exploits.

Every blink recalls another moment, like a series of polaroids imprinted in her brain. She suffers for her freedom, and that's what makes it so fucking good. The pain reminds her this was real, not a dream, not a fantasy. Pure fucking whoredom in its most delectable throws. Freedom inside her restraints, to enjoy.

To give herself fully, without shame or guilt. She rejects her subconscious 'desperate final attempts at turning her against herself with absolute conviction.

She runs her hands over her body, feeling the welts and marks fading slightly now. The pain still feels good, but this time in memory. The bruising on her wrists reminds her. She flashes back to her reflections. Watching herself be devoured. A dopey grin and a lip bite, she closes her eyes and embraces her memory.

As always, a quick shower, the alarm reminder rings - *protein shake and scrambled egg* now, and obviously *'stay hydrated'* she mocks Rizzy's irritating repetitive reinforcement. Consuming the prescribed nutrition and hydration, she grabs her bag and heads over to Dev's.

The 5am crew are in and working as normal, but there's no Rizz. Dev takes control of the session, with the same competency but not the same *fire*, he doesn't command the room the same. He doesn't emanate fear. Everyone still works hard, focused and determined. Bee included.

His voice lives in her head rent free. Every correction, every piece of sage advice. The training plans. She trains as if he's stood behind her... *like he was the other night*. Shaking the thought from her head, she puts another round kick into the bag.

Smoke, wearing a t-shirt to train for the first time in forever *I know what you did the other night* she giggles internally. He's putting a shift in, he's working hard on alternating waves on the battle ropes. Completely focused as sweat pours down the back of his head.

Chiz strolls in, trousers and a shirt, black shoes. Hands in his pockets, walking straight through people's workspaces. He couldn't be more out of place, or look more of a dick, if he tried. As soon as he acquires his target he beelines. Not even waiting for the round to finish, and with no inclination to indulge upon social decorum, pleasantries, or even manners.

"You seen Rizz?"

Smoke doesn't respond, his *"fuck off, prick"* glare speaks for him.

"Know where he is?" Chiz continues

"Probably sorting the fight" - without interrupting his flow

"Hassan's asking" - the name drop entirely deliberate, the delivery slow and intentional

"Anything I can help with?" Dev asks, walking in from the store room - clearly having missed Chiz's appearance in the 2 minutes he was away from the desk.

"Nah it's good, bro" barely even acknowledging Dev, and he leaves with his hands still in his pockets, looking impatient yet somehow still smug.

After finishing her session, Bee heads over to the shop for her shift. Ash looks fatigued and worn down, but he still wears his genuine, but slipping, warm uncle smile and greeting *"Beta, I nearly started moving the papers myself!"*, in a mock scold.

"Mamu, I'm 90 seconds late, of all your winters I'm surprised you noticed!" she comically retorts with a wink.

Every morning, once they finish moving newspapers and milk in, they stop at the counter. Like clockwork, Meena brings their morning chai and stops for a gossip. *"Good morning Ammi"* with a genuine smile *"Bitiya"* she greets with heartfelt warmth, a quick soft inspection, and a tight hug. Bee winces, kink inflicted injuries rearing their heads. *"Aye, he training you too harshly eh?"*

"Yeah you could say that" Bee quickly and awkwardly replies, brushing her hair behind her ear.

Cupping her Chai in both hands, enjoying its aroma, and her proximity to such familial love, she looks over the steam at her kind of adopted, kind of in-law, parents. The devil is in the details. They look *tired*, like they didn't sleep, or are bearing some burden they are not sharing.

"Rizz wasn't at training this morning" her statement comes across as an inquiry, and says more than she spoke. Sure, she's missing him. She's not pining. She's concerned.

"Ah my sweet, don't worry. He's a busy boy, I'm sure he's fine" comes Ash's response, Meena's mutual concern unaired. *Is he trying to convince me, or himself?*

The familiar jingle of the customer entrance door breaks the uneasy silence. *"Hey, Pa?"* comes Rizz's voice.

With speed shocking for her age and demeanour, Meena bolts to the front of the shop. *"Rizvar, you bloody menace - you trying to give your Ma a heart attack? Where've you been? No text, no phone call? Abandoning your mother for days... days! No bloody words!"* she smacks him repeatedly on the tops of the arms with each hand in turn. He doesn't try to stop her. He wraps his hands around her, pulls her close, and sits his chin atop her head.

Over his mother's comforting embrace, he looks at Ash. It's a serious look. An "uncomfortable conversation imminent", kind of look. *"Ma, I'm here, everything's fine, don't worry. I'm starving, have we got any samosas?"*. Smart. Weaponising her love language. His own mother. He's here on business. Bee observes, no doubt in her mind, that Ash has noticed the same. Whether Meena knows or not is immaterial, really.

He nearly walks straight past Bee, but his eyes stick to hers. *"Hey, lil Bee"*, a finger under her chin and a thumb in front of it, he gives her a fast, firm peck. Before going towards the store room with Ash.

Okay, now I'm pining.

He's like heroin to her. No matter how much she gets, she's hooked. Gets none? Withdrawal. *This fucking man.*

Their conversation, unheard, is seen. Ash pinching the middle of his nose, stroking his beard in contemplation, listening intently to what he's being told. Rizz speaks leaning in, with his arms folded. Delivering information. Ash receives, listens, processes. Whatever they're talking about must be heavy.

Bee's never seen it before, but Rizz takes the nape of Ash's head and pushes his forehead against it, in a show of strength and camaraderie, before putting Ash's head onto his shoulder and holding him for just a moment. She can almost hear him, *"Don't worry Pa, it'll be fine. I've got this, I'll handle it"*.

Ash heads back to the store room, probably to check the temperatures in the fridge.

Straightening the collar on his leather jacket, Rizzy walks back with very-nearly his usual charm. *"Little Bee, what're you doing tonight?"* - she doesn't get a chance to answer, because the answer isn't relevant *"I've got a promotion on tonight, Smoke's on the fight card"* as if she didn't already know Smoke was fighting tonight *"You're not riding with the boys tonight. You're riding with me. I've got you something, I'll drop it by later"*. A quick kiss on her forehead, and the door jingles again - marking his exit.

No sooner is he gone than Meena returns with a plate of Samosas. In a moment of kettle whistling fury *"Bloody Rizvar!"* shaking the plate hard enough it might snap, or spill the snacks. Quickly regaining her cool, she turns to Bee - "Samosa?"

Back at the flat and still burping spicy onion from the plateful of Samosas. Bee and Jade are getting ready *#GlamAF* - it's several hours too early, but obviously the sacred ritual of pre-drinks, gossip, and dancing must not be broken. *We have*

Rioja and Root Beer for starters, and Captain Morgan's - spiced, obviously - for mains. Throwing absolute carnage performances to *Waiting All Night* by *Rudamental ft Ella Eyre.*

With his usual charm and wit, Green bursts through the front door, carrying a bag of the usual essentials - the fancy crisps, breath mints, chocolate, and Red Bulls for the morning - in one hand, and an unlabelled expensive looking bag in the other. *"It must be Crufts in here because these are THE finest bitchesssss to grace our good King's shores!".* Dopamine strikes hard for Green as the girls lose their shit at that particular chat up line. He drops off the groceries, gives Jade a little more than a "peck", then turns his attention to Bee.

He enacts a royal messenger *"Good lady, our fearless leader sends this gift in exchange for her courtship at tonight's main event".*

She takes it to the sofa and has a look. It's a very expensive dress, with all the class of a ball gown, but absolutely none of the length. Shoes, handbag, earrings; and another wrapped package underneath. Lingerie. A really cute boneless basque, suspender belt and stockings.

He's going to have as much fun unwrapping me, as I had unwrapping this.

Catching reality for a second. *"Honey, I'm already dressed!"* she motions to her fabulous outfit.

"Then get changed" deadpan - dropping all acts and entertainment entirely, this isn't a negotiation. And he sure as shit ain't going back to Rizz with anything other than good news.

She ponders for a second, *it's not worth the argument, and Rizz isn't a negotiable kind of guy.* She silently agrees.

"Anyways ladies, some of us work for a living, y'all stay fabulous, keep slaying and all that good stuff..." he looks directly to Jade *"... I'll see you later"*

After getting herself dressed up... *again*... for him. She sends him a couple of cheeky selfies. With the caption - spending what seems like hours agonising over what to say and how to pose - *"Maybe I'll let you take them off later"*

She gets a reply back, almost instantly

☐ 😺 **Rizzy** ☐ ☐☐

Don't pretend you've got a choice, little Bee

Stomach drops. Fanny flutters. *"Shots!"*

Chapter Eighteen

At 8pm on the dot, a pristine, all white Range Rover Sport pulls up outside. The driver is smartly dressed, with a discreet earpiece just visible at the right angle. The rear windows are completely tinted and allow no visibility of the occupants from the outside.

Standing on the curb, feeling rather overdressed for the high street, Bee stands. Looking like a glamour model, in the outfit Rizzy chose. Passers by slow down and look. They are not discreet, which gets one old husband in trouble with his wife.

The opposing door, not visible, opens. Rizzy appears from the rear of the car, he dips his glasses to get a true eye's view of his trophy before placing his hand on the small of her back, subtly taking a hint of her scent. He opens the rear door, and kisses her hand as he guides her in. He closes the door firmly behind her and returns to his seat. As soon as his door shuts, the car is in motion.

Inside the tinted darkness of the luxury vehicle, even in the short time it took Rizzy to walk back round, the first thing Bee notices was how the constant influx of notifications on his phone illuminated the cream leather interior.

There's no conversation on the drive. Plenty of talking, but all small conversations directed at their devices. The driver through his bluetooth, and Rizzy through his handset. Everyone wants to talk to Rizzy tonight. He manages to make time to make her feel seen. His eyes crawling up her legs, his gaze brushing her chest. His smoulder heating her through her eyes.

"Robbie, bell Daz, see if he's got a replacement for Faizal" no more than 5 seconds later Robbie's on the phone "Faizal's out, you got... yep... 75kg.... uhuh... yep... he's made weight.... wicked... inabit"

Simultaneously, Rizzy is back on the phone. "Brother... stop taking bets on Faizal-Hammer... he's out... yeah I'll let you know" and he hangs up.

Phone calls move fast in Rizzy's world. Bee observes.

"Rizz, Daz says Assassin Jones can do it, he's made weight already" Robbie relays back, the instant Rizz hangs up.

A rapid fire text sent, Rizzy answers another call. "Go... yeah... nah... no... tell him if he makes me tell him myself, I'll fucking body the cunt". Click, end of call. A single bead of sweat forms in his hairline.

After about 30 minutes of intense fuck all, they pull into the world's biggest abandoned shithole of an industrial estate. In the very corner, through some security gates - which are manned and opened for them without check - they head to a particularly large warehouse. Outside it's nothing to look at, at all. She feels like she's about to be murdered on a red carpet. The only thing pristine are the completely black windows.

There are a few other vehicles parked up, a couple of luxury coaches, and a couple of expensive cars - AMGs, top end BMWs - luxurious and discreet is the dress code on the cars. Nothing too flash, but nothing that says "hasn't made it yet".

Rizzy gets out of the car, phone still to his ear. He opens Bee's door, and offers his hand to guide her out. He offers his arm to walk her, never detaching from his phone.

Robbie is already out of the car, talking to someone who looks like security. "Has Swansea arrived yet? ... Where are they?"

Rizzy is back on the phone. "The fuck do I care if there's a crash on the M6, if he's not here on time that's on him - did I not say to come up last night? Did you listen? Nah that's what I thought... nah... nah fuck off" Click. "Oh you did? Fucking mint. Nah that's great. Told you it was good, catch you in there later mate, alright nice one, bye" Complete tonal shift. "Yes... yes... absolutely, my guy.... really? ... Nah I get it I do, but have I ever let you down? That's what I thought.... You legend, thanks mate, I owe you" the tiniest air punch when he hangs up.

Through all of these exchanges, he never missed a step. He doesn't slow down, he walks the exact pace that Bee can just about keep up with, without falling in her heels. He doesn't look up, approaching the steel, handleless fire door. Yet it opens as if automatic, he slides his phone into his pocket, shakes hands and gives a nod to the doorman without slowing down.

A smartly dressed man waits, in a typical "stood easy" pose.

"Rizz" he says, requesting permission to speak. The only thing letting down his glamour is the transparent coiled cable to his earpiece. His eyes portray some levity. Rizz nods at him, before he leans in and says very few words, directly into Rizz ' ear. Rizz 'jaw clenches as he listens. "Alright" he agrees.

"I've gotta go, I'll catch up with you later. Robbie will look after you" he gives her a peck on the cheek and is gone. Robbie seems to be checking things with people stationed around, she waits patiently and has a look around.

Holy fucking shit, what is this place?

She glances from right to left, they've clearly not come in through the public entrance. It's the size of a small aeroplane hangar, but organised - with a small village of people busy at work. From where she is directly to her right is a corridor that looks like it goes to changing rooms. Velvet ropes separate a walkway towards an MMA cage, centrally positioned. Around this half of the cage are a series of black-tie tables. Champagne ice buckets are already on the table, as are place settings including the full 3 forks. There's a couple of long desks facing the cage, with a couple of microphones, note pads and laptops. That must be for commentators and judges.

The staff/fighter door opens, and a small army of models of some description walk through together. Busy and ushered by some kind of manager whilst being directed to where they can finalise hair and makeup. *This is them not done up?!*

"Excuse me, Aria?" Robbie approaches, busy but careful not to appear rude, she smiles politely at him, not really sure what to say. He motions to a lady in her 30s, well put together in a pant suit. *"This is Carla, she's going to show you around, please excuse me"*

With that, Carla comes to life. Polished and professional. *"Hi, I'm Carla. I run the executive experience team, we look after our VIPs and ensure our most important guests are well cared for, comfortable, and connected. If now is a good time, I'd love to show you around, and escort you to your table?"*

Bee can do nothing but gawk. Carla smiles sweetly, gently steering her with subtle gestures — never breaking stride or blocking the view — all while delivering a perfectly practiced tour speech.

"Welcome to SFD - Sanjay's Fighting Dream. London's premier unlicensed combat sport venue. Before us now is the cage where all of our action happens, surrounded by our premium VIP tables - where you will receive your complimentary 5 course meal and bottle service.

If you make your way to the right here, you'll see our Tatami Bar - closest to the action with a range of wines, champagnes, and spirits. Your host will ensure your throat is never dry.

Should your tastes desire, you'll find our Bookmakers in this office here. Beat the odds and the queues with our VIP lane, or alternatively your host can take and place bets from your table. Please be aware that all wagers exceeding £100,000 must be pre-approved by our Executive Sporting Commissioner and may be subject to different odds."

Looking through the windows into the bookies, Ree notices a familiar face - albeit dripping in finesse. Well that's where Green fits in. He is clearly organising and co-ordinating the flow of illicit money for this whole venture.

"As we make our way around the venue, you will notice our industry leading Audio Visual setup, so that you don't miss a moment of action. Keep an eye on these screens for close ups of the action, referee scorecards, betting odds, and live replays."

"Continuing past our highly trained safety colleagues" - oh so that's corporate speak for 'terrifying security henchmen '- *'we climb into a world of pure indulgence. This is our VIP lounge, where your party is welcome to spend the evening with us - before, during, and after the evening's entertainment.*

Our hospitality team is on hand to ensure you have an unforgettable experience, for all the right reasons.

Through those doors you will find our Gentleman's Lounge, and our Casino is along the balcony to the right. The balconies here can be used to view the action, but we strongly advise that any drinks are left at your table. We remind guests that there is to be no photography or videography in the venue at any time and wish to caution that violations of any of our House Rules may result in the refusal of future bookings and immediate ejection from the House. That concludes our tour, if you have any questions, I'd be happy to answer them for you now"

With a prepared smile, Carla awaits questions or dismissal. *I wonder how long she'd stay there if I just maintained the peep?*

"That's all, thank you so much Carla" Bee opts for dismissal, she'll get the tea from someone less trained later.

Bee makes her way to the balcony and observes. She sees the casino team, identifiable by their monkey suits, head into the casino room. Teams of stewards and security are briefed. Trolleys and carts are pushed around. Catering teams buzz around the kitchen doors by the VIP seating. The barmaid in the VIP lounge ensures the mirror topped bar is gleaming. Fighters and their entourages make their way into the prep rooms. *This is one hell of an operation.*

Down at the Tatami bar a few early comers order their drinks. In a sparkly green minidress stands a familiar ebony goddess, fully channelling her Island Queen. Thank fuck for that. There's no need to ask why she's not in VIP, she 100% has the clout, just not the inclination. Bee makes her way to her bestie, and some familiarity in this alien world. And a breath of fresh air, realest of the real, my girl.

"Giiiiiiiiirl" Bee exclaims from behind Jade, who turns to face her and gives one of those signature could-pop-your-neck hugs. *"What the FUCK"* Bee silently mouths behind a hand.

"I know right" Jade silently replies in kind.

They do what they do best, and complete the earlier-started ritual. They've had pre-drinks, now it's time for pre-fight drinks, before the fight drinks, and the post fight drinks.

While sharing their drinks Temu-McGreggor decides it is wise to advance. If ever there was a man who knew what crayons tasted like, this is him. He tries to spark conversation, but it's flat. The man's got less chat than Classic FM. Trying to casually ignore this fucking creep, he keeps just chirping up into their conversation. Eye rolls and body language cannot penetrate this level of social density.

"Hi Chad" - Bee decides to show some bare faced audacity of her own

"Erm, my name's Kevin"

"Yeah, didn't ask, but thanks for confirming your name isn't on the list. As hints clearly aren't your specialty, let me spell it out: We're not interested"

He's not deterred. Clearly his wrapped hands and fight team hoodie are giving this man superhuman testicles.

"I'm fighting tonight, after I win, I could do with some company - what you girls saying then?" dripping with cheap "game".

"Yo, Tate from Wish. You're not listening. Your ears got more cauliflower than my Mum's roast dinners, but it's sweet of you to ask", in a mocking gesture she rubs the top of his arm, faux-flirting, *"so when you're finished playing in that cage, how about we find one for that little slug you call a cock?"*

He steps closer, towering above her, menacing. Looking down into her eyes. *"You're nothing special, just another skank in a nice dress"*

"Yeah this isn't where you scare me into giving you a kiss. Take your protein breath and your sexual frustration elsewhere, it's giving incel with a side of rapist sweetie" through a smile and a fluttering of her - perfectly applied, by the way - false eyelashes *"buh-bye Chad"* blowing him a kiss.

"I'll see you later" he gives her a wink and takes his leave. Clearly thinking his ego, reputation, and pride are intact.

Jade finally lets go of a monstrous cacophony of hysterical laughter. *"No fucking crumbs.... Tate from Wish... slug cage.... girl, for real"* she cries and squeezes her legs together, holding her stomach.

The pair laugh until their cheeks and abdomens ache in equal measure. Until they clock him.

Rizzy. He pulls his phone from his ear, silences the room and shatters the fun, flipping the razor edge danger of the room. His eyes radiate the kind of danger that make you leave the fucking country. *The fuck did I do?* Perplexed, with a nauseating concoction of fear and anxiety, she stands there. Deer in dangerous spotlights. Confused as fuck. He ends his phone call, taps on his phone, makes another and walks away.

☐ 😼 Rizzy ☐ ☐☐

You'll pay for that.

Pay for fucking what? She shows Jade, confused.

"Ooooh weeee.... sucks to be you girl, I'm gunna go count cash with Green... love yas" and she disappears. *Girl are you joking?*

The evening goes on, Jade eventually sticks her head above the trench line and returns to Bee's side. They sit in the VIP and have a few drinks, watching the fights, the ring girls, the people.

"He's on, it's Smoke!" They are clearly the most excited about his walk out. It's fucking eerie, seeing him like this. They weren't allowed to see him before the fight while he was preparing. In the zone or something apparently.

Now he stands, a warrior god about to take another poor soul to meet Hades. He'll fuss Cerberus while he's down there, and return like nothing happened. He stands, majestic. Looking out at the crowd. Completely still, for the whole intro of In The Air Tonight by Phil Collins. Only taking his first step towards the cage at the iconic drum solo. Even then he's calm,

collected, surgical. Ready to fucking GO. Once he's ring-side he has his gloves checked, gum shield put in, vaseline applied to his cheeks. Dev's behind him, giving quiet pointers. Smoke lightly limbers up, and enters the cage. He gives a Muay Thai wai to the officials and shakes himself off. Staring at the floor. His opponent goes through a similar ritual, but honestly it's just not as impressive. What a nobody.

They go through the formalities and the fight begins. Fairly slow at first, testing the waters, its footworks and feints. Smoke is so much faster than he was last time they trained. He moves like a cloud. Barely taking shots, let alone damage. *Rizz has done a magical job there.*

Through the first round, he's just moving. 90 seconds in, his opponent is slowing down considerably. He wasn't accurate to start with, not against Smoke's movement, but the live stat readers on the jumbotron confirm he's tanking on accuracy and significant strikes. Smoke's opponent only really takes body jabs and leg kicks, but they're working.

Then they come out for the second, a lazy kick gives Smoke the opportunity. Smoke detonates, with the force of Hiroshima and the accuracy of a Rolex Superlative. One right hand, to the jaw and the job's done. His victim staggers backwards, momentum keeping him upright ish until he hits the cage wall. In the absence of a referee stoppage, Smoke's assault continues with the sustained ferocity of the Blitzkreig. Bomb after bomb. Oppo's guard may as well not exist, he's just curled up at this point. Where's the ref? What's he waiting for?!

With full intention and malice, Smoke throws a right hand straight, allowing the switch of his feet leaving his right foot leading. And then he puts his left shin through this corpse's face. No need for the ref stoppage now. After the recoil of the shot, he falls lifelessly forwards. Laid on the canvas like a murder scene chalk outline. *That was fucking brutal.*

Smoke honours his fallen adversary with a wai. He hangs around as the medical team enters, and carts his victim out. The formalities need concluding. The announcer does his job, declaring Smoke the winner as the replays of the final shot, in 1000fps quality, show the deciding shots.

Then comes his carnage. A guttural roar. An uproar somewhere in the VIP seats. Smoke points gun fingers before charging the cage wall, jumping up and straddling it with striking agility for a man so large and powerful. He points at the commotion. *"You're next!"* he yells, pointing at the next contender, set to challenge. He climbs so he's stood balanced on the wall, before doing a backflip and landing in the true superhero pose with one knee on the floor inside the cage. A menacing throat slit with his thumb and a curled lip. Playing for the jumbotrons, but goddamn he knows how to put on a show.

That's why Smoke being on the card is so important. Bee observes, as the crowd goes absolutely wild for his theatrics. What they didn't see was how he dropped the bullshit the moment he got out of view. Walked back to his changing room, and slipped back into his bootcuts.

A tap on her shoulder, it's the 'safety team'. *"Miss Waters, Rizz has requested your attention in his changing room"*

Why the fuck has he got a changing room? She follows the henchman through the crowd, past the ropes, and into a changing room. There Rizz skips casually without a rope, doing dance moves and fuckery. Dev's got the pads on, Rizz is shirtless, in Thai shorts with the word "RUINER" along the elastic.

"Turns out we're both working tonight" he coolly says. She can't respond, because she hasn't a clue what's going on. Sensing this, he casually continues. *"I saw you liked that Scouse slag at the bar, he didn't recognise my territory. It was an error on both of your parts. I paid triple his opponent's purse, and stepped in. I'm going to dismantle him. You're going to watch. You're my ring girl - and everyone will know it."*

So many questions. She opens her mouth to explain but is interrupted and silenced, *"ah ah ah, I'm warming up - take your dress off, what's underneath will work"*.

She looks to Dev, to be the voice of reason, to offer some semblance of sanity into this absolute shit show. He won't look at her. He knows what Rizz's like when he's in this mood.

She contemplates. She swallows. She weighs up her options. She doesn't like them. So she does it. She reaches behind and undoes the zip on her dress and steps out of it. Now she stands there, ivory g-string, basque, heels, stockings and suspenders. *At least my pants are clean.*

Her stomach churns at the thought of standing in front of what, *2000 people? In fucking lingerie? He will not see me wilt. He wants to play this game, I'll make him regret it.*

Three sharp knocks on the door and *"time"* comes the call from some kind of usher. The whole entourage - Smoke, Green, Jade, and a few of the lads from the gym, meet them in the corridor and they make the walk down the corridor to *DNA* by *Kendrick Lamar*.

When they get to the curtain, the track changes with a record scratch to *Out Of Nowhere* by *Bugzy Malone*. The announcer calls his name, and between his name and the track - the House shakes with anticipation, with the crowd. They're carnal, blood thirsty, whipped into a frenzy.

The iconic intro is met with the lights cut low, flashing red strobe lighting, and ambient smoke.

As soon as the lyric *"no such thing as turning back right now"* drops, they start the walk. It's fucking fierce. He's a God. She's his Goddess. Security are stopping people from high five-ing and touching them. He walks like a man who knows he's about to add another skull to his collection. She fucking works it. All eyes on her. She even stops for a pose or two. *He wants a ring girl? I'll be the best fucking ring girl he's ever had.*

They go through the formalities. The glove check, vaseline, gum shields. When Chad/Kevin sees her, his face drops. He spots the fuse he lit earlier. And it's too late.

Bee climbs onto the outer edge stage of the cage. She works it, hard, holding the "Round 1" placard. Pausing every few seconds to pose provocatively. Letting the crowd light her fire, admire her, desire her.

Then the bell goes. Rizz is... different. He leaves his hands down, puts his chin out, and relies on his head movement. Dances like fire. Slapping embarrassing counters on this clown. You can taste his arrogance, him thinking *'Touch me if you can, cunt"*. And boy does he try. He really tries, and he's good. But Rizz makes him look downright average. Rizz barely punches him, he slaps him. Humiliates him. Makes it seem comically mismatched. He's not beating this boy. He's destroying him, ego first.

Then Rizz starts to go to work, his counters start to sting. He never over-capitalises. He draws some blood, he causes some damage. Hurts him. But it's not time for the finish yet. Then he starts to "chop wood", hard leg kick after hard leg kick. Pure damage. He's already too slow to catch you, why are you chopping wood?

Rizz senses that he's about to get a TKO on the leg damage, and switches up. His limping opponent tries to chase him. Rizz makes him look like he's stood still. Then with a series of clever feints, misdirects and footwork he lands a single clean shot to Chad's eye. It swells near shut almost immediately.

Why didn't he finish him, the KO was there?

He carries on dancing against his wounded foe. With only half of his visibility left, and only one leg, he's almost defenceless. Still playing the high-IQ game, feints and setups, this time planting the ball of his foot with a sidekick - clearly breaking his nose. Blood goes everywhere.

The end of the bell rings, and it's Bee's turn again. She takes her placard, puts on her biggest smile, this time she doesn't just stop to pose. She dances like she's on a podium inspired by the DJ's choice - *Pour Some Sugar On Me by Def Leppard*. She's working it like a pro - the crowd don't know what they're more worked up by - her entertainment or Rizz's.

This whole thing is so fucking hot unhinged.

The second round starts, and Rizz comes straight in. Lead leg side kick after another, punishing Chad's abdomen. He looks like he might vomit and Rizz explodes with a boxing combo, he throws the overhand and pulls it short. It doesn't matter. The damage is done as Chad flinches and curls up, showing the world - through the jumbotron - how terrified he is.

That's the point. This is all for the optics. It's the picture he's painting.

Rizz laughs and literally dances away. Every feint, tactical advance, making Chad flinch or over-react. He's limping, can't see, covered in his own blood, defenceless, and terrified.

In his final act of absolute dominance, he turns to the crowd, even with the audacity of spitting out his gum shield, he screams and poses *"Are you not entertained?!"* - his Gladiator moment, and this is his coliseum.

Bladed on, he points at Chad, and begins his assassination. Jab, overhand, hook, uppercut, leaving Chad fully rocked. Credit to him, he gets his hands back up and tries to walk Rizz down. To be met with a flying knee to the chin. The suffering ends.

The savagery is a huge turn on. Being adored amplifies it.

Bee bounces up and down clapping, whooping, and hollering. The medical team do their thing, putting Chad on a stretcher as he's regaining consciousness. Looking harmless in victory Rizz approaches the stretcher - it's designed to look like he's offering words of camaraderie. In fact he tells him *"talk to her again, and I'll take your fucking tongue"*.

She climbs into the cage, ready to see her man crowned. *"And your winner by knockout, Ruinous Riiiiizzzzzyyyyyyyy"* and the crowd goes absolutely mental.

Now his real spectacle begins.

He raises Bee's hand, to the crowd's approval. He gives her a twirl, presents her to his loving audience. Then, standing behind her, he places a hand on her throat, and his forearm between her legs. Lifting her off her feet as if she were a child on a bicycle. He shows the crowd his trophy. Through chokes she asks *"Rizz.... What... what're you doing?"*

Everything he does, the crowd reacts. His puppets in the show where he pulls every string and controls every stage. He places her back down.

In the centre of the cage, he stands behind her, hand still on her throat, and plants his teeth on her breast, aiming to create a love bite as quickly as possible. The more they cheer, the more awe they sit in, the more inspired he becomes to make his statement. *"She's fucking mine, adore her, admire her, but don't fucking touch her"*

He pulls down her basque, allowing the admiration of her bare breasts. He slides his hand from her throat to cover her mouth. Pulling her head back, he bites her neck, sucking painfully. Bruising instantly. When he releases the lioness from his bite, she looks up to notice herself on the jumbotron. Looking out into the crowd she can't see much, the spot lights on her make the crowd invisible, but not inaudible.

"You like to dance for them, don't you...? It turns you on, knowing how much they want you...? You want everyone to look so much, you got it little Bee"

With that he releases her neck, and she stands there. Looking at the crowd. Once again a deer in headlights. Once again refusing to back down, and owning it. He's kinda right. She concedes. She stands there, still, feeling the burn of a thousand eyes. Basking in their heat. He snaps her g-string off and holds it in the air like a prize.

Taking her mouth with the cup of his hand once more, he pulls her head onto his shoulder. He slides the other hand between her thighs, and guides them open. Drunk on the power he has over her, and they have over the crowd. He runs his hand from her ass right up to her clit. He starts to play, with everyone watching. Holding her up, making the whole room, the whole world, watch her submission.

She loses herself in the motions, coming close to climax. He's learnt her body so well already. The rhythm, the pressure, the motions, everything she loves. She's putty in his hands. Just as she reaches the brink, getting close to the point of no return, he stops. The jarring end to the pleasure without release awakens her harshly. He leaves a trail of her excitement from her naval, to her chin. He holds his hand in front of her face, and she already knows what he wants. She over-acts, licking all around his fingers from base to tip. The act is performative. The arousal is real.

But he's not finished yet. He takes her wrists and puts them behind her back and marches her to the cage wall, the one with the best view from the camera. Pushing her against it, she can feel the side of her face and her breasts pushing through the chainlink.

"Smile for the camera, little Bee." The hook from *Trapt - Headstrong* hits full momentum.

With her face still pushed to the wall, and her still bent almost all the way over, he puts his knee between hers, forcing them open. She doesn't resist. She arches her back. Uninterested in the scraping of her face and bare breasts against the chain.

"You wouldn't fucking dare" she challenges. Her eyes adjusting to life slightly outside of the stage lighting, she can see the ocean of faces. Some obsessed, some shocked, some crazed. All captivated, nobody looks away.

Slipping his Thai shorts down far enough to expose his glutes, she feels the heat of him behind her. She stares straight into the little red light of the camera.

She feels the heat of his head rubbing up and down her. Preparing. She squirms with anticipation.

And he does it. He rams straight into her. There's no fragility tonight. Before she catches her breath from the first thrust, he's already pushing in with everything he has again. She can't brace against the wall, with him holding her wrists behind her back. So she has no choice but to take it as she is. She's never been fucked this hard. Certainly never like this. She pushes back, over and over again, opposing his rhythm for maximum depth.

She needs him, every part of him. The man, the myth, and the monster. She, the willing participant, in his depraved game. The object of his obsession, him the object of hers.

"Fuck me, Rizz. Show the world I'm yours" and she pushes back harder, her ass cheeks rippling with the force of his thrusts meeting her pushes. The world starts to blur as her senses begin to give way to the mounting pressure inside her. She agonisingly aches for release. Hers and his.

She needs to feel him fill her, and breed her. Marked, bruised, full of his cum, fucked in front of the world. She pushes back harder and harder, as he releases her wrists, she grabs the chain link. Her finger tips whiten with the force she's gripping.

He pulls her hair hard, forcing her head back, and her back arching more. Making his strokes deeper and a direct hit to the epicentre of her aching desires. He spanks her more, hand shaped whelps appearing on her ass cheeks, releasing tension before he releases everything.

"Make it hurt, let them see.... let them see the monster......"

With a deafening scream, the sounds of her climaxing fills the room. She shakes, her vision blurs. Her body burns and freezes. As soon as she finishes the first, he carries on, forcing another. And another. Until she's a hot mess of sweaty hair, ruined makeup. Stood naked, abused, before her adoring, cheering crowd.

Legs still weak and vision only just returning to focus, she turns to look at Rizzy. He smiles: act complete. He catches her as she falls into him. Scooping her up, a leg either side of hips. She melts into his warmth. As is becoming ritual, she buries her face in his neck. Not from shame, just exhaustion. His hands underneath her ass, holding half her weight in each cheek.

He does a full 360 of the cage, before ducking his head to leave through the door. He carries her back to his changing room. When he gets there, he wraps her in his robe.

Nobody that was there that night can remember who fought next.

Chapter Nineteen

After being carried from the cage last night, everything became something of a blur. An adrenaline crash like no other. In the dark of night, she was only really aware of passing streetlights, and the re-emergence of civilization. It takes moments for this memory to return to her consciousness.

Upon awakening, she's only really aware of the softness of the bed. A mattress that provides just the right amount of comfort and heat. That cuddles you coolly to sleep, then wakes you gently, like a mother with a babe. Bed sheets that make you shuffle and snuggle because the movement feels just so damn soft.

Her eyes slowly adjust to the daylight streaming in, bathing her in the glory of awaking naturally, to the smell of bacon. She stands and takes in the bedroom - something she barely had energy for last night, being carried to bed basically guarantees instant sleep. The pristine laminate floors, the ceiling is unusually high. Everything is white. Clinical and sterile. Everything in its place and a place for everything. Like the watches on the dresser, he might have actually lined them up with a ruler and a spirit level. She could give this place the white glove treatment and find nothing. This isn't clean, this is

"the Corporal is gunna chuck my shit out of the window" clean.

Glancing out of the window she realises she's no longer in Top Boy London, this is My Fair Lady London. Ornate street lights, over-wide footpaths.

Completely naked, yet entirely unbothered, she waltzes out to find Rizzy. Following the scent of the bacon. The acute awareness that she's never been in his house before, or seen him in this setting, suddenly unnerving. She walks to the doorway, catches sight of him, and leans against the doorframe. Observing the beast in his natural habitat.

He's preparing bacon medallions, scrambled eggs, greek yoghurt and granola. A combination that only makes sense to people who have fought or cut weight and had to manage their macros.

Rizzy doesn't look up at Bee before addressing her.

"Morning, Bee. Come, breakfast is ready. 500 calories, 49g protein, 18g fat, 30g carbs" - he doesn't have to look at anything to know that, it's from memory. That's precision she notices, then realising he's shared the information with her for a reason - and that's his love language.

She'd never let on that she knows what's going on, but that doesn't mean she hasn't noticed. He wears a very thin robe that covers about the same amount of leg as the Thai shorts, and leaves his chest mostly exposed. She takes a seat on the high stool opposite him on the island, breakfast bar side.

So... Do we talk about last night? Or us? Or why I'm here and not at Jade's?

Rizz can tell what's going through her head, he just chooses to not engage with it. Instead, he opts to pass her a cup of tea - strong with milk and 2 sugars - just how she likes it. Where does this man get his information?

She takes the honey from the side, and starts to drizzle it onto her granola. She's really not focusing. But there's a very interesting reaction from Rizz. He watches it pile on. His eyes open wide, they fixate. He shifts uncomfortably. She's clearly pouring too much on. She capitalises whole heartedly, committing to the fuckery.

"What's the matter, Rizz?" she asks... honey still piling, maintaining eye contact as the honey continues to layer down.

"Alright, that's enough honey, don't you think?"

"Nah, not yet"

"You don't need any more than that"

A moment's pause. Her deliberate micro-chaos continues with a smirk, until he bursts. He vaults the kitchen counter, and bear hugs her - pinning her arms to her sides, forcing her to drop the honey. "Aw, are we protective of our honey, Pooh Bear?"

He doesn't react. He just holds her. He's been caught in her scent. Caught dangerously close. She's like a proximity mine, detonating his feelings.

"Pooh Bear giving big cuddles for honey?" she teases relentlessly, before continuing "excuse me, Bear, my medallions are going cold".

He releases her.

"Oh wow, you let me go" she jokes

"I told you, little Bee, all you gotta do is fly away" comes his deadpan response, very matter-of-fact. Her intuition says that would hurt him way more than he'd ever admit. And he'd probably burn the city down in response.

"Yeah right, a display like last night - because you'd just let me walk..." she probes, wishing she's added something, anything that told him she doesn't want to

He's still for a second. Contemplating. Deep down he knows he could never let her go. He also knows the right thing to do would be to let her go if she wanted to. He'd let her go, probably. But he'd destroy the whole world so there was nothing but desolation waiting for her.

"Also, what the fuck is this?" she says, pointing to a love bite on her chest "every bloody time, Rizz. Between you and training, I'm always covered in bruises"

"Yeah, they're like a Bee's stripes, warning people they can sting. They're my claim, mark my territory. What do you want from me?" almost joking with the last part.

Everything. Is her gut response, not that she'd hand him that power without a fight.

"Maybe I should put a more permanent claim on your skin" Rizz ponders "like a brand"

"I'm not fucking cattle" she laughs.

She's right, but that did give him an idea. "C'mon lil Bee, throw your stripes on, we're going out".

As is perfectly normal for London, it takes exactly 84 seconds to walk from My Fair Lady back into Top Boy London. Trickle down economics, there's no wealth gap she jokes to herself in observation to the starkness of the change of culture.

Dutifully, Bee follows him wherever he goes, which is into a Skull & Cross Piercings - an edgy, black exterior building. Perfectly gothic. **

"You're getting a tattoo?" she asks him.

"Nah, you are" with a wink.

"You're serious?" she knows she's being challenged to back down again, and she still refuses... and being marked as his forever? There are worse fates.

"Trixie, sweetie, you got a slot in this afternoon" he asks the nonchalant ultra-edgy girl behind the counter, with the bright blue pixie haircut, 4 piercings in each ear, tiny ripped jean shorts with fishnets

"For you, Rizzy, always" she says, all goth-chic seductive.

You're not jealous, Ree. You're not.. nah fuck that, I'll bang her in her face.

"Well, not for me" he nods towards Bee.

"First time?" Trixie asks. Judgey much?

"Mmhhmm" is the only reply she can muster.

"What you after?" it's all cold business between the girls now

Bee looks to Rizz, realising she doesn't actually know.

"Anything you want, wherever you want. But you'll look hot with ink"

Is this permission, a gift, a test or what kind of game is this man playing?

"Follow me" with a fake smile, and they head into the chair room.

Some discussion, some "girl, you sure?" with actual concern and warmth. The girls, without Rizzy's influence, actually get on quite well. The stencil goes on and they approve the design, size and placement and get to work.

Wow, the buzz feels good. Even after a while when it starts to sting, it's enjoyable for her. She's relaxed, laid back. Bee and Trixie exchange anecdotes and gossip, but nothing too heavy.

Finally, the work is done. Bee admires Trixie's handiwork in the mirror, feeling empowered and sexy.

She covers herself with a cushion, Trixie heads to the door "Alright, you can come in now" before returning to stand behind the chair, invited to observe the reveal. Rizz stands there, eyebrow raised, awaiting the reveal. They all maintain the peep long enough for Rizz 'impatience to show through, just a little "well?"

Then she shows him. In Gothic script, right where only he will ever see. A warning, a promise, a prophecy, a reality. Ruinous.

His jaw clenches instantly. Eyes widen like a madman. He glances between ink and eyes.

"I'll give you two a minute" Trixie makes her exit, leaving them together. The ruinous and the ruined.

If he could fall to his knees right now, and thank the Gods for the prophetess delivered before him, he would. Instead, he walks to the tattoo chair with restrained calm. He takes her face in his right hand, and kisses her on the lips. It's not ferocious, but it is forceful.

He lingers there a while, before spreading her legs so she's straddling the bench. He puts his face between her legs. His arms under her knees, hands holding her hips. He kisses her thighs, her lips. He teases with his tongue, finding every nerve ending at the perfect pace and pressure to have her swooning and swaying. Needing him.

One finger then two, effortlessly. Telling her pleasure to come hither, never neglecting her clit with his tongue, and never working hard enough to incite an orgasm, yet. Just pleasure rolling over her.

He takes her hands, and moves them to behind the head rest so she can steady herself. Without command, prompt, or encouragement, she opens her legs wide for him. Returning to the foot end, basking in her glory, named as his own. He prowls towards her end of the bench. She raises her chin, opening her mouth slightly.

His heat meets her moisture, and they groan together. Before their lips reunite and reignite with carnal and eternal passion.

Returning his hands above hers, behind her head, being encased by him adds to her arousal. He's not physically holding her in place. But she can never move. Channeling her obsession into her grinding and gyrating. Seeking gratification in the slippage of his control, and she finds it.

His eyes, locked onto hers, tell a different story. His body, the cage, for him and her, his eyes reveal the monster.

She watches the veins appear on his neck and shoulders, his chest tense, as she pulls him in close. A venus fly trap that will never let him escape. Wrapping him with her arms and legs she pulls him in as far as she can as his whole body slams into her with gradually declining pace, and rapidly inclining intensity.

The heat of his ownership now as evident inside her as her marking is outside. She looks him dead in the eye, and makes her own advance, kissing him - sweetly this time. Gauging his reaction he didn't hate it. But he'd never admit to needing it, or to how his soul decays without it.

She dresses her top half, Trixie comes in to clean and cling film the artwork. Not before dropping a knowing "you'll ruin it", in a deadpan tone and with a flat sarcastic facial expression.

It's not long before they're strolling back towards Rizzy's, he's got some work to do.

"Can I come?"

"Sure"

She clings to his arm, her armour. Her demon in dark jeans. No matter where they are, he'll keep her safe. They jump in the car, no chauffeur today, and no ringing phones. "Just a quick errand, maybe 15 minutes", and they drive for about an hour. Eventually pulling out of the city, into one of those rural looking towns, that brags about how close it is to London.

They pull up to an old dilapidated church that probably has a congregation of at least 4 pensioners. Walking down the faded gravel towards the door Rizz holds her hand, interlacing their fingers, before moving his arm over her head, so it hangs over her shoulder. Their small show of affection hangs over her like a noose.

"You sure we won't burst into flames as we walk through the door?" she jokes

"Not unless you brought petrol bombs" he flatly retorts

The clergyman is at the end of the isle, Rizz motions Bee to take a seat in one of the rear pews. The men take a walk, talking quietly. There's a discreet exchange of envelopes, quickly tucked into pockets, and Rizz makes his way back down from the altar.

"Paying off your sins? Smart"

"There's not enough money in the world, little Bee"

They meander outside, for once purposeless. "I love graveyards" she tells him. Though this isn't much of a graveyard, more a series of old stone pimples adorning a long forgotten lawn. No flowers or ornaments, just moss covered names and the inevitability of dying the second time.

"My birth parents are here"

"Oh... I'm sorry, Rizz. I didn't realise"

"Don't worry about it, fuck 'em. They're lucky they still have their lying headstone - 'loving parents'" and he laughs, as strong men do when their soul feels pain.

She holds his hand and grips his arm as they walk. Holding him close. He won't reveal his pain to her, but she can reveal her nurture. They come to a slow stop, and he stands at the foot of a grave. He gives their joint headstone a little kick, as if selling a used car - definitely 'sold as seen'.

"Sperm Cunt, Egg Cunt - Bee. Bee, the cunts" entirely indifferent in his demeanour and tone, even if portraying a lack of emotional resolution. He continues, "not sorry I've not been to visit, didn't want to. Bye then".

"Rizz" she calls, still holding his hand and refusing to move as he goes to walk away. "It's OK," she reassures.

"Bee, honestly, I'm not arsed. They did fuck all for me when they were here. Getting in the car was the most responsible thing they did. It was landing in the system that got me close to Ma and Pa. Their ridiculous irresponsibility led me to my family. They died for what they loved. We should all be so lucky.".

She stops for a minute, and just gets it.

He, meanwhile, looks his ruinous prophecy up and down. The hunger returning to his eyes. He smirks

Really, again? ...Really - here?!

His look does not falter. Pushing her with his forehead on hers, she walks backwards until she's sat atop the headstone of the failures that used to haunt him. They were legacy, she is prophecy.

She lifts her ass and slips her leggings and frenchies off, as he chokes her, biting her lower lip. Growling as his nervous system processes everything - trauma, testosterone, and her. He possesses her as property, she possesses him as pure demonic energy.

She spreads her legs, and opens herself at the lips with an upside down "V" sign, a spectacle for his enjoyment.
Seductively licking her finger, giving him a show. Reclaiming this hallowed ground as their desecrated temple. She slides

her middle finger in. He stands, motionless. Watching the performance.

She grinds her naked ass on the memory of those who could not do what she does - dedicate to him wholeheartedly. The crumbling stone grazes bite at her skin, but it's a fraction of the pain he's held over the years.

"She stops, a hand either side of her on the stone." tempting him, daring him "What, you're going to make me play by myself? Not going to come and claim what you own?"

Realising she's the sacrifice at this altar, she embraces it.

Turning around, legs as wide as they'll go, fingers still inviting him in. When his hands lands on her hip, and another runs under her t-shirt up and down her back, she braces against the headstone. She hears him unzip, and he slaps her ass cheeks - one side with his palm, the back of his hand on the other.

The familiar heat, this time shaking - quivering. He doesn't put it in yet. Instead reaching around to her nipples. Groping, squeezing, pulling - hard. Pain close to her heart. Then holding them, firmly and tenderly. Changing between the two.

He pulls away slightly, lining himself up for the grandest desecration.

"Own it, Bear" and he slams into her, and he stays there. For seconds. He's big enough to rearrange her insides for her. Still he strains, pushing to go deeper. She gasps, whether she can take it or not, she's going to.

With every fatal thrust, slow and purposeful, she comes closer to the edge. His reach-around torture of her clit, forcing her to tense and release, pulls him in deeper. She pushes back away from the headstone and gets down on all fours, before putting her face sideways on the floor, arching her back properly.

Using her now free hand, she takes over working the front, while he focuses on deep, powerful thrusts into her. There's no rushing today. This builds and builds internally. Relentlessly.

Oh my God, I'm going to pee...

And then she screams. The birds fly from the trees. Critters flee. Grass fills her fists, and dirty her fingernails.

Rattling the gates of hell themselves she lets out a soul searing orgasm, for the first time in her life she squirts, covering the desecrated ground. A beautiful mixture of both of their essence fertilises the land of the forsaken dead.

Realising he's just made her squirt for the first time he laughs

"well I definitely own you now"

Without missing a beat, she looks straight into his soul "in this life and the next".

Comfortably in each other's silence, they get dressed. To get in the car. The seats of the Range Rover are treated with more reverence than the resting place of the dead. She laughs to herself.

They climb into the car and begin the drive home. Getting onto the motorway he changes into 6th gear, puts his hand on her thigh, squeezing slightly. Keeping his eyes on the road, he casually asks;

"Starbucks?"

Chapter Twenty

Post-squad training session debrief. There's always a few days rest after a big fight night. The important business of training is done, so the whole crew lounge on the sofas. Rizz and Bee, Jade and Green, Smoke and Dev.

"A fucking superhero landing, surprised you didn't break the floor, tubs!" Rizz fires at Smoke through laughter

"My brother, give me a call when you fight a challenging opponent" Smoke retorts

"How about you boys give Green a call when you handle the real business" Jade pulls a reluctant Green into the banter, making a money gesture with her fingers and thumbs

"Oh Rizzy handled his buuuuusiness" Smoke defends, standing up and making exaggerated hip thrusts with his hands behind his head

Jumping in, defending Ree from inadvertent embarrassment, *"Yeah, get it girl"* and she high fives Bee

"All I'm gunna say is I'm the only one here that can handle that man in the cage" Bee owns it, making everyone - and herself - laugh.

Dev is busy looking at his phone, and uses the laughter as an opportunity to leave the conversation, answering a call.

"Awh, I didn't mean it, Dev - I'm sure you could hold your own with Rizz" Bee continues her joke, but it doesn't really land. There's a few exchanged glances. Jade, in true Jade style, commentates the scenario with a pantomime grimace and eye roll.

"Oh you reckon so, do you?" Rizz fires back, cool but challenging

As if he's punched her windpipe, she realises she's said something she shouldn't have. *Shit biscuits. I'm sure he'll "correct" me later.*

The jokes and chat continue. They discuss various parts of the night, fight highlights, interclub gossip. Just a general debrief. As the time creeps on, people naturally depart. Leaving just Bee and her Bear. He looks thoughtful, not quite distracted. He keeps glancing at Dev's desk, but Dev doesn't return.

"You okay? she asks him, he silently nods, dismissively

"There's obviously something on your mind, babe"

He doesn't react well to being called babe, apparently. He maintains his stoicism, he doesn't tell her it's none of her business, but he may as well have.

They don't talk much in the car ride back to his place. She starts preparing the sweet potato and steak they've got for dinner when they get back. Weird pride that she's been both allowed to cook *and* allowed to touch the steak.

He goes into his office to take a call, and comes back out. Visibly tense. Deep in thought.

"What's going on? Looks serious" he doesn't answer. It's kind of hard making *'how was your day, honey?'* but she's intrigued, worried, and she's got a bit of FOMO. *"Rizz? What's going on"*

"It's none of your fucking business. If I wanted you to know, you'd know"

Startled at his change of tone, and *the audacity of this man,* she snaps back

"Sir..." with the hand gesture *"respectfully, don't talk to the woman cooking your fucking steak like that"*

He fixes his posture and walks his way to the other side of the makeshift battle line that is the kitchen island.

*"You're giving **me** orders now? That's not brave, it's stupid"*

"Oh fuck off Rizz.." and she starts to mock *"I'm a big bad bear, do as I say or I'll huff and I'll puff and I'll fuck you over there"*. The humour is laced with some audacity of her own.

Stonewalled. He walks over to the kitchen sink and washes his hands. She smirks, embracing her victory. Until he pulls at her pony tail, dragging her to the sink. He turns her to face him, pulling her hair tight exposing her throat, making her look down her cheeks at him. *"Reconsider your tone, little Bee..."*

"Oh no, he's gunna fuck me over there" she feigns boredom at the trope, inside she's shivering with fear and anticipation. *He can probably see my pulse through my neck.* But while he's focusing up top, he won't notice what's going on for her down below. Being man handled has a certain effect on her. His grip doesn't loosen.

"Last chance, and you're getting a final chance because I'm in such a good fucking mood"

"I've got to cook dinner" she replies, ignoring his behaviour like you would a toddler throwing an attention-craving tantrum.

In one swift movement he steps back, turns her, and puts her face in the ice cold water. The sink is plugged and nearly overflowing. He holds her face under the water for a couple of seconds, and pulls her back up. As soon as her lungs fill with air, she begins a tirade. 2 syllables in, she's under again.

She's still in her little shorts, and he pulls them down with his spare hand. When he runs out of reach, he pulls her up again. Using her position to extend his reach and push them further down. He roughly separates her legs with his knee and thigh. Holding her above water for a second, and roughly shoves two fingers inside her. He was expecting some friction and resistance, but there was none. She was ready for it.

He doesn't waste time waiting for the third finger, essentially punching her pelvis the level of force he's destroying her with. Periodically dunking her and allowing her breath. She's gasping, not choking. *"Like pushing limits, don't we, little Bee?"* he rhetorically asks in an oxygen-allowing pause. He pushes her head back in, and in goes the fourth finger.

He's not just thrusting in and out, he's simultaneously motioning his fingers. Her screams of pleasure and pain are only audible through the bubbles of air escaping her lungs in the sink.

"Make me take it - that's what you said, wasn't it?" he keeps her above water level for this one, as he pushes his thumb into the first nickel. The stretch starting to burn in the best possible way. She prepares for the ice cold plunge, and down she goes.

He works his fist further and further in, in a sequence of micro-punches. Destroying her pussy, owning her soul. Pulling her back up just in time for her to splutter a little. She endures the torture. Fights for survival. He opens and closes his digits inside her. Inciting yet more response.

The widest part of his hand still inside her, he pulls her up. After a gasp, she takes a deeper couple of breaths. *'Have we finished being a little brat?"*

'Fuck...'' he doesn't wait for the second word. He dunks her deeper, ears covered by the water. And forces his fist in, all the way to the wrist. He rotates, opens and closes his hand, and pulses in and out until the bubbles nearly stop.

He pulls her out, spluttering. Before she's caught her breath, she finishes her statement *"...you"*. She goes in again. He goes hard, destroying her insides and her soul with a tsunami of pain and orgasms.

Wrenching her back out, she laughs, *"fucking do it"*, he doesn't wait. He submerges her again, violently pounding her, she pushes against him forcing his fist deeper, when he pulls her up, she doesn't splutter; she maintains a stoic silence.

He dunks her again, and he holds her down, he can feel her climax building. He's not going to let her up until she cums. Holding her up by her hair, she tries to steady her weight on the worktop. *'Finished?"* he teases.

She throws her head back and laughs, he rips his fist out and she winces. Embracing the stomach churning sense of being emptied at such pace. Legs still unsteady.

"Thank me" he demands.

Her delay triggers him applying pressure on the back of her ahead again, she breaks - *"thank you"*.

"There's a good girl" he slaps her ass *"now finish the dinner, and stop asking so many questions",* giving her a kiss on the cheek. She blushes, he doesn't break stride, fetching his phone, tapping the screen and heading into the office.

She eavesdrops his call, not taking her eye off of the steak.

"... shit... okay..... right..... how much? .... and you're fucking sure? .... alright, see you there"

She decides not to tell him; but he didn't wash his hands before making the call. *Sir, my pussy juice is on your phone.*

Chapter Twenty One

They pull up outside Chiz's club.

This is not the night for jokes. Green, Smoke, and now Rizzy. The atmosphere is tense, Green carries a backpack.

Rizzy addresses the pair as soon as he approaches *"boys, before we go in, are we fucking sure?"*

Nobody stops him, so he turns and walks in. He's holding Bee's hand, but almost dragging her. The boys are only a step behind them. No handshakes and fistbumps tonight. No pre-prepared rounds of drinks. They don't stop until they get past the dancefloor, down the little run off corridor and to an office door.

Outside it stands Ali, and a supposed-to-be-intimidating "bouncer". Ali steps in front of the door handle. *"Just you"* he says to Rizz, not even acknowledging the others.

"Says who?" Rizz questions

"Me"

"Oh, well in that case" and he pushes his way past and waltzes in. The bouncer looked like he might do something, but Smoke does his Jedi mind trick and convinces him otherwise.

"Come in, take a seat" Chiz sarcastically decorates the scene with faux-hospitality.

With a nod from Rizz, Smoke allows Ali in. The rest of the crew take up positions around the edge of the room. There are two chairs facing Chiz's desk, Rizz motions for Bee to sit in one. Before taking a seat himself. Green stands close to Smoke, Ali takes a seat in the back of the office.

"What can I do for you then?" Chiz politely asks, 99% sure he knows the answer, but better safe than sorry. He decants a glass of whisky from the crystal bottle into his glass, neat.

Rizz motions Green, who opens the backpack and puts some paperwork in front of Chiz on the desk.

"We're short, a lot short" Rizz explains

"Ah yes, about that. I should've called."

"Well we're here now. That's a lot of money, start talking"

"Your recent... indiscretions... have not gone unnoticed. Given the recent changes in the provision of talent to SFD events, Mr Hassan has deemed it prudent to implement a haraam-tax. That's the perceived discrepancy in your paperwork there" dropping Hassan's name has clearly given him a false sense of security.

"A haraam tax, really?" Rizz chuckles darkly

"She's fucking haraam, bro" Ali chirps in, uninvited. Rizz shoots him a look like fire, and nods to Smoke.

Smoke calmly proceeds to Ali's chair and punches him in the face, before picking him up by his collar, and turfing him out the door. Chiz is unflinching in the face of this enforcement, noticing the obvious chink in Rizz's armour.

"He wants to fucking haraam tax me? Don't bullshit, it's got nothing to do with my 'indiscretions', he's just pissed I won't use his workforce, 'cause he fucking trafficking them - that wasn't part of the deal. Working girls, strippers, escorts - that's fine. Fucking sex slaves, get a grip, Chiz. And I'm the one that's full of sin, really?"

"It's not just you that's haraam, it's her" he nods in Bee's direction "she's fucking with your business, and with your head". Chiz looks for support around the room, but there's none to be found. Hearts and minds mission aborted.

"Sorry, maybe I'm not understanding the rules. We don't eat bacon, but we do lines and drink. We won't fuck free women, but we'll enslave them to be fucked by someone else. We make deals then change the terms when we feel like it? Get off your *high horse, your God doesn't give you a free pass here on Earth. You're taking a liberty and you know it."*

"Mr Hassan says get rid of the Gori Randi, and we'll renegotiate"

Green audibly gasps and lunges forwards, stopped by Smoke, who grabs him by the collar, snapping him back to his senses. Smoke returns to his place, blocking the office door.

Rizz turns to ice. He sits on Chiz 'desk.

Slowly, he takes an upturned glass from Chiz 'desk, and pours himself a drink. He takes a swig and swirls it before swallowing. *"That's a nice glass that"*, pouring himself another.

Reaching over to the cigar box, he takes a cigar and lighter. He lights the cigar, and leans forward to replace the lighter. Like lightning he smashes the whisky decanter on the side of Chiz's face.

"Now, I guess we have two problems. I don't have a business problem, you do. But you do not sit there, using Hassan's name or not, and call her that. You can't uncross that line, but you can beg..."

This time, translating to English for full effect, Chiz composes himself and continues; *"Unholy White Whore"*. He barely finishes the sentence before Rizz jams a 3 inch piece of glass in his throat. His eyes widen with shock. He chokes a little on his blood.

"Now, now, don't take it out. Right now it's plugging the hole in your artery. Keeping you alive that piece of glass..."

Chiz clutches at his neck, with nothing to hand to stop the bleeding.

Rizz gives Smoke and Green a nod, and they discreetly depart. No doubt waiting outside of the door.

Bee isn't terrified this time. *Chiz was rude, and kinda fucking racist.* She's a mixture of intrigued, and turned on. *Oh god, that's FUCKED.*

"Come here, my little whore" she offers him her hand, and stands *"our little incel friend here is jealous... and, well he should be... let's show him why"*

Oh God. Really? Biting her lip and smiling.

Chiz has clambered his way to the wall behind his desk now. Propped up against the wall, clutching at his neck. Unable to call for help in such a loud nightclub, and a soundproofed room. With his phone in its holder on the desk.

Rizz makes Chiz watch as he exposes all of Bee's naked beauty. As he kisses her breast, to her areola, taking her nipple in his mouth.

'Don't look a way, my little incel. You might learn something, what a shame you'll die without feeling the flesh of a woman that wants you"

But he does avert his eyes, to be showered in shattered glass as Rizz throws a glass at the wall above his head.

'Look at her eyes, look how beautiful they are. Look how they sparkle for me. Just admit you're jealous habibi, we'll save you"

Chiz locks eyes with hers, while Rizz showers her with increasingly lustful affections. She can't help herself getting fucking turned on. She turns to the desk, facing Chiz head on. Her breasts swing freely as she takes Rizz 'glass, and enjoys some of Chiz 'whisky.

She makes a show of how good it tastes, and does the same with the cigar. There she is, smoking his cigars, drinking his whisky. While he bleeds out, and she's about to get violated, violating his office.

I'm an actual fucking demon.

"You ready, baby?" Rizz asks her, kissing her neck from behind.

"Yeah Daddy, do it"

Chiz is beyond horrified at this violation he's forced to endure, but he can't look away. Even as his consciousness fades he maintains eye contact. Perhaps in some false hope that Rizz will show mercy and save him, but it's too late for that.

They fuck with more urgency than usual. Rizz pounding her ass, her whole body reverberating off of Chizz's desk.

He doesn't violate her like usual, but she's still so tender from the fisting earlier. Her insides are alive with his cock now. The whole situation is so intense, she needs this.

"There's my good girl" as he pulls her hair to the side, exposing her neck. Increasing the pace. With everything burning thrust, hurting so fucking good, she comes close. Panting, sweat forming and running between her breasts. She plays with them for Chiz. Thumbing her nipples and groping her tits.

"Tell him how good it feels"

"It's amazing, your cock feels so good in my pussy. I love knowing that you railing me on his desk is the last thing he's ever going to see"

Oop, there's a kink I didn't know I had. Almost ashamed.

She nears her climax as Chiz nears his end. *"Fuck me harder, make me cum, make me cum for you"* she rapidly pants.

Her eyes widen, her soul ignites, as he expires. She climaxes, and finally orgasms to the sound of his agonal breath. Their eyes close at the same time, as Rizz fills her.

He pulls out and zips up his trousers. She quickly redressed. Clearly more panicked about being at a murder scene than he is.

Rizz takes the whisky in the glass, and pours it on Chiz's face. He was already covered, so a bit more doesn't hurt. Then he lights it. It serves a dual purpose, ensures he's dead, and sends a message.

"Alvida, Habibi" he spits, and guides Bee out by the hand.

Chapter Twenty Two

Meena plays beat-the-knock, but her intention is different this time. Everyone is greeted with the same warmth, hugs, and inspections. But this time there's an unspoken rush to not stand on the doorstep too long. Meena tries her best, feeding everyone, remembering their tastes and preferences.

The air feels different. The chats tonight are not punctuated with laughter, they're punctuated with sighs, knowing nods, and caution.

Ash is grey in the face, and Meena's wrinkles run like valleys through her tired face. Even Jade is zoning in and out. Green's jokes lack their usual energy, and they land to a flat crowd. Smoke's the one trying to lift the mood, but he doesn't carry Rizz's gravity, or Green's wit.

Bee doesn't know exactly who knows what. But bad news travels fast, and she gets the impression there are some consequences for last night.

Everyone sits down at their usual spots; Ash and Meena opposite each other at either end of the table, Jade and Bee next to Meena, with their respective partners next to them. Dev's seat - empty by seeming default these days - between Rizz and Ash, and Smoke sitting opposite.

Meena serves the plates, not removing the cloches and lids. Much to the shock of everybody at the table, except Ash. She stands behind her chair, places a hand on her chest and slightly raises the other, in an age-old gesture that says *Aunty is speaking*. Everyone silences, and pays attention.

"In my mother's house we offered thanks before every meal. Not just for food, but for breath and blood: life and family. Waheguru gives and takes - but we are here, together." Everyone bows their heads, Bee takes a tenth of a second to realise, and does the same.

Meena continues *"May this food give us strength to our hearts and courage to our hands. May we act with honour, even when the world does not. May karma return our deeds, and light guide our way each day".*

A beat of silence before she continues *"now tuck in everybody, I didn't slave away all bloody day for the food to go cold before it's tasted!"*

They start on the appetisers, the mood lightens a little. Some jokes and small talk start to creep their way into the interactions. Smiles start to grace the room, like critters returning to the forests after a fire.

With food in full flow, the front door goes. *"Sorry I'm late"* calls Dev's voice, he heads in, gives Meena a quick hug and kiss on the cheek before taking his seat between Rizz and Ash. Conversation, food and drink carries on until the late evening.

With a stretch and some finality, Ash pushes himself out from the table. *'Thank you, everybody, for your company. Jaan, you have outdone yourself again with a beautiful meal and time for family old and new. It is time to get you off your feet, and if I eat one more bite I'll bloody burst. You've eaten and managed a smile or a laugh, now it's time for you to find your beds"*

Chapter Twenty Three

Motivation runs out, it's discipline that gets you through.

Rizz's words echoing in her head, again, as she leaves the gym and heads to the shop. Having chai with Ash and Meena has become a sacred little routine on its own, and she's so here for it.

The sun is rising, setting a beautiful day out ahead of her. Much the same as Meena laying out a hearty feast for the family. She breathes in the fresh air, filling her lungs. Post workout cold air hitting you just feels different. Today, today she's thankful. Reflective, her life is so different now.

Dysfunctional, sure. Kind of fucked, absolutely. Beautiful in its imperfection - 100%.

Wow, find the clutch.

A loud van revving, *another one of those dickhead delivery drivers, honestly they're a menace, they don't give a fuck.*

Then she sees it screech to a stop only a few feet from her. Doors fly open. Balaclavas rush towards her. She turns to run back to the gym, and the doors open on another car. More balaclavas. *"Dev! Help!"* she screams back at the gym, pleading for backup. Hands and arms grabbing. She brings her hands up to protect her head. *Fight and move.* Her fist hits something. Something hits her. Dizzy. *Stay standing.* Blackness. Claustrophobia. Panic. Feet flailing. Arms pinned. Mouth held shut.

"Get the fuck in there, Gori Randi"

She smashes her shin on something solid, probably a tow bar. She hits another person, or body, as she lands on her side in the van. The doors slam shut and she's thrown around in the back as it speeds away. *Fuck. Breathe, breathe.*

She rolls around as they take corners at breakneck speed. *Who the fuck is that?* A particularly hard turn has her hit the van wall, and hit by the other body. This seems to stir them and they groan. *They're alive.* She knees them some more before hearing "what the fuck?" from a familiar voice. It's Green. He's not exactly conscious.

She starts to calm a little, though extremely car sick. There's a bag over her head, her ankles have been bound, and her wrists bound behind her back. *Fuck.*

Almost succumbing to desperation, but refusing to feel fear. *My Bear is gunna fuck these cunts up.*

Then darkness and realisation starts to set in; *Who else have they come for?*

The van slows and comes to a stop. The doors open and the pair are dragged out and forced into a very small space. *It's a fucking dog crate.* Green is forced in with her too. There's just enough space to sit with their backs against opposing walls, with the knees at 90 degree angles.

A bucket of ice cold water is thrown over the pair of them.

"Sit tight in there, we'll see if lover boy wants you back"

Over the next few hours people kick the crate, laugh at them and hurl verbal abuse.

"Why don't we sell this one? Pretty little whore like her, just stick her in the container, they'll never find her. It's what she deserves"

"Sell the bitch boy too. I hear he sucks dick anyway. Maybe we'll cut him up and leave him at the shop. Fasiq!" and it sounds like they spit on him *"we don't need to sell him, we could just get the Yardies in, let them fuck him one after another"*.

Threats and verbal abuse, with a side of physical intimidation are almost constant. They shiver, still soaking wet, and the water doesn't drain. Leaving them to slowly decompose.

"Aww, he's shivering. Open up, Munafiq!" The smell and splashes of warmth let Bee know that they've decided to urinate on Green.

They're going to fucking pay, I'll rip their throats out myself.

She can do nothing to help him, except push her body closer for warmth. *"Green. Don't listen. We're going to be fine. They're going to come and get us. Stay strong, I've got you, then we're going to fucking get them"*. She whispers in moments of silence from their captors. She hears him sniffing, she's sure he's crying. He doesn't say a word before her reassurance.

He breaks his silence with defiance, he whispers his prayers
"Ya Allah, forgive me. I am weak. I am afraid. If I have not strayed too far to be heard; if you can hear me, please. I have not always been loyal or true. I accept the errors of my ways. Bee has not felt your grace, she deserves your forgiveness. Don't let her die here. La hawla wa la quwwata illa billah"

"I've got you, babe. And so do the others. We're getting out of this together"

Chapter Twenty Four

Rizz's Range Rover screeches to a halt outside the shop. About thirty seconds later Smoke's Golf GTi does the same. Neither of them park, they just finish driving. Leaving the keys in the ignition, the cars running, and the doors open they jump out, and look at Ash's shop.

Every window has been smashed. Remnants of glass and bullet holes. Nobody's hurt. *Thank God.* The damage is unbelievable. Rizz heads in *"Ma, pa?!"* he calls out. They both emerge tentatively from the store room. Ash holds Meena protectively. Her face marred with tears. Sniffling uncontrollably.

The three of them have an intense embrace. Rizzy inspecting them for harm this time. Barely a word is spoken. The shop is full of damage where rounds have hit things. It's no accident that nobody was hit.

If the shop's been hit, they've probably done the gym too. Shit, Dev!

"Smoke, go check the gym, make sure Dev's alright"

He nods and dutifully heads over there with urgency.

"Did you see anything? Hear anything?"

"We heard a commotion outside so went to see, there was a car parked outside. The men had balaclavas. They pushed us out the way and shot all the windows."

"Then what?"

"Then they got in their car and left"

"And that's it, nothing else?"

"Nothing my boy, absolutely nothing. It's Hassan, isn't it?"

Rizz doesn't answer, but he knows Ash is probably right. *"And you're both okay, you're not hurt?"*

"We're okay"

"Alright, I'm going to call Green, he's going to get you somewhere safe to stay okay, just until this blows over"

Ash holds Meena tight. Rizz dials Smoke to make sure Dev and the gym are alright. The call is answered, but Smoke doesn't answer. Just agonising breaths.

Rizz sprints to the gym. Bursting through the door. *"Smoke!"* he calls, he can't see him anywhere. Panic rising through his chest, but staying calm he calls again *"Smoke, where you at?"*.

Nothing. He runs into the office. It's like a warzone. Nothing is where it should be. Filing cabinets dipped over, computer smashed, everything.

Oh my God. Smoke's hit. There's blood everywhere. Smoke's head rolls slightly. He's still breathing. Rizz calls Ash and puts him on speaker. As soon as he answers *"get the car - Smoke needs the hospital"*.

"C'mon fat boy, you're fine, you've got gallons left, you're gunna be fine, you're gunna be fine" trying to find the wound and apply pressure. *"You're gunna be fine big boy, and we're gunna fucking get them"*.

In a final moment of fight he manages *"Dev..."* before he succumbs and loses consciousness. *Shit, they've got Dev, too.* He just can't get enough weight on the wound, he's pushing his whole body on him. *"C'mon Smoke, hey, you're gunna be fine. Smoke? Hey!"*

It seems to take an age before Ash bursts in *"we've got to get him to the car"*, they grab an ankle each and drag him to the car. It's a huge effort. They bang him on every step and piece of furniture on the way. Rizz reassures him the whole time. *"Stay with us Smoke, it's going to be okay brother, we've got you"*. They get to Ash's car and manage to pull him into laying across the back seats with sheer adrenaline and will power.

"Call the hospital - tell them you're coming"

Ash screeches down the road and disappears out of site. Rizz can still hear the car going full throttle and the traffic complaining several streets away.

He squats down at the street, in the last of the blood puddles. Resting his forehead between his blood soaked thumb and trigger finger for a second. With the other hand he grabs his phone, shaking stained fingers putting his passcode in. He calls Green - no answer. He tries again - no answer. He calls Bee - no answer. He tries again - no answer. He sprints to the shop.

"Ma? Ma?!" she's sweeping the floor *"Have you heard from Bee or Green today? Have you seen them?!"* she shakes her head. The weight of the morning is dawning on her.

The scale of the assault dawns on him.

His phone rings. A cold voice on the line.

"Had a rough morning, have we?"

Chapter Twenty Five

Waking to the rattle of the cage being kicked, and the stench of piss. Her spine aching unbearably from the position they've been stuck in.

"Good morning, shitbags" as he kicks the cage again.

The door of the cage opens, and Bee is dragged out by her elbow, hands still bound behind her. She tries to straighten her legs but they're dead from the lack of circulation. They "accidentally" drop her on the floor. With no arms to save her, she hits her head, nearly knocking her unconscious.

In her groggy state, she's aware of painful noises coming from the cage, and a snarling voice *"Come on hijra fuckboy"*, with a thud. He refuses to groan in pain, but she knows they've just stuck a boot in him.

She dazes out of consciousness.

Awoken to a bright light, a torch being shone directly in her eyes as they hold her eyelids open. She pulls her face away. It takes her eyes a long time to adjust.

Her captors look exactly as she'd expect. Roid-munching thundercunts, dressed like shitty SAS wannabes. There are three of them, and a man in a suit. He's old. Refined. She recognises him. From the photos, the ones with Chiz, Ali,

Smoke, Rizz and Sanjay. This is Hassan. *This is fucking Hassan, I'll kill that motherfucker.*

One of them pulls his hand back to hit her in the face, and is stopped by the other. *"No. That one"* he motions to Green.

Vicious Bitch Guard hits Green hard in the ribs with a heavy duty flashlight. Causing him to cough hard.

"Do we have your attention now?" Hassan asks, nonchalantly.

They both look at him, waiting to find out what he wants.

"Rizvar has committed some grave indiscretions. They must be paid for. There are debts owed and blood feuds to be settled. That's where you two come in. Between you, you are in a position to fulfil either of those, at my instruction. You just might save Rizvar, and dear old Ashok and Meena. Should you choose not to cooperate, your stay here will be..... uncomfortable."

Well that's one hell of a position to put us in.

"Mr Green, I am willing to overlook your... lifestyle choices... but you must prove yourself useful to me. I understand you are Rizvar's accountant, and hold the keys to his financial operations"

Green sits in silence. Hassan nods to Vicious Bitch Guard, who kicks his chair over onto its back. Green catches his breath.

"Mr Green, your cooperation would significantly lessen the suffering of... well yourself... and everyone else"

Still, nothing. A sharp penalty kick in his ribs surely breaks them.

"Lift him up". They stand the chair back in its original position, affixing Green back where he's supposed to be.

"Mr Green, let us start again. You are responsible for the financial affairs of Rizvar, and more importantly Sanjay's Fight Dream. I knew Sanjay. He wouldn't like the recent state of affairs. You are also responsible for the cleaning of money that comes in from SFD, through various ventures, the night club, the gym, Ash's shop. You have the ability to repay this debt and end all of this foolishness?"

Well that's a revelation, but it makes sense.

Struggling with the pain, he looks at the floor until Hassan grabs his face. *"Listen to me, Fasiq. You can stop this suffering. You can repay Rizvar's debt and just maybe save his life. Instead, you choose this, what, vow of silence? You are a fool and a traitor"*

Green's silence is really grating Hassan now. Who stands, slips on a brass knuckle and punches him straight in the cheek bone. The crunch suggests it's just shattered. Green cries out in pain.

Bee struggles at her restraints, desperate to help her friend. Desperate to hurt his assailant.

"Aww, found our voice now have we? Say something... say SOMETHING"

Green breathes in, and prepares to speak. Hassan gets close to listen. Green turns his head, and spits out his blood.

With Hassan's full attention, Green speaks slowly and purposefully *'Hasbunallahu wa ni'mal wakeel"*

This causes an almighty detonation from Hassan. "Allah will deal with us? Will he! And not you!? Filthy fuck. A believer?! But you do not attend Mosque, you mix with the non-believers. And Allah will deal with us?!" before taking the flashlight and smashing it across Green's temple. Rendering him unconscious immediately.

They are dragged to a new room now, it's damp and solid concrete, small like a cleaner's closet. Discarded and the door bolted, Bee sits, with unconscious Green in the darkness. In awe of his strength and wishing she could take his pain away.

Green stirs, a broken body houses a soul in tatters. *'Green, it's me, I'm here, we're okay"*

He adjusts and puts his head on her lap, and silently but uncontrollably sobs. *'I've got you, we're okay, we're gunna get out of here. I'm so proud of you"* she places the gentlest of kisses on his hair *"you're none of those things. You're you, and we love you"*. His chest heaves and creaks with the sobs and his broken ribs. *'We're going to get out of here, and we're going to get them. You'll be cracking jokes in no time, you hear me? You'll be back with Jade, she's waiting for us both out there. It's going to be fine.".*

She rests her face on his hair - the best cuddle she can offer - until his sobs stop, and they both fall asleep. Her tears fall too. Silently. And they taste of vengeance.

Chapter Twenty Six

'Don't worry it's not for long, and you don't want to be here while the crew are in sprucing the place up" Rizzy reassures Meena with a hug just before she climbs into Rizzy's Range Rover. Her eyes have barely dried since D day. It's a strong hug, and a *'look after her for me"* for Ash as he too is prepared to be evacuated from the carnage. He hands Robbie his phone, *'if it goes off, let me know".* Robbie nods dutifully. He gives a double tap on the back of the car, and lets Robbie know they're ready to go.

They're off to a safehouse. It's not too shabby, an upgrade in luxury from the house and shop. Rizzy's been trying to get them to move for years, but they won't have it. Now it's for their safety its mandatory - for a short while, anyway.

"You ready to stand on business?" he asks his accomplice *'this is deep, and it's a line you can't un-cross. You'll go down with the rest of us if shit goes sideways"*

'Don't give me the responsible brother act, let's get this shit done" comes Jade's reply, no sass today.

They both pat down their knee length black leather jackets, and make sure they've got everything.

Love conquers all, and these two are ready to burn London down if they have to.

"You sure you can handle it?"

"I've trained with you for years, I've been shooting with Green more times that I've sparred with you. Spare me the damsel act, I'm in my Demon era"

They get into the car and start driving. Calm, sensible, not breaking a single speed limit. Jade raises her eyebrow at Rizz, and he imparts some sage advice

"One crime at a time. You wanna explain to Green we couldn't rescue him because we got tugged for speeding, then they found everything that's in the car?"

Acknowledging his point, Jade makes no more jokes.

They pull up at their first stop of the day *Kings Street Phone Unlocks*. Rizz looks at Jade, and she nods. She plays her part perfectly, luring the sales girl out to the handset aisles - and away from the desk, so she can't trigger the alarm. *"Call him in, get your boss"* Jade quietly instructs.

"Keith, there's a customer here that wants to see you" the poor girl calls, shaking. Keith emerges, looking exactly as you'd expect. In his 40s, fat, receding hairline, shirt tucked in *way* too tight. He's an indignant little cockroach of a man.

"Your boss here is a dirty, dirty cunt. Did you know that?" Jade whispers to the shop girl. *"Do you know what he's into, or how this shop survives, despite doing basically no business? Well, you know the Netflix documentaries, about those girls who get trafficked? Well this guy here, makes sure the gangs doing that always have international phones, that they can't be triangulated by families or the feds, but that those poor girls can always be found by their owners - yes, owners, owners of slaves"*. The shop girl looks like she might be sick, so Jade finishes the job - *"so, how about, you take this and disappear, and don't tell anybody you saw us"* - Jade hands over a stack of cash, enough to cover her wages for probably 6 months. She nods, pale as a ghost, and leaves. Jade locks the door behind her.

Meanwhile, in the middle of the floor - away from the alarms. Keith is held at a subtle knifepoint. Jade closes the blinds on the door, changes the sign to "closed", turns off the tacky LED lighting on the outside, and locks the door. She then makes her way out the back, to make sure nobody else is in. It's all clear, and she gives Rizzy the nod. Keeping lookout, and watching the action unfold.

"Keith Keith Keith... you are a naughty bastard, aren't you?" Rizzy starts, ending with a series of tuts. *"Today, it's not a good day for you mate, but you might be able to lessen your own suffering here"* and he bounces his head off of a security glass cabinet full of stolen iPhones. Keith blubbers like a baby. Rizzy doesn't care.

"I've not got time to fuck around. So this is your one and only chance before I grow impatient... Where are the pair that Hassan's had kidnapped?"

"I don't know"

"That doesn't make you very useful to me alive, you know that don't you Keithy? Sister, would you please provide some encouragement"

Jade drops an L-shaped wheelbrace from the sleeve of her jacket, and starts smashing everything within range.

"Please! I don't know anything!" he cries

"I dunno Keith mate, I'm just not buying it", he man handles Keith to the security case, and puts his hand on it, holding him there by the wrist. Jade doesn't hesitate, she gives him enough time to answer, and when he fails to do so, she smashes his hand. He tries to scream, but quickly has a silicone phone case shoved in his mouth, and Rizz's hand over it.

"Open the fucking safe", he roughly handles Keith to the back, where he opens a small green safe. He struggles, having to do it with his weaker hand, due to the damage to his dominant one.

The SIM cards here are very important to Hassan. The cash is, well it's just cash. Rizz grabs the few stacks in there. *"Take all the money you want - all of it, have all of it!"* Keith tries to negotiate.

"Do I look like a common fucking thief to you?" he grabs a bottle of lighter fluid from his pocket and sprays the various phone paraphernalia with fluid, before lighting it. *Fuck knows what that's going to cost Hassan - but it's not enough. "I've got to send a message, you understand? It's not personal, but you are complicit".*

"Please! I've got more money, loads of money, as much money as you want, I can steal it from Hassan"

He would've continued begging if not interrupted by Rizzy ramming his elbow across Keith's face, popping his nose with impressive efficiency. *"Oh, sorry about that, here let me help"* he uses a fistful of cash to clean up Keith's nose. *"I don't want this money now, it's got blood on it... Tell me Keith, it's going to be pretty hard for you to fix phone screens and rip off pensioners for tech support without the use of your hands, isn't it?"*

Keith's eyes widen as Rizzy pulls a meat cleaver from the inside of his coat. *"Now hold still, okay, this is probably gunna hurt..."*. Jade grabs Keith's arm and pins it to the back office desk. Keith struggles and panics, and wets his pants. Jade curls her nose.

"Last chance big dog, where is he keeping them?"

"I swear I don't know" Keith cries, so Rizzy promptly hacks through his wrist cutting his hand off. Grabbing some of the cash and using it as a makeshift bandage for the wound.

When the blood is sufficiently soaked, Rizz grabs Keith by the jaw and forces his mouth open, and starts stuffing blood soaked notes in. Keith's eyes go wide, and Rizz keeps shoving them in. Slowly suffocating and bleeding out, Keith's panic turns into resignation. They leave before he takes his last breath.

Jade wipes down the surfaces the pair touched, and they clean the blood from their hands on their way out the door.

They climb back in the car, Jade necks some of her Red Bull trying to steady her nerves. Rizz lights a cigarette, offering Jade one. She takes it. Ramming a banana in his mouth and checking his wing mirrors, they head off to their next destination.

It's only a few minutes before they pull up to "Pressed and Blessed Dry Cleaners".

"For a money launderer, isn't a literal laundrette a bit on the fucking nose?" Jade quips, Rizzy smirks.

"This place is important though, everyone who's anyone goes through here, because they can leave notes and shit in the pockets of the coats. Burner phones can still be triangulated

to your normal phone - and they can use those phones in court cases to prove they're yours"

They casually decamp from the car, and walk into the dry cleaners, Jade filling her pockets with coins, and grabbing a big laundry bag. This time it's Rizzy being the distraction

"Hey, I was wondering, are you good with dry cleaning leather coats - this one's covered in blood".

In the meantime, Jade is unloading her bag. One brick per machine. Once she's been round just about all the machines, she goes round again - putting a coin in each.

"Madame, I'm very sorry. We need to get out the back, right now. I'm afraid it can't wait."

She shakes her head emphatically. So she turns a machine on, the brick destroying the drum in seconds. The sound is horrendous as the revenue stream disappears.

"What are you doing?!" comes out the screaming owner, an older East Asian woman. She looks at the carnage Jade has caused.

Rizzy then calmly explains how Hassan's gang are exploiting her little business and naivety. They explain in some detail how Hassan makes his money. Her disgust is palpable, and she leads them out the back. Searching through the coats, they find some useful information. It turns out the lady had heard some conversation in the cleaners - they talk next to the washing machines because the noise prevents any recordings or wires - and she thinks she knows where they are - Habibi's Shihsha Lounge on Camden Road.

Rizzy thanks her, and apologises profusely before handing her a large stack of cash to cover the machine and the inconvenience. He then takes all the coats she has, dumps them in the outside bin - along with his burner phone, and sets light to them. *That's going to be very inconvenient for him.*

They go to the boot of the car and check their bags and stock their various pockets before climbing back in.

The car comes to a slow, controlled stop on the red lines a few doors down on the other side of the road from Habibis. He checks the time, and tells Jade they've got a few hours before opening. The clock on the dash reads *1:11* - *"oh Angel number, make a wish"* Jade comments, before realising the absolute absurdity. Rizzy does make a wish.

Checking across the street there are only a couple of people milling around inside. The street is clear, no real foot traffic. *Perfect.* He pulls out a burner phone, does some quick tapping, and puts it back in his pocket.

He then nods to Jade, and they pull and don Ghost Face masks. Checking hers is on, he redlines the car before releasing the handbrake and the car screeches off its mark. He aims it straight at the glass front of house, and within seconds crashes straight through it, all the way into the bar. Pinning some henchman to it. The chaos and destruction caused gives them time to unbuckle and jump out. The melee begins.

Jade is immediately jumped by an absolute unit of a man, swinging arms like tree trunks at her. She fires an exceptional sidekick straight through his kneecap, inverting it completely. He hits the ground unaware of the damage he's sustained, and she stamps on his face with her full weight.

Rizzy flies at the men on his side. They're bigger than him, but nowhere near as crazed or intent on violence. The first one swings a punch, as Rizzy rolls underneath it his attacker catches hold of his coat. Rizz headbutts him once, sending him off balance. Pinning him to the bar with both hands he headbutts him three more times. Noticing the second getting closer, he spinning side kicks him straight in the chest, from where he was in the bar. Effectively clotheslining him, landing him on his back gasping for breath. Raising his knee all the way to his own chest, Rizzy stomps through the sternum of his attacker.

The third and final feels he's no fool, he pulls out a knife. Rizz looks at him and smiles. Unnerving the knifeman and causing a delay. A long enough delay for Rizz to pull out his hatchet. Risking the chance of mercy, he turns and runs away.

With the upstairs threats handled, they head to the back of the car. Jade takes out a double barrelled shotgun, and Rizz checks and sticks a Glock in his belt, and checks and sheaths his hunting knife. Finally, he grabs his huge maglite torch.

Jade contemplates throwing the shotgun over her shoulder for the aesthetic, but remembers Green's scolding. *Gun safety isn't a joke, babe.* With that in mind, she honours his teachings. Gun pointed at the floor, finger not on the trigger, running along the guard above.

"*Cellar?*" Rizz calls to Jade

"*Cellar*" she confirms

The jump over the bar and prime, Jade on the hinge-side of the trapdoor to the cellar. Finger in the hook, ready. Rizz brings his maglite up with his left hand, and puts it on rapid flash. He rests his Glock hand atop his torch hand and takes aim at where the cellar door is going to open.

Jade watches Rizz intently, and when he gives the nod, she rips the door open. The flashing light illuminating for Rizz, and blinding for anyone down there. But there is nobody. Jade, shotgun still in hand, follows Rizz down the uncomfortably narrow staircase. His torch and firearm stay true as he scans for threats. Nothing.

They come to the end of the cellar, which runs narrow like a corridor. And find another door, it has a lock, but there's nothing on the latch. Jade primes behind the door, Rizz ready. She waits for his nod, and he primes. He gives the nod, and she rips the door open. Nothing can be heard but some kind of Arabic speaking. *It can't be call to prayer at this time - Dhurh was an hour ago and Asr isn't for a few hours yet, what the fuck is this?*

Rizz cautiously enters the room, scanning for dangers. Jade follows in after him. No sign of humans anywhere. Until there is. He sees a dog cage, full of piss and water. With no other signs of dogs around. *They better not have fucking put them in there. But we're getting warmer.*

A machete swings from behind Rizz, he doesn't see it coming. Jade does. She blasts him in the chest with the shotgun. Shattering the eery quiet. Alive, but gasping and still reaching for weaponry, Rizz puts a foot on his chest and shoots him twice in the face, just to be sure.

Following the noise, muffled screams can be heard. Garbled and frantic.

Rizz and Jade pick up the pace heading directly for it. They see a bolted door, and it starts shaking and banging. Outside is a speaker, the source of the Arabic. *That's them.*

They get to the door and open it. The stench of body odour and human waste is thick. They gasp for air as the door opens. The room is no more than a few feet in any direction. They are too weak to stand properly or even really move themselves. Green is in the foetal position, being held by Bee, between her thighs and abdomen.

Rizz and Jade, despite their acts of horror violence today, take a few seconds to absorb the level of cruelty.

"Kill... the speaker...." Bee manages to beg their heroes.

Jade stomps it silent immediately, suddenly realising what it was doing. She crawls into the space, and lays herself gently atop Green. *"Baby, it's me. We've got you, you're safe"*. Bee is pinned in by this, but she allows it, for Green. Tears run down Jade's face, as she starts to accept the reality the pair have been forced to endure for the last couple of days.

A sound. From the other room. Rizz 'ears prick up. *"Watch them"* he instructs Jade. He raises his gun and investigates the source of the sound. While Jade is with them, she takes her knife, cutting their restraints.

He enters the room to find some wannabe henchman, dressed like a valour thief, hiding. Realising he's been caught, he puts his hands in the air in a show of peace. *"One wrong move and I'll fucking end you"* instructs Rizz keeping him at gunpoint. He walks towards him and hits him with the handle of the gun, before taking physical control of him, grabbing his throat and pointing the gun at his forehead.

When Rizz and his captive return. Green is stood, barely. He's crying uncontrollably into Jade's chest. She's soothing him and holding him close. He notices that Jade stops to look at Rizzy. Green turns to look as well. Green's eyes go like a man possessed.

262

"Want the honours, brother?"

Green nods, with full resolve. *"Tie him up"*

Rizz doesn't ask questions, retribution is a bitch, and so is therapy. This is much faster.

He tries to make a run for it, and Jade shoots his kneecap. He screams in agony, rolling around. Rizz pins him, and ties his arms behind his back. Rolling him onto his back he nods to Green. Rizz keeps his eyes on him, and Jade keeps her gun trained on him, just in case.

"Knife" Green requests, and Rizz hands Green his hunting knife.

Rizz keeps his Glock in his hand, and puts his arm around Ree. She doesn't respond much. She's as invested in this retribution as Green is.

"You talk too much. Your words are poison, they do not spread the message of Allah, they spread hate". He mounts the chest of his oppressor, striking him in the top of his jaw with the butt of the knife before forcing his mouth open. He rams the knife in there and wiggles it around, and when he's made enough space to handle the knife properly. He cuts out his tongue. Over his now incoherent screams, Green begins his retribution. He holds the knife, blade pointed downwards, in both hands. He ends every sentence with a stab. Emotion building with every sentence.

"You will not enter Paradise until you believe, and you will not believe until you love one another.

As you sow, so shall you reap.

In the name of, the Most Gracious, the Most Merciful."

With that, he raises his arms, and stabs him in the throat. Inspired and blood crazed, he stabs him again and again and again. Crazed, a man possessed. He keeps stabbing. Until his rage processes to despair, and finally sadness - at what he was forced to endure.

He stands, and turns to Jade. Bursting into tears and collapsing into her arms. *"I've got you, boo".*

Sirens approach. Jade and Rizz exchange glances. Rizz fireman lifts Green, who groans in pain *"my ribs".*

"I know brother, but right now we gotta get you out of here"

They make their way up through an alternative fire escape. Outside Robbie is waiting in a BMW X5, they all climb in. Rizz in the front, the other 3 in the back. The doors aren't closed before he speeds off.

Rizz makes a quick call, doesn't wait for it to answer. He wipes it clean with alcohol wipes and throws it out the window.

In the bar, the car remains in situ. The henchman pinned to the bar is awake. Emergency services are closing in. An old

Nokia vibrates, and the first fuse is lit. Smoke pours from the car.

'Everyone out! To the outer cordon!" a Police officer shouts, the emergency response teams follow the order and evacuate. The henchman, pinned, is helpless to escape. 30 seconds later the second fuse ignites. The car detonates, destroying Habibi's, the henchman, and the evidence. And all the windows of the cars parked on Camden Road. There are no civilian or first responder casualties.

The first fuse was for theatre and effect, to give a chance for the evacuation. The second sent the message. One to scare, one to scorch. Killing civilians and emergency crews brings too much heat. And fire fucks forensics.

Chapter Twenty Seven

The drive from the wreckage of Habibi's prison is near silent.

The drive isn't short, it takes them out of London to the South East and into Kent. They pull up on the pressed gravel to a manor house, with a few cottages attached.

Battle scarred they head inside. Meena and Ash are there, they greet Rizz and Jade with hugs and inspections.

Bee seems too normal, too okay. Green is silent, his eyes are the definition of what was once called "shell shock". He

doesn't speak, and doesn't make eye contact. Everyone notices both of them.

The last to enter the safe house are Rizz and Jade. He stops her.

"I know you're a tough cookie. What we did out there was no

joke. If you're not okay, today, in a week, in a month. If it haunts your dreams or your blinks. You let me know, alright?"

Normally, this kind of tenderness would've been rejected and laughed at. But Jade feels heavy with the weight of all the lines they crossed. She looks at him, showing a rare glimpse of vulnerability. Instead she takes a pause and a deep breath. *"I appreciate it - right now we need to help Green. After that, maybe I'll feel something"*.

Once they're all in and have eaten, the pairs head their separate ways.

"I need to shower, come with me?" Bee pines for her Bear.

"Of course" he takes her hand and leads her to their room, and en suite.

He gently helps her undress, and guides her into the shower. Stripping out of his own clothes, knowing he has to burn them later. They step into the water together. Scolding hot.

She doesn't react to the heat. Doesn't react to his touch. She's a shell of a person right now. The weight of what she's just been through is sitting on her. She's stayed strong for Green this whole time, even when they opened that door the relief didn't hit her.

He's unsure of how to support or what to do, but he's damn sure she's going to know he's there. She turns to face him, under the rainfall shower head, desperate to wash away the dirt and filth. He takes the shower pouffe, lathers it in way too much shower creme. And starts to help her clean. Methodically and tenderly.

He starts at her neck, and works through her shoulders, down her arms, her hands, her armpits, chest, and abdomen. *"Turn around"* he instructs, the gentlest he's ever spoken to her. He washes her shoulders and down to her butt. Every body part gets a mini massage and a gentle scrub. She doesn't react much, but he knows she can feel it.

He turns her back round to face him. Then he moves onto her face, with a gentle mint refreshing cleanser. He places his hand on the nape of her neck, she leans her head back, allowing the water in, and he gently scrubs across her face, using it as an opportunity to cup her head in his hands. He wipes the suds away with one thumb at a time. He feels her start to breathe again.

The face wash gave the perfect time for her hair to soak through, he grabs the shampoo and starts to work it through her scalp and to her ends. Another excuse for a micro-affection, a little head massage.

When he's done, she's facing him, free of all the dirt and filth. She looks up at him and tries to talk, but no words come out. She tries this a few times. He doesn't need to hear the words to

understand she's in pain. Under the shower's warm atmosphere he pulls her in, cradling her face against his chest. The water somehow makes them feel closer than they've ever been before.

Eventually, she pulls away just slightly, her chin a couple of inches from his chest. She looks up at him, finally able to articulate, just a little *"I'm so glad you came for me"*

"Little Bee, we've never been apart. We've been soulmates for eternity, and will be for an eternity more"

"You went through all that, to get us back"

"I'd do it all again. I would burn the world for you"

With that she forces their bodies as close together as she can. Not even water can come between them. And then they open. The flood gates, her defences from everything she's felt. She cries demurely at first. Before succumbing to full blown, hysterical ugly crying. Sobbing onto him, he holds her tight enough that her ribcage can still move. He quietly reassures her, knowing all he can do right now is let her get it out, and be there when she's done.

A single tear rolls down his face as he tries to comprehend the density of emotion she must be feeling. After the crying, and her breathing resettles, she asks him;

"Bear...?"

"Yeah...?

"... I love you"

"I love you too, little Bee" almost a whisper

Their bodies mould together, as intertwined as their souls.

Eventually, they turn off the water and climb out. Rizz hands her 3 towels in turn. One for her hair, one for her shoulders, one to wrap around her chest.

"Hey, I wanna show you something" Rizz softly mentions

"I'm really too tired for games"

"I think you'll like it"

Reluctantly she follows, holding his hand just to feel near to him.

In a frame on the wall is a commissioned painting. A brown bear sits with his back against a gnarled old olive tree, a bumble bee sitting atop his nose. The bumble bee is staring straight into the bear's eyes, stinger raised like a warning. As you follow his upper legs down, you see a sticky paw, and a jar of honey.

Bee stands there taking it in, and everything it symbolises. She hugs around his waist, and he holds her tight around her shoulders. She doesn't take her eyes off the painting, her face from his chest, or his scent from her nostrils for minutes.

A few days pass, and the family is mostly healing. Physically, at least. There are daily efforts from Rizz and Ash to locate Dev or find out what happened. There's been no contact from anyone who knows anything. Every lead, every favour they've called in, it's all led to nothing.

Jade, Meena, and Bee's efforts have been directed at trying to encourage Green back to the land of the living. With no success. He will eat now. In that he will consume nourishment. No enjoyment. He'll stare at a TV, or the ceiling, or the wall.

The four have started taking walks around the grounds. He accompanies them but says little to nothing.

"I've got to pop out, I'll be back in a few hours" Rizzy declares to the group at lunch to a cacophony of questions, all of which he evades. Nobody is comfortable about him going out solo, but that doesn't mean they have any choice.

Several hours later, a minivan pulls up through the crushed gravel. Everybody, except Green, twitches curtains and prepares for the intruder.

The driver's door opens, it's Rizz. He goes to the boot and is there for a while. Then he appears, walking backwards pulling something. As he moves away from the boot, what he's pulling becomes clearer. It's a wheelchair, containing a heavily medicated Smoke.

The anxiety vanishes in an instant as the family fights to be the first ones out the door. A blur of greetings and well wishes overwhelms a pretty grumpy Smoke.

"Alright you lot, we love you, but back the fuck up. Give the brother some space, would ya?" Rizzy commands, his usual servant-leader self.

Over the next few days Smoke gradually, with the help of several professionals visiting night and day, heals and recovers. Not to his usual self just yet, but the progress is evident. He spends time in his wheelchair sitting with Green. The first time they saw each other was the only emotional reaction anyone's seen from him since getting to the house. A genuine smile and hug. Then he switched off again.

Smoke spends time with Green every day. He eventually stops monologuing, but never stops showing up.

Another week passes, everyone gradually moving into their own cottages. Space to breathe, close enough to feel safe, and not yet returning to London. Green has barely eaten, barely spoken. Between everyone, they've run out of strategies and options. Jade knows her man, and she knows he isn't right, and he's spiralling. He's not getting better right now, internally, he's declining.

Sat on chairs in the living room are the whole family, and two esteemed guests. Imam Haris Anwar, and Dr Zayn. They sit patiently, sharing chai with Meena, and discussing life and culture. The chairs are all angled towards the sofa, and are all occupied.

Jade walks into the bedroom, where Green lays, shrouded in darkness, desolation, and destitution.

"Come on babe, I know you don't want to get up, and that's okay. But today we have guests, and I really want you to see them"

Still no answer.

"I don't wanna be harsh with you here babes, but it's either you come out, or I bring them in here. And you don't want people in your space."

He agrees, not in words, in actions. He has a quick wash in the sink and puts fresh clothes on. Before brokenly walking to the living room. He looks up, and confusion distorts his face. Jade guides him to an empty seat on the sofa, and sits next to him, folding her legs underneath her, and holding his hand on his thigh.

Jade looks around the circle for silent confirmation that everyone's ready before starting. Her monologue is rehearsed, she's slow, and let's each part of the message sink in before continuing.

"Baby, we know you've been to hell, and we've seen hell. But we didn't have to feel it or endure it. We are all here today *because we love you, and we want to help. We know we can't do it alone, and that's why we have Imam Haris and Dr Zayn, who would love to speak to you."*

Green starts to soften, he listens to Imam, and pays him the respect that is due. Imam begins to speak

"As-salāmu 'alaykum, Green" - he doesn't wait for the correct formal response, prioritising Green's emotional welfare -

'your family have called upon us, and Allah has provided us to you, in your hour of need. I do not come to preach, I come to sit beside you as a brother." His words are genuine and sincere, from a place of love and compassion rather than dogma. He continues *"As imam, I have a message to deliver to you, and I pray that you are ready to hear it. The men who treated you as they did, are not the messengers of Islam, and they are not the bearers of Allah's will, they dishonour qadr.*

Not one verse in the Qur'an commands cruelty. Not one hadith condones what was done to you. Their behaviour was oppression, so far past zulm, their actions were haraam, brother. Not yours.

Allah teaches us to love and respect. In your darkest hour you prayed, you did not ask Allah for mercy for yourself, you prayed to save your friend. This is not weakness, habibi, this is divine strength. Allah sends to you ummah in your family here, and through mas-jid. I have survived at the hands of cruelty from those who believed I was no longer worthy of Islam, simply for embracing compassion towards people who walk different paths. But this is what Allah teaches us, this is his gift; rahma, to love with mercy and sabr, to stand with patience, even and especially when it is hard.

I have sat where you sit, and felt how you feel. The journey ahead of you is painful and long now, just as in the Journey to Ta'if, but we stand with you, and know you have the strength. But even the Prophet bled on that road. And still, he rose again, with grace."

During his speech, Green begins to humanise. Silent tears roll down his cheeks, he nods, his soul and his faith healing with every sentence.

Giving him time to sit with everything he's just heard, Meena silently hands Green a cup of chai. Which he accepts. He closes his eyes tight, and allows tears to roll. He smells the tea, and takes a sip. Exhaling some relaxation for the first time.

Dr Zayn now speaks up, *"Green, I'm not a preacher, and I sit here today not as a fixer, for you are not broken. Profoundly injured, yes, but never broken and never beyond help and love. And none of us except imam can understand how that feels as you do. What was done to you wasn't just violence, it was a defilement, it was psychological warfare weaponising your faith. You do not have to talk to us, you do not have to share anything you do not want to, ever. I'm not here to try to coax you into telling us anything. What I am here to do is make sure that you know how strong you are. And how many of us there are that deeply know how to help people understand and overcome the darkest violations that others do to us. I'm here as a brother, as a drinker of chai, and as a*

Muslim, to offer to you ummah, and every tool we have between us. To help you feel, however you want to feel. It is okay to feel, with extreme force, it is okay to shed the shackles and to cry if that is what you need. This does not make you weak, it makes you human. Tears do not mean we are not strong, it means we have been too strong, for too long".

The tears roll down Green's face now, Zayn's words and Imam's faith have cracked him. He breaks eye contact and slumps into his own hands. Everyone watches as Jade wraps her arms around him. *"It's okay boo, we've got you, we've all got you"*. The floodgates open, and his family old and new support. The love and care in the room is palpable. Still holding his hand. *"Shall we ask everyone to leave? If you're comfy for them to stay, squeeze my hand twice"*. He does.

One by one, not to crowd, but to show their presence, the chairs empty towards Green. They all deliver their own messages.

"We love you brother, we've got you" - Rizz, with a hand on his back and a kiss on his head

"You're so brave, Green, love you" - Bee, with an embrace around his head

"Brother I'm so sorry I wasn't there, but I am now, always" - Smoke leans out of his wheelchair, to speak directly to Green's ear his own tear running down his face

"You're a good boy, Green, with a solid heart" - Ashok, who puts his forehead on the top of Green's head

"You light up every room, and you have always honoured our hearts and homes, Baccha. You are our family, and we are so glad to have you home." - Meena, at eye level, with a warm and tight cuddle

After everyone has returned to their seats, Green finally speaks. He looks around the room, feeling broken still, but today was the strongest of steps. Overwhelmed by their love and effort.

"Thank you... I love you all... imam, can you say prayers with me?"

"Of course, where shall we pray?"

"We've laid out a prayer room, imam" Meena informs

"I'll take you there" offers Ash, quietly guiding imam and Green

Once they're out of the room, Jade addresses everyone remaining. *"Thank you..."* as her hand comes to clap her own mouth and nose, and she finally lets go. Her emotions and tears come in tsunamis, and she is held - Bee and Meena hold her tight. For as long as she needs.

Chapter Twenty Eight

Robbie bursts into the living room, Bee quickly pockets her phone. He doesn't waste time, but isn't rude.

"Where's Rizz?"

Bee shrugs, and Robbie continues searching, finding him in the library with Ash.

"Remember the laptop from Chiz 'office?" Robbie asks Rizz without pause

Rizz gives him a look that says *"obviously, go on"*

"It's just come back, Dimos 'guy cracked it. You're going to want to see this". He proceeds to guide Rizz through the findings. Rizz listens intently, giving nothing away in his facial expression. After the findings, Rizz thinks for a second, then speaks.

"Call a conference, get everyone into the dining room. You're a good kid, Robbie, you did good"

Everyone takes their seats around the table, Rizz at the head, surrounded by Bee, Smoke, Green, Ash, Jade, and Robbie.

Calling the meeting to order, without pomp or circumstance; Rizz begins

"Smoke, can you tell us about what happened before you went into hospital?"

"Yeah, so I head over to Dev's to check the gym and make sure he's good. I catch him on the phone to Hassan, he's talking about Sanjay's, he's telling him all kinds of stuff man about his Dad's legacy and that, but like I was just there to check in on him, I didn't even know Ree and Green were gone. He looks at me and fucking flips, telling me he didn't know they were gunna take her, I didn't know what the fuck was going on. He tried to bolt for the door and I grabbed him, started shaking him like 'what did you do?!' and I chuck him back into the office. Before I know it he's swinging for me, I socked him, and then boom, I got hit. Motherfucker had pulled a glock on me, man. I didn't even see it, he shot me point blank through the stomach and fucking left me there. He gets back on the phone and splits, that's when you turned up"

Rizz puts his hand on Smoke's shoulder, in both thanks and solidarity, before continuing.

"So we got Chiz' laptop back from Dimos' guy, and there are some revelations, and some problems... We know that Chiz was a piece of shit, but watch this..." he then hits play on a recording on a laptop, and turns it so everyone can see.

The recording plays, it's from a camera at a low angle on Chiz' desk. We can see him sitting in his chair. You can hear Ali sitting on the other side, preaching extremist shit; *"Islam gives us rules to follow for a reason. You think Allah approves of a woman uncovered, defiling sacred spaces? This is why empires fall. Why our people suffer. Because we've allowed devils like her to walk freely among us."*. Chiz goes along with what he's saying, nodding and agreeing, before Chiz adds *"I spoke to Uncle Hassan, he agrees. He's starting to believe brother, we've saved him. And he's saving Dev. As I told Dev and Hassan - the Prophet (peace be upon him) stood against corruption with strength. He didn't tolerate fitna in his house. You want to be a man of deen? You stand up. You cleanse what's impure. Rizvar does not respect Sanjay's legacy, does not respect Allah. Ash is complicit, he allows a generation's work to be thrown away for some cheap whore"*.

The video finishes. The room sits, in stunned silence. But Rizz must interject.

"Yeah, that's not all of it..." he opens another file, this one a voice recording and plays it. There are two voices;

Chiz: *I'm trying, but he doesn't trust me yet*

Man: *Well you'd better try harder*

Chiz: *What do you want me to do, man? I'm stuck in a rock and a hard place here*

Man: *We want both*

Chiz: *That'll take time, Hassan's turning - then you can tie them both together. Just give me a few more months*

Man: *You can have all the time you need if that case comes back to bite you, huh?*

Chiz: *C'mon bro, you know they'll kill me*

Man: *We wanted Hassan, and you found an extremist recruiting and radicalising. You know how many years it takes to get that kind of penetration? Go deeper, and get the evidence, or your shining recommendation from the NCA and the Metropolitan Police Force might just disappear, that won't look good when the CPS decides to push on those rape-murder charges, huh?*

Chiz: *You're going to get me killed*

Man: *Don't break your cover, and don't try to disappear*

The line goes dead. The audio recording finishes.

The room doesn't speak as everyone tries to wrap their head around everything that's just happened. The gravity of it all sinking in.

Jade, nearly back to her usual self, breaks the silence *"So wait, sorry, rewind, recap... the fuck?"*

Rizz summarises for everybody *"So, piecing together everything we now know...*

Ali is an extremist, and he's been recruiting for radicalised prison gangs here on the outside. He's been making connections between the outside organisations and the gangs on the inside.

That's how he gets in so tight with Hassan and gets in his ear, and starts trying to radicalise Hassan himself.

Yes, and he uses Chiz to do Hassan's dirty work. Chiz has the street level connections, but Hassan has the infrastructure and reputation.

Hassan is infuriated when Rizz cancels the girls for Sanjay's - he's losing money. He would've kept everything else sweet though, if not for Ali's constant preaching. Eventually Hassan implements the haraam tax, because Ali's been going on and on about everything that happened at Sanjay's.

This is where Dev comes in. We're not sure how or why they got into Dev's ear. What we do know is that there have been a lot of calls made from Hassan and Chiz to Dev.

My best guess is, Ali and Hassan have convinced Dev that there's some moral dishonour in how Sanjay's is being run - and they're using Sanjay's legacy as the way to leverage Dev. Hassan wants the business, Ali wants a recruit - and to undermine my position to fight back.

This leaves us with a couple of pretty big problems; 1. Dev's still out there, we don't know what he's up to now. But we need to have a.... conversation... and figure out what's going on. 2. We know Chiz, Hassan, and Ali were all being actively monitored by the Police. And we don't know what Chiz told them about us. And 3, a pretty big one, we killed a fucking 'Covert Human Intelligence Source'. Met or NCA, whoever's onto it, aren't going to let that one go. If we've already been under surveillance, and now everything else has happened."

Variations of "fuck", temple rubs, and general shock reverberate around the table.

"So, what do we do now?" Bee asks

"Yeah, tell us how to help" Jade adds

"Well, Green, Smoke you boys have earned some rest, and you're not exactly battle ready right now. Ash, do you think you can get through to Dev?" - Ash, with folded arms, nods his head in a way that says *'I'll try my best'.*

Rizz continues *"We've got to find Ali, and we've got to get to Hassan - maybe if we deliver the same as Chiz was going to they'll let us off the hook, and we'll solve both problems in one go"*

To everyone's surprise, Robbie chirps up *"I'm in - Sanjay's is everything to me, man. Let me know what to do, I know how deep this is going to get, so don't try to talk me out of it, just let me help"*

Chapter Twenty Nine

In the grounds, using trees and cans. Robbie, Bee, and Jade are firing down range. *"Breathe, squeeze, and move. Hard cover, engine blocks, something the rounds won't pass through"* Rizz recites Dimos 'teachings, which Dimos 'recited from his learnings in his time in the military. He was pretty shady about what he did in the military, and it's hard with him and his demeanour to know if he's joking, full of shit, or serious. But *the gun stuff works.*

Robbie clearly spent his time in the Army Reserves wisely. He might not have deployed, but it's a hell of a lot better than nothing.

"Rizz, we've got a location - he's at Sanjay's, right now..." Green's voice is urgent but controlled.

"Alright guys, ready up. Bee with me, Jade in with Robbie"

"... Rizz, I think Ali's with him" Green adds. Rizz sighs.

Two G-Wagons are loaded and ready to go, keys already in the ignitions when their crews climb in. They start and depart in unison, barely 3 feet between them.

Green, laptop still across his forearm, watches them depart. Smoke hobbles out of the front door with his crutches. *"Oh, bye then"*, pulling a pouty face.

In a rare moment of spark Green retorts, without missing a beat, in his most fabulous voice *"Can't wait all dayy, got baddies to slayy"* before doing his very best "sashay away".

Smoke laughs so hard one of his stitches starts to leak. Noticing the blood appearing through Smoke's shirt, Green continues *"Brother, you can't be both - a blood and a cripple"*, Smoke's wheezing now as Green helps him into the house. The medical team will be round soon anyway.

On the way back into London, Bee checks her kit again. She's already checked it a hundred times, but one more can't hurt.

They're taking a pretty scenic route, avoiding all the main A and B roads. No sense in getting hit by ANPR or anyone else that might be lurking.

"You good, little Bee?" Rizz asks

"Prior preparation..."

"... prevents piss poor performance, I know. That's not what I asked"

"I feel... weird..."

"Nervous and a bit tense, that makes sense, maybe a bit scared?"

*"No, that's not it. I feel fucking **powerful**"*

Rizz raises his eyebrows, giving her some side eye before she continues *"...it's making me kinda hot"* as she casually counts the rounds in the mag for her Glock, slapping the mag back in with a satisfying *click*.

Rizz eyebrows hit his hairline, as his mind is sharp, but so is his recall. *"That mouth"* he thinks.

Like she's reading his mind, she licks her lips. It's intentional. He keeps his eyes on the road. Rewarding her with only the occasional side eye.

"Ready your weapon, soldier" she jokes at his expense, putting her hand firmly on his crotch. The joke takes a turn, when she feels him twitch. *Oh, this might be a **thing**.*

She takes out her Glock, staring at him. She turns it on herself. His stomach *drops*. She takes the barrel with both hands, and licks it from trigger guard to muzzle. He gulps, they both know this is crazy. She knows she's in control. She knows he's twitching - sitting on the line between sexy and dangerous. She holsters the Glock, and turns her attention to her comrade-soulmate.

He shifts his hips as she puts her hand down his boxers, he's already got a semi, but she works it hard. It takes seconds. *"Safety off, make ready"* she commands him, flipping him up into his waistband.

"Standby" he complies, lifting his ass from the seat so he can use his free land to pull his trousers and boxers down, keeping one on the wheel. With himself freed, and realising just how tense he is. He sits back, two hands on the wheel.

She unclips her seatbelt and rotates, her knees on her seat, she licks him from base to tip. *"Weapons hot"* with a smirk, before taking him in her mouth. The taste of his precum quickly overrides the bitter taste of burned gunpowder residue lingering on her tongue.

She works up and down, doing the best she can in the confined space, but feeling connected to him in a way that's different. Highly aroused by her power and control she controls the pace. When he throbs, she stops. When he gasps, she slows down. Teasing him out. When he tries to take a hand off the wheel, she replaces it. His hips try to push upwards, she withdraws.

He can do nothing but enjoy, and make sure the car stays right way up and on the tarmac.

Deciding she's teased him enough, and his balls almost disappearing as his scrotum retracts, desperate for release. She buries her face all the way in, taking his full length in her throat. She stays there, working his head deep in her throat.

When she feels the inevitable coming, she pulls out half way. Enthusiastically taking spurt after spurt of his cum in her mouth.

She sits back up, swallows and looks at him. She takes a mouthful of Red Bull to wash the taste of him away. He relaxes in his seat for a second, before shuffling his trousers and boxers back up.

When they're both adequately redressed, the absurdity of their act sits silently between them before she breaks the awkwardness. *"Weapons hot?"* and she burst into laughter, quickly followed by him.

Chapter Thirty

Night falls before the G-Wagons roll to a stop, exactly a quarter mile from their destination. Tucked down an access road on the abandoned industrial estate. The four dismount from their vehicles and make ready. Weapons systems checked and loaded. Earpieces put in place.

"No fancy tactics, we roll in dark - no headlights, no phone screens, nothing. I'll park up by the fighter's entrance, Robbie you park up the main side. Green says Dev's still in there, we don't know about Ali, and we don't know about backup. Keep your eyes open, and don't discharge your weapons unless you can see who you're shooting. We don't need a blue on blue. No kills unless absolutely necessary. Aria, Jade - you breach the doors. Robbie, you and I are the first ones in. Breach is at 22-hundred. Understood?"

They all nod.

"Sync watches; 21:55" the final instruction.

Ghostface masks go on. Every team member silently fist bumps each of the others. There's no hugs. No space for warmth here. The wagons pull off. It's on.

21:58. Silently, almost invisibly, the wagons roll to a gentle stop at their respective drop points. Their operators, shrouded in black, make their way to their entry points.

21:59. Prepare to breach. Rizz looks at Bee. Robbie looks at Jade.

22:00 nods, the doors open as quietly as possible. The teams enter, resting Glocks on maglights, scanning for life.

As quietly as possible, they clear the areas and rooms, one by one. The building is eerie dark when not full of staff, fighters, and fans. They rendez-vous at the stairs to VIP as planned.

Rizz takes the lead up the stairs, covering the straight ahead. Robbie watches the peripherals, scanning balconies. Bee climbs in the middle, ensuring the human chain doesn't break. Jade guards the rear.

The check and clear the VIP lounge. Rizz signals for Robbie and Jade to clear the Casino, Rizz and Bee to clear the Gentleman's Lounge. They prime at their respective doors. Hand signals between Rizz and Robbie... 3.... 2... 1... they move through.

Jade kicks open the door for the Casino, Robbie primed to move in. He doesn't see it. Neither does Jade. The trip detonator on the top of the door triggers an explosion that throws the pair back, Jade is thrown against the bar, Robbie against the balcony cracking the safety glass with his head. Both unconscious.

Rizz spotted it half a second before Robbie breached the door, and threw himself over Bee, shielding them in a corner.

Smoke and dust fills the air.

From the gentleman's lounge, Ali appears. Clearly pleased with himself. Clapping slowly. He turns straight to where Rizz and Bee are reeling from the force of the explosion.

"So you found me, what now?" With that, he kicks Rizz in the face, the toe of his winklepicker shoe landing firmly in his eye, sending him into the wall. He lifts his foot, and stomps on Rizz 'head. Bee uses the moment's opportunity to spear him, driving her shoulders into his hip while she grabs his thigh. Causing him to topple over. As soon as he lands on his back, he grabs her head and drives his thumbs into her eyes while she blindly rains semi-accurate punches at him.

It doesn't last long before Rizz is back in the fight, he rips Bee off - sending her to the bar, and puts his foot on Ali's throat, holding him in place while he squirms. *You little cunt. I should fucking kill you for everything you've caused.*

But he remembers the plan, they need to hand him over. So he gives him a quick kick in the face, and while he's recoiling rolls him onto his front, using his cable tie cuffs to secure his wrists, then pulling out his limb restraints and securing Ali's ankles and just above his knees.

Rizz pulls his Glock, putting it under Ali's chin, his face touching Ali's.

"Are there any more traps in here?"

Ali laughs. Rizz decides he's probably not more than a 1 trick pony.

"Where's Dev?"

Ali laughs maniacally. *"You think you can stop what's been written? Urah At-Tawbah, verse five: Kill the polytheists wherever you find them. It's in the Book. His will. You'll all burn, Insha'Allah. Especially her."*

Rizz's jaw tightens. *Fuck it.* He paces back to the bar, and finds the blow torch. He grabs a metal spirit measurer. He heats it until it's red. Grabbing some ice cube tongs, he picks it up. Bee sees what's coming. She's feeling it. She holds Ali's nose, and punches him in the balls. Forcing his mouth open. Rizz puts the red-hot measurer into his mouth, narrow end first.

"Your filthy tongue has caused enough fucking problems"

They laugh watching him rolling around, trying to spit it out, the wider end too big to fit past his teeth with the natural range of his jaw.

Jade's consciousness starts to return, and she sees what's unfolding. She hears Ali's fanatical bullshit, as soon as she can, she's on her feet. She rejoices at "Bizzy's" hot tongue trick. But it's not enough. Not for what he forced her Green through.

She walks to the bar, calling to Rizz *"hold him"*, grabbing a grapefruit spoon. Rizz decides Jade deserves her catharsis, and Ali deserves whatever the fuck he gets. Rizz holds Ali in place. As Jade takes a knee in front of him.

She rams the grapefruit spoon into the bottom of his eye socket, before scooping it all the way around, completely removing his eye, the squelching and popping sound is satisfying, against the backdrop of the crackling burn coming from the Casino. She takes his other eye in a similar fashion. *"Perhaps losing your sight will help you see the error of your ways, you hateful fucker"*.

Robbie appears behind Jade, he puts his hand on her shoulder. *"He's had enough. Living like that is a fate worse than death"*. Jade nods.

"Get him out of here, drop him outside the emergency room, we've gotta find Dev". With his arms bound behind him, they link through the gap between his ribs and elbow. Pulling him backwards, they disappear from sight.

They head into the Gentleman's Lounge in search of clues. There they see Dev. Sitting on the sofa. His elbows on his thighs, his head in his hands. The fire is starting to rage hotter in the main room now.

"Dev, what's going on?" Rizz asks

"You ruined everything, you filthy bastard" he spits back. Rizz is shocked to hear it coming from his mouth, but he's not surprised. Until he continues *"We had it all, we had everything. My father's legacy, you ruined it, with that dirty whore. You threw it all away."*

"So you had her kidnapped?! You tried to kill Smoke?! Why?! Why wouldn't you talk to me, to Ash?"

Dev is crazed now, climbing to his feet *"Talk to Ash?! My Uncle by blood, he took you in off the street, eating rubbish like a rat. He's not even your family, but he treats you as a son and me as an afterthought! It should've been me, it all should've been me. Instead it's you. You taking my father's name and throwing it to every non-believer whore in the land, Sanjay's?! Ha! Sinners paradise, and it's Jahannam for you, your whores and your infidel demon siblings!"*

Shit, how do we even try to talk him out of this?

He stands, and lunges for Rizz. So far into his ideological fanaticism he's forgotten everything. His father's training, Rizz's capability, the lot. With the fire burning getting out of control, and Bee clearly getting nervous. It's now or never time. Rizz drives him back into the sofa, grabs him by the head and screams in his face

'Dev, brother. You've got to snap out of this. And you've got to do it now! We can help you - we can save you, but not like this. You cannot hold this much hate. We love you, but you've got less than a minute to make the right choice - please!"

Dev shoves Rizz back, who trips on the podium around the pole, catching the pole to prevent his fall; he feels how warm it is to the touch. *We've got to get out of here, we've not got long.*

He's too far gone. Rizz knows it, and he has seconds to make the right call. Dev lunges to grab Bee, Rizz can't risk it. He draws and opens fire, 3 rounds penetrate Dev's rib cage. He still has enough fight in him to make his final words poisonous, hateful, and radical.

Bee stands there, splattered in the blood of her enemies. Looking... **alive.**

Rizz is caught, between hate, bitter disappointment, disloyalty, betrayal. The release he needs isn't yet fulfilled. Ripping his shirt off over his head. He pulls his Ghostface mask back over his face. And stalks towards his prey, undoing his belt. He's not going to let the inevitability of the burning world collapsing around them ruin this.

He takes her by the throat, and pushes her onto the podium.

"Dance for me little Bee" - the electrics are still working right now, so he turns on *Cute Girl* by *Diggy Graves*. She dances around the pole seductively. He can see the light from the flames illuminating her body as she pulls up her top to expose her breasts, and pulls down her cargos, showing her ass.

She dances loving how he watches. Turned on by the mask, the flames, the hell behind them and the apocalypse in front of them. Being so close to death reminds you how alive you are.

He's seen enough. He pounces when her back is turned. Grabbing her throat from behind, grabbing and groping, spanking her ass hard. Tactical gloves leaving a special mark. He turns her round and pushes her onto the floor on her back.

He sees the word "RUINOUS", and loses his composure. He jumps on her like a man possessed, holding her by her throat, he penetrates her soul. She scratches his chest and back until they bleed. He grabs her wrists and pins them down.

"Do it... command me... make me march to the gates of hell with you... fuck me so good the Devil herself will clutch her pearls"

And he does, pelvis and cervix bruising hard, dirty primal fucking. She feels it all. The heat from the impending doom, every vein, every bump, every pulse, every throb, every thrust.

The roof cracks as a beam falls, the exposure of oxygen makes the fire roar. Flames licking everything around them. The danger heightens their excitement. And they climax together, their roar matching the inferno. After they finish, he slides his mask off, pins her by her jaw and kisses her. One final ferocious kiss. A slow motion minute shared.

Then the world comes back into focus. *It's time to get the fuck out of here.*

They soak their compression shirts in water and wrap them around their faces. Tipping as much water as they can over themselves.

"Ready lil Bee?"

"Let's get the fuck out of here"

And they sprint, dodging falling debris. Using their makeshift gas masks to full advantage as they pump their arms and legs as hard as they possibly can. Their route across to the balconies is fine. When they get to the main room, however. Flames dance on the ceiling, the cage looks like an invitation to spar Hades.

Seeing what has become of his lifelong dream catches Rizz off guard, and chokes him up.

"Bear, we've got to go, now". He freezes. She punches him in the cheek, as hard as she can manage. It stumbles him and reactivates him, and the race resumes.

Just as they get to the bottom of the VIP one of the jumbotrons fails - 16x 52" TV screens fall to the ground, raining fiery chaos. Pieces of burning plastic rain down around them. They bolt through the main entrance, the door is closed, it's solid wood and charred, glowing red hot. Rizzy charges it shoulder first, taking the brunt of the impact and the burns along the right hand side of his body as he hits the floor, compounding the crash of heat upon his skin. Bee runs through unharmed, and they get out into the fresh air. Coughing, spluttering, but safe from the inferno.

They sprint to the car and disappear as quickly as possible.

Rizz and Bee pull up at the house. There's a downstairs light still on. Meena and Ashok sit at the dining table, waiting for their return. They walk through the door, bruises, battered, and burned.

Meena runs to the door and inspects them, then holds them tight. Tears dripping down her face, *"I'm so glad you're okay"*.

Ashok quietly approaches next. *"Did you find him?"* he asks Rizz directly, his eyes begging the universe for mercy.

"We did, yeah" Rizz replies, dread in his voice, looking his Pa in the eye.

"...?"

Rizz's silence is his response.

"Is he....?" not managing to say the words

".... Pa, I'm so sorry" in the smallest voice any of them have ever heard from him.

Tears roll down Ash's face. He places his hands on Rizz's shoulders and looks him in the eye *"Son, look at me. I know, I just know you did everything you could"*

After sending Rizz and Bee to get cleaned off and get to bed, leaving just Meena and Ashok alone again. *"I promised Sanjay I would do everything I could, I would protect his only son. What an awful job I have done"*. The weight of guilt and remorse sitting heavy in his soul. He sheds more tears that night than in the last 20 years combined.

Chapter Thirty One

Early hours of the morning. 6 hours since Sanjay's burned. A lone black 3 series sits in an empty car park by the river. A man in a long coat smokes a cigarette under the brick archway of a small bridge.

A blacked out G Wagon pulls into the car park. Its driver silently decamps, and walks to the bridge.

"Sir", greets the newcomer

"Want to tell me what the fuck is going on?" challenges the smoker

"I don't know what you mean"

"I've got a tortured half dead terrorist, several destroyed buildings, a dozen dead bodies - including a Covert Human Intelligence Source, with your mark's name over them all of them. Yet no call for assistance, no intelligence reported, seemingly no attempts to prevent serious and violent offences. Some could even argue conspiracy to commit war crimes. You better talk, and you better talk now"

"What you've got is a severely disrupted extremist network, an organised crime syndicate on the mattresses, and a prolific radical recruiter unable to do so. That's not to

mention the city's largest illicit fight organiser unable to run any more events"

"Yet you haven't brought a single person in for questioning, haven't provided a single case file, and have sat by as London's been half burned to the ground. Why?"

"The remit of my assignment, sir. Was to monitor the clients and network that attend Sanjay's, not to close it down, not to take down extremist networks or prevent kidnappings"

"Instead you've left a trail of blood and rubble, I can see how that works"

"It's not in the public interest to prosecute, sir."

"That's not your call to make, Sergeant. You better make getting some prosecutions in your interest real soon"

"Leave it with me, I won't let you down"

"You're a good detective, don't end up behind bars, Robbie"

Chapter Thirty Two

Summer Jam by *The Underdog Project* kicks through the boombox. The barbecue is sizzling with a range of beef, chicken, and vegetarian options. All flame grilled with the perfect grill lines.

The whole family is together, and starting to become whole again. Meena prepares and does everything except the grilling itself, that's Ash and Rizzy's job.

Jade and Bee sit on the grass drinking Sangria, it's maybe not an Instagram Hot Girl Summer, but they're enjoying themselves.

Smoke is nearly able to walk without sticks, Green's humour is slowly but surely returning to form.

Rizzy and Robbie talk quietly by the barbecue. There's been fallout since Sanjay's. Hassan's gone to ground. The Police are sniffing.

"Yo, burgers! C'mon fat boy, I know you want one" Rizzy calls to everyone, and firing a shot in Smoke's direction

They sit around the picnic benches, joyfully eating as much as they can fit, enjoying each other's company. There is laughter. There are anecdotes. There are a few drinks flowing. There are hugs.

This is family.

And for a sweet, tender moment. They believed it might all be over.

Chapter Thirty Three

"It's time, we've got a ping" Robbie calls to Rizz, passing him the address. Rizz and Bee jump in the car, kitted and ready. *"It's an address on South Street, the building's still under construction, but the penthouse is finished. That's where he is".*

Not far from home, Rizz thinks. Longing for the simpler days, but determined to set everything right and get the family back where they belong.

Tyres screech as they high-tail their way back to London, as always avoiding motorways and A-roads, and any unwanted attention. The route is getting more familiar now, cutting travel time considerably.

Scaffolding and blue tarpaulin covers much of the building, with a few floors seemingly complete. They pull into the underground parking structure and kill the engine. The advantage for Hassan of this building is that nobody knows to look there. The disadvantage is in the absence of it being inhabited there are none of the security amenities that the future residents will enjoy. The penthouse looks to be on the 35th floor, they opt to take the lift to the 33rd and then make their way by stairs. They use the lift ride to ready their weapons, check their kit, and generally eye each other up. No need for masks tonight.

They tactically climb the two sets of stairs, Rizz in the front, Bee monitoring peripherals and the rear. Cautiously approaching the penthouse, unsure what to expect, their nerves are alight. Hairs on end. *Is he alone? Does he know we're coming? It doesn't matter. He's going to die anyway.*

The entrance door isn't locked, and they silently make their way in. It's mostly open plan, super spacious, high ceiling, modern white chic. They clear the bathroom, bedroom and ensuite, and work their way through the luxurious marble-laden residence. It's been lived in. It's been lived in recently. The coffee on the counter is stone cold. *Fuck.* Closer investigation reveals they're too late. He probably left a couple of hours ago. *Shit.*

They head out onto the balcony, from this height it feels like they can see the whole city. Streetlights are like tiny LEDs. They feel the weight of it. Every bedroom light, every set of headlights, living lives as complex as their own. *Well, maybe not quite as complex as ours.*

In the absence of danger, Rizz and Bee become acutely aware of how little time they've had alone recently. Living in the safe house is great. So is living alone. Even moving out into the cottages, everyone's just *right there.* You never know when your front door will knock.

Stood looking out at the skyline, Rizz realises how Bee doesn't actually know the area very well. So he points out some landmarks. *"And over there, that's the shop, and the gym".* It's a sweet moment. While his arm is raised, pointing, she sneaks in to snuggle under his armpit.

Her Bear isn't really the cuddly type, he's not an affection-phobe, but it doesn't often occur to him in the same way it does to her. She muscles her way between him and the hip-high glass railing, playing the spoilt-sweet brat for a second. She may as well have bounced up and down and screamed *"pay attention to me"*. Instead, she holds the front of his t-shirt, and kisses his chin.

He looks down at her and smoulders. She melts. Every part of her melts.

The peck is returned, on the lips this time. She gives him one back, *"I win"*. He looks beyond perplexed at this.

"What do you mean 'I win?'"

"I mean this..." kissing him again *"... see? I win"*

He leans in, kissing her more forcefully now, and it's not just a peck. She returns the kiss, with some. *"I win"*

"... I don't get it"

"Well, I did it better, so I win."

"I always win, little Bee"

"Hmm... I dunno, I'm winning so far..." with a wink, and a full french kiss.

He takes her face in his hand, and gives her a steamier french kiss back. Her lip quivers as he pulls away. *"Yeah... I think I win"* he adds.

She gives her own red-hot, seductive, tongue teasing kiss. Pushing her body against his, making sure he can feel all of her against his body. She looks up at him, no competition this time. He smiles at her, brushes her hair behind her ear, takes the back of her neck in his hand, and kisses the side of her neck. Her breathing becomes heavier. She takes her top off, and he undoes her bra, leaving her topless on the balcony. Feeling the gentle breeze brush across her chest. She steps out of her bottoms and frenchies. Loving the freedom.

"See, I win" she taunts. He stands behind her, wrapping his arms around her waist, and kissing her neck as she grinds on him. His hands move up and down her body. From cupping her breasts, to teasing her clit. Never lingering long enough. Keeping her guessing.

She turns to face him, placing his hands on her hips. *"Don't let go, okay?"* she tells him. He looks perplexed, as she places her hands on the railing, and jumps herself up to sit on it. Nothing between her and 35 floors of descent.

Keeping her hands on the railing, she leans backwards, and his hands tighten. She giggles, and takes her hands in his, interlacing their fingers. She opens her legs, and pulls him close. The tension between their arms preventing her plummet.

"Why don't you do it, Bear? You know you want to..."

It's true, he aches from the constraints of his boxers. She releases his hands and takes hold of the railing, leaning forward slightly, so her ass is past the railing, and her shoulders are balcony side. Rizz watches her intently. Partly because she looks amazing against the night sky, partly because he's terrified she'll fall. Wholly because he's entirely obsessed with her.

He stalks back towards her, ready to go. She wraps her arms around his shoulders. They kiss as he rubs himself against her, and finally feels her warmth as she feels his heat. She wraps her legs around his waist, as he intentionally slowly gains depth.

She takes his hands again as before, and leans backwards. Adding to the fear, adding to the pleasure. She grinds up and down, feeling him perfectly hit the target deep within her. And it feels amazing. They do not break eye contact the whole time. Her life being literally in his hands is the biggest thrill she's ever experienced.

The ride together over waves and waves of heightened euphoria. Free of the world's troubles. Gradually he gains confidence in holding her up, and starts to push harder. The metal topper on the railing gripping and slipping on her bare ass.

They slowly climb towards their climax, not rushing, embracing the journey rather than the destination. A couple of times she slips so slightly, their sudden tension causing a climaxing tightness. Every movement a worship, every slip a gasp.

She leans back as far as she dare, as her senses alight, and her courage grows. A gravity defying orgasm rocks through her body as she feels him finish inside her with the force of a man who's been unable to indulge for some time. The night stars align, she screams to the world, body convulsing as Rizz holds her in place.

After his moment of extreme tension, his sweaty hands twitch, and his grip slips, he dives forward and catches her by the small of her back. Eyes wide with adrenaline. She throws her head onto his shoulders as he stands upright.

The near miss leaves them laughing, she feigns a backwards fall again, and when he catches her makes cheesy reference to *Titanic* with "I'm flying, Jack!" arms outstretched.

He lifts her, and places her on solid ground. *"Scientifically speaking, Bumble Bees aren't supposed to be able to fly, apparently"* he adds.

"*Hmmmm*" with a mock frown, pulling her lips to one side of her face. She can't retort quickly enough, so bails *"I'm going for a wee!"* and skips off. Knowing full well he's watching her ass jiggle.

Hearing her footsteps return, Rizz turns to face her, to be confronted with a balaclava, looking down the barrel of a handgun. Instinctively Rizz knows there's no chance of winning a fight at several feet against someone with a gun. His first thoughts go to Bee. What's going to happen to her after he gets shot? Her clothes and everything are still on the balcony with Rizz. She's completely naked and unarmed.

She waltzes out, and stops in her tracks, seeing Rizz's predicament. The advantage of being barefoot, the pads on the balls of your feet make little to no noise as you walk across hard flooring. She squats down to prevent shadows or any other movements causing attention her way. Rizz keeps attention on himself *"Bro, really? ... What Hassan sent you up here did he? ... Couldn't do it himself? ... You killed before?"* evidently, this assassin is not very experienced. If he was, they'd both be dead already.

Instead, he gets a screaming spider monkey jump on his back as Rizz dives out the firing line as his natural startle response squeezes the trigger, discharging the round. *No trigger discipline.* She rams a wooden-handled corkscrew through his eyeball, she rips it out and goes again, and again. She keeps hold as he falls backwards, onto her own back, the would-be assassin on top of her.

He's still squirming and trying to fight, Rizz walks over as she scrambles out from beneath him. Rizz puts two rounds in his head. *Hassan knows we're here.* Like a hive mind they run to the balcony and get dressed and kitted again.

That's when they hear it. Two almighty explosions in quick succession. *What the fuck.* They had both dived for cover instinctively. They stand back up trying to see what's going on when they see it.

Following all the car alarms going off, like morbid indicators, they see the glow. The shop. The gym. Ablaze. Soon to be gone.

A chorus of sirens can be heard, and blue lights seen from all around the city. Descending on the area. They watch with morbid curiosity as their stomachs return to their normal positions. *They're going the wrong way. Why aren't they turning off?!*

Then it hits them. The blue lights are coming here.

Chapter Thirty Four

Rizz stands on the balcony, consumed. By the wreckage of their life. The blue lights closing in. His jaw tightens, then his fists, then his chest. *"How do we even get out of this?"*.

He turns to Bee. *She can't get caught up in this.*

"Take the car, go!" throwing her the keys, and checking the magazine in his gun. He has murder in his eyes.

She does not do as commanded.

"Aria, get out of here, now" more firmly this time. She realises his intentions. He's not going down without a fight.

"Rizz, I've got a plan" he pays no attention. Determined to go out in a final display of defiance and destruction. He's moving his kit behind a concrete wall. Preparing for his final stand.

She grabs her gear and puts it with his, making her weapon ready. He stops and pauses.

"We go down together, or we get out together" she tells him. Matter of fact, matching his determination.

He stops and stares her dead in the eyes. Behind the grit, behind the determination, and the fight. She knows he's hurting, and she knows he would never risk her.

"I've got a plan, but you've got to fucking trust me" she tells him again, his silence is compliance. *"You get us out of here, and I'll get us to safety"*

He stops and thinks for about 0.47 seconds. He runs to the kitchen and starts tearing the cupboards apart. He slaps a bottle of cooking oil on the slide, and then finds a bottle of 70% proof Rum and slaps it down. He chucks the bottle of cooking oil to Bee *"soak him"* he instructs, motioning to the inept assassin's body.

He then takes the rum, and soaks the bedroom carpet, the sofa, and any other soft surfaces he can find. Before tipping it over the oil Bee has poured onto the corpse.

He drags the corpse to the balcony, and lights it. The rum catches quickly, as the heat increases the oil flashes. And he dumps the body, falling 35 feet to the ground. A raging fireball sure to distract the Police when they arrive and buy some time. He closes the balcony door behind him.

He turns the gas on the hob. Then lights the other rooms.

"Cardio?" he asks her.

"Ugh!" she groans

They grab their stuff, and sprint. Down the concrete stairwell, jumping 3 stairs at a time. Eventually dropping half-story blocks one at a time and using their shoulders to stop them at the corner walls. Legs burning and lungs on fire they get to the car and bundle in.

No time for seatbelts. Rizz redlines and dumps the clutch. Launch control throws them forwards and he gets airtime flying out of the underground parking almost sideways. The car rocks violently as it hits the tarmac sideways and Rizz floors it. The blue lights are behind them, but he doesn't think they've noticed his escape. Thanks to the flaming corpse trick.

Checking his rear-view mirror, they don't seem to be stopping. *BANG*. The windows from the penthouse blow out as the gas finds the fire. Not a big explosion, but enough chaos to keep everyone else distracted.

"I got us out, what's your plan?" he asks, still driving like he's straight out of GTA.

"I thought we'd end up having to get out of London"

"What did you do?" he shoots

"I arranged an exit strategy" she calmly replies

"For who?" showing his care and concern for all in his charge

"All of us" feeling smug

"How?" seeming suspicious

"I spoke to Dimos"

"..." he doesn't reply

"Passports and safe passage are sorted" feeling even more smug now

"We're going to Rhodes?" a little sceptically

"Yup"

"Make the call"

Chapter Thirty Five

The sun rises on sleepy London. The second G-wagon pulls up to the docks, the doors open and a crowd of mixed emotions emerges. Ash from the driver's seat, looking tired. Meena from the passenger's seat, cheeks barely dry. Jade from the rear passenger seat, in a haze. Green from the same door, looking sharper than he has in days. Smoke thumping and groaning trying to disembark. *"Yo, what's a busted up fat man gotta do to get some help around here?"* Ash had forgotten to pull his seat forwards, making an impossible space for a semi-capable but still mountainous Smoke.

One holdall each. To start a new life. Everything left behind. No weight to carry forwards.

Bee fuels the dinghies, needed to get to deeper water for their awaiting transports.

Rizz pulls everyone into a huddle. A group hug, where they hold their family tight. They all feel the gravity. They barely go a few days without seeing each other. Now? Who knows when they'll see each other again. It wrenches at their guts. Feeling their heads all together is all they can do to control the vomit and hysterics that will definitely arrive later.

In the distance, hidden in a side road off the industrial estate, a lone BMW X5 opens the window and discards a cigarette. An emotionless face, takes a deep breath, and exhales.

The driver checks and cocks his Glock 17. He listens to his radio, officers dispatched to a "fail to stop", another unit calls for a shift-swap on a scene guard on South Street.

He maintains his observation of the approach road to the dock. And lights another cigarette.

Adjusting his seating position and stretching his back, he slides his hand into his back pocket, removing his warrant card. He looks at it, thumbing over the metallic *Metropolitan Police* crest.

Robert Smith Detective Sergeant Collar no 7846

The vehicle approaches the docks on the access road. Black Mercedes G-Wagon. 5 occupants. *Positive identification.*

Clutch in, first gear. The loose stones and dust kick up behind him.

Startled by the sound of a high revving, large diesel engine, the group turns to face the road from which they came. A black SUV speeds towards them.

Almost like a hive-mind, *what the fuck* spreads throughout the group. *This is definitely not good.*

The car approaches at high speed. It's sunrise, the sun is glaring off the windscreen. They can't see the driver.

The SUV handbrake turns, pointing it at a 45 degree angle, blocking the road. The side windows open. Automatic rounds spray everywhere.

The group dives for cover. Ash throws himself on Meena behind a metal barrel. Green rugby tackles Jade, into cover behind the engine block of the G Wagon.

Smoke falls over trying to run. He's in the open. Rounds are raining all around them. Rizz has already seen him, he grabs the shoulders of his shirt and drags him, Smoke kicking his legs pushing them further. They fall behind a shipping container.

Rizz glances, and lets off rounds from his Glock. He's too far away for small arms to be accurate, especially under automatic rifle rife.

One hitman carries on with suppressing fire as the other reloads. *They're pros. No gap for me to fire back. Shit, Bee!* He looks to the dinghies, Bee isn't there. He looks to where the overs shield from the gunfire, she's not there either.

Taking cover and formulating a plan. His thought process disturbed by a loud smash.

DS Robert "Robbie" Smith bounces off the rev limiter, fighting to keep the car straight on the poor surface. Hard shift to 2nd, and up to 3rd. The handbrake turns and the firefight rages in front of him. Feet away from the car the muzzle points in his direction and goes off, rounds firing in his directions. He braces himself for impact, and smashes straight into the side of the shooter's car. Gun shots ring out, and then they stop.

Dropping into 2nd gear. He doesn't let off the power. He pushes it sideways, nailing it against a shipping container. *Two occupants, armed.*

He fights to remove the airbag from obstructing his view. His door won't open. The car has crumpled with the impact. *Suspects are unconscious.*

He looks around. Shell casings and bullet holes. No visible casualties. The steering wheel has done something to his ribs though.

He glances down. *Aww, shit.*

One casualty. That's a lot of blood.

He sees the blood leaking from the holes in his torso. Glancing through his passenger window, he sees Rizz firing off rounds at their attacker. Bee sprinting to catch up with him.

They're all safe. He takes comfort in that thought.

His vision fades to black.

Petrol-can still in hand, Bee sprints when she sees Rizz tactically moving and shooting. The whole scene unfolded before her eyes from her viewpoint. *These motherfuckers!*

They're not shooting any more, but still hellfire fuelled rage consumes her. She uses the front bumper as a step to jump onto the bonnet and up onto the roof.

With full fury in flow she stomps the sunroof in. Checking they're still unconscious, she leans in and grabs the gun from the shooter and puts it on the car roof. They're pinned in, but their stirring tells her they're still alive.

She starts pouring the petrol can in, waking them up with the splash and the smell.

'Good morning, fuckers!"

She empties the can in, and waits for their consciousness to regain.

Rizz sprints to the X5 embedded into the side and sees Robbie. He sees the warrant card, and the gun. He feels the weight of Robbie's actions, his sacrifice, and his loyalty.

Rizz shouts for help, Ash, Green and Jade all begin their sprint. The passenger door won't open. He tries the rear door, which opens much easier. He climbs in through the rear passenger door. Robbie's seatbelt pins him in place. Rizz unsheathes his knife and cuts it.

"Round the other side, pull the seat back" he shouts at anyone who will listen. Jade's the fastest to understand and move. She's quickly in position.

Rizz crawls through to the front, feet still on the rear passenger seat. Head in the footwell, he rips up the manual seat slide. *"Pull!"* he shouts Jade, and she does, the sudden spacing dropping Rizz into the footwell a bit more. He does a pushup-esque walk backwards against the steering wheel, base of the seat, and centre console getting him back into position.

Now released, he gets his arms under Robbie's armpits and bear hugs his ribcage. *"Now pull me out"*. Hands grab Rizz's legs and waist, and they pull him out like a human chain, dragging Robbie with him. It's not gracious, it's not pretty. They both get knocked, bumped and scraped on every piece of interior furniture and gizmo on the way out.

They drag Robbie out the car, realising the scale of his injuries. Green notices the radio and looks to Rizz, who nods his approval.

Meanwhile, screams ring out. Deafening, agonising, soul wrenching screams. As flames lick out from the inside of the other SUV.

Bee stands in front of the flames. Watching, listening, and enjoying them burn.

Green uses the radio *"Officer Down, multiple gunshot wounds"* copying what he's seen on TV. He gives the location.

The screams eventually stop, and the sirens start to close in. *"It's time"* Rizz instructs, and they all make their way to the dinghies without delay.

Picking up their holdalls, very quick hugs, with Rizz's constant *"guys, we've gotta go"* they climb into three dinghies. Rizz and Bee in one. Ash, and Meena in another. Smoke, Jade and Green in the final.

Ree and Rizz head East and the others head West. There are larger vessels and alternative routes waiting for them all. Some are heading to fishing vessels, some to canal boats. Rizz are Bee are heading to the estuary where a fishing boat awaits; their departure is more urgent.

The dinghies make one last look at each other as they depart. So much left unspoken, so much that didn't need saying.

Bouncing on the rough currents and dodging other vessels, it's a white knuckle ride, which they navigate without incident or attention. Arriving at a blue and white fishing boat, they climb aboard and abandon the dinghy.

As soon as they were visible, an M16 was aimed at them. When they're onboard, still at gun point from the Skipper and his deckhand. The skipper barks, in a thick Greek accent *"how's the weather?"*, Bee responds quickly *"dry in the shade"* and the skipper lowers his weapon, placing it on the side. He moves forwards and shakes their hands in turn. They all greet each other.

Skipper hands them both small envelopes with Euros, a few Passports each and a few other bits.

Transponder off, to prevent tracking. GPS preloaded. Panama flag flying, which clearly catches the eyes of Rizz and Bee. The Skipper laughs and explains *"Nobody stops a Panama flag sailing west"*. He carries on, explaining his part in the plan *"We sail to Nice, your onward journey to Rhodes isn't my problem and I don't want to know"*.

This clearly concerns Rizzy, so Bee explains *"we dock in Nice in about 10 days. We drive from France to Greece via the Balkans. Then we do a quick hop from Lavrio to Rhodes and meet Dimos"*.

He pulls an "I'm impressed" face. Then the skipper tells them to get changed, they don't look like fisherman. They take a seat, looking back at an awakening, and disappearing, London.

As the sun sets, Rizz and Bee look at an illuminated Brighton. Behind them, home. Ahead of them, who knows.

Fuck you, find us.

Epilogue

The warm wooden interior glows with soft lightning. Meena waters the house plants. Ash takes a deep breath of fresh, Welsh air. The Langlollen canal is a stunning place to retire. Quiet, peaceful, and surrounded by tranquility.

He finishes his Chai and walks back in, Meena already tucked up. He climbs into bed, puts his arm around her and snuggles closer. She snuggles back, always feeling content in his arms.

Maybe not how they planned it, but what a beautiful way to live.

In a rental apartment outside Rome, *Who Knows* by *Proteje, ShyFX and Chronixx* plays.

Smoke stands with a shit-eating grin on his face holding a holdall.

"How much did we make?" Green asks Smoke.

Smoke stands like a statue, still grinning. He shakes the bag a bit like a toddler.

"Smoke, I swear I will bust your fat fucking head, how much?!" cries out Jade, sipping her root beer.

Instead of answering them, he walks over to the dining table, and upends the bag. Stacks of Euro notes pile, mountain, and fall to the floor.

Jade rips the volume knob all the way up and starts dancing. Getting sexier when she realises Green is looking at her and not the money. He grabs a stack and rips the rubber band off. Making it rain for Jade, who plays along.

'That's it baby, dance for that money!" throwing more notes at her.

They all join in for the chorus, screaming at the top of their lungs and dancing wildly *'WHO KNOWS, WHO KNOWS, WHO KNOWS, WHO KNOWS, I JUST GO WHERE THE TRADE WIND BLOWS, SENDING LOVE TO MY FRIENDS AND FOES"*

Jade moves towards Green, teasing him, grabbing his shirt, pulling him to the bedroom, the door kicking shut between them.

Smoke turns the music down a bit, and goes back to the front door where he left his carrier bag.

He sits down, with his bucket of cheat day chicken and his bottle of Henny. Contentment fills him. A small smile across his face.

He pulls out his phone and taps the screen a few times, Facetime comes up, waiting for connection

☐ **Brizzy** ☐

Connecting...

☐ **Smoke** ☐

Incoming call

"Yes my brother, what you saying?!" Smoke starts, face full of chicken, smile beaming

"My guy! You good? How's Italy treating you?" Rizz answers

"Is that Smoke?!" Bee screams, running through from the pool through the villa, nearly slipping over on the tiled floor before swinging her arms around Rizz's neck from behind, so they can both talk to the fam

"Italy's good, just checking in, how's the happy couple?"

They don't answer, Bee just plants a kiss on Rizz's cheek.

"As happy as these ones then" and Smoke points the FaceTime at the bedroom door, where the soundtrack of Jade's seduction is getting louder by the second

Rizz and Bee laugh *"everyone's good then?"*

"Yeah man, it's good"

"When you coming out to see us? Rhodes is peng, and Dimos has got a sweet setup here"

"Y know what man, soon, real soon... we miss you guys... Aite, anyways, love and bless"

Not one to be overtly sentimental or affectionate, that call was full of love.

A luxurious bedroom, silk sheets and fancy furnishings. A wife lays in bed, rolling over and taking comfort in the absence of her husband. Bruises adorn her arms and legs, where nobody would ever see them. The darkness of the room broken only by the dim glow from the en suite and the moon shining in from the balcony.

Looking at her with disgust. He closes the door behind him, leaving her there.

"The shipment?"

"Complete, 36 delivered. 4 didn't make it"

"Acceptable"

"One more thing"

"Go on"

"We found them"

"Where?"

"Rhodes"

Dimos, that fat fuck.

"Okay, make arrangements" he clicks, ending the call.

He walks back into the bedroom, turning the light on with disregard to her sleeping. She throws the pillow over her head, she's all too used to this kind of nonsense.

He calmly dresses and tightens his tie in front of the mirror.

Suitcase packed, gun neatly on top. He zips it up and walks out the door.

You got to the end, you filthy little smut slut, you!

Love that for you. How was it?! We are **deadass dying** to know what you think!

Post about it and message us: Tag us @drjhnorris on TikTok, Instagram, or wherever you spill your thoughts

Use the hashtags: #BetweenTheRopes #BeeAndRizzy #DarkRomanceUnderground

Leave your reaction or review on Goodreads or your socials. We love to see it, and we'll do our best to repost and stitch as much as we can (unless you ask us not to!)

You can always email us at author@jhnorris.co.uk

Oh, you thought that was the end?

AGAINST THE ROPES
Fighting your way home never hurt so good

DARKER & DIRTIER COMING SUMMER 2025

J H NORRIS

Printed in Dunstable, United Kingdom